ELIXIR

CHRIS ROOK

ISBN 978-1-99930-830-8

Contents

Acknowledgements

I would like to thank my amazingly supportive wife for giving me the time and space to chase a dream. My sons for being my motivation, for being the drive behind me completing this novel, I love you boys.

Additionally, thank you to my closest friends Mike & Matthew for offering their support and helping me refine this novel.

Finally, thank you. Thank you for taking the time to read my work and I wholeheartedly hope you enjoyed your time with every page.

Chapter 1

"Good Morning Tobias." a warm female voice rings throughout the habitat, "It is time to wake up, you have 59 minutes until you are expected at work, would you like me to play the newscast?"

Tobias, a tall middle-aged man with his short brown hair askew from another restless night's sleep, slowly crawls his way from under a fabrisilk quilt, his skinny, almost gaunt frame naked as the artificial weather simulator blows a gentle warm breeze throughout the room. The bedroom is fairly typical of any in the middle level habitats, whilst small and functional there is little 'homely' about it, a small digital alarm clock sits on a bedside table alongside a half drank glass of water, the Viewmaster showing a green countryside with the sun freshly rising over the horizon but simultaneously working to hide the stark contrast of the outside world. He spares a moment to look over at the photo on one of the cabinets, him as a toddler next to his biological parents, one of the only pictures he has of them, his mind wanders to them as it often does in the morning as he stands up and approaches the mirrored wall, it slides open automatically, granting access to his wardrobe, the familiar view of cleanly pressed grey suits and white shirts, whilst in the corner sits the standard holographic simulator. As he reaches for one of the suits, the house interjects, "Would you care to see this outfit in the holosim before you change into it Tobias?"

"No thank you, Amanda, I will take that newscast, however," he replies, his tone flat and bored with the drudgery of repeat encounters,

Tobias busies himself with the morning routine as the house reads out the headlines collated from various different media corporations, the soft voice of the habitat's AI following him as he moves around.

"The High Council has passed a new law further banning the creation and use of the super drug, eliXir. New harsh punishments for those who are caught are to be implemented immediately and include the death penalty. Activists outside the Mayor's office are calling the punishments outlined inhumane and antiquated. Mayor Lewis's popularity figures are at an all-time high however during his current fight for a second term, with his firm new policies against superpowers and eliXir the spearhead of his campaign. Police Captain Avalos offers *"No comment"* to rumours a large operation in the low habs is due to happen later today,"

Tobias enters the kitchen, the cold chromium floor hard against his feet causes him to shudder momentarily. The lights immediately buzz to life, mirrored by a click as the coffee maker activates automatically.

"Congratulations to Mrs. Hawkes who won the "To the Top" lottery last night, her family bound for a new life in the upper habitats, all expenses paid by the Pro Life Corporation."

"Lucky bastards," Tobias curses as he takes a sip from his coffee, cursing again as he burns his lips on the drink, the restraint of not spitting it out clear on his face.

The house interrupts its broadcast, the voice still warm and calm, "My apologies Tobias, I will re-tune the coffee maker to a lower temperature next time."

"Don't worry about it Amanda, end newscasts. I'll have breakfast option one today please." Tobias mutters flatly.

"Very good Tobias, it will be ready in 2 minutes, you have 35 minutes until you are expected at work. Would you like me to bring the car to street level?" The house artificial intelligence offers.

"That won't be necessary, thank you, Amanda. I think I would prefer to walk today." He replies curtly, waiting by the food dispenser unit as the smell of bread being cooked fills the kitchen.

With an accuracy born through repetition, mirrored in the sound of cogs and gears, a plate of toast arrives in the food dispenser. Tobias methodically works his jaw until the house chirps once again, "You currently have 30 minutes until you are due at work."

"Thank you, Amanda, deactivate notifications."

"Permanently?"

"Just for today." he pauses, "actually, I suppose yes, permanently." Tobias's tone lowers, his shoulders slump, a sense of defeat is evident on his entire frame. He slides his hand against the cold metal of the biometric scanner and after a few seconds, there is a cheerful ping as the door slides open. "Have a great day Tobias," the house calls out as he is thrown once more into the chaos of the middle habs during the morning rush hour.

The streets bustle with the morning crowd, people destined for another day at the office, Tobias sighs as he joins the stream towards the Future Plus Bank. Sparing a moment to look up at the sky, another perfect morning, sun breaking through the clouds like every other day, the SkyCast set to summer time and displaying to everyone in the middle habitats a beautiful day to be out despite the cold biting wind betraying the picturesque scene. The sound when hitting the streets is practically an assault, the conversations of other citizens drowned by the constant unrelenting adverts projected on various holoscreens and vid feeds, almost immediately his subdermal communication chip causes an advert to start playing in his ear, pressing a finger to the side of his head, "End all advert streams," is all he can say to maintain at least some control of the array of stimulus bombarding him. A vidscreen hums to life as he passes by, a young Chinese girl talking almost incomprehensibly about the latest DNAAR technology and why everyone should invest. A half-naked holo woman dances in the middle of the street, an advertisement for a nearby drinking establishment, flickering out occasionally as cars pass through it. Ignoring the cacophony takes a conscious effort but it is one Tobias has become accustomed to making.

His journey is methodical, placing one fancy loafer in front of the other as he traverses the streets to work for the last time, he makes an effort to take it all in, the sector never sleeps and even with the artificial day and night cycle, the heady aroma of spices and herbs from the cooking stands fill his nostrils, he allows the sound of advertisements, conversations of the masses and the whistling winds, the din of the middle habs to wash over him as he turns a corner, his destination just a short distance ahead of him.

Future Plus Bank is one of many in this sector, a tall building, festooned with the usual bright signs and logos so prevalent on all the buildings. As he ascends the few sturdy polished stone steps upwards, an automatic door slides open and he cringes expectantly as a soothing voice announces over the entry speakers, "Welcome Mar. Barton, have a pleasant shift and remember, here at Future Plus Bank the future of your life is safe in our hands."

"Hey Toby," greets a bold deep voice belonging to a Hispanic man wearing the traditional navy blue bank security uniform, his shirt seems ill-fitting atop all the growth stim muscles, he wears a holster complete with sidearm, the digital readout making it clear the gun is armed, active and loaded "Did you hear the news?"

"Morning Elliot, about the new eliXir laws? Caught it on the newsfeed this morning. I've been saying for a while that the government needed to step up and do something about it, incidents have been on the rise for months now." Tobias replies, now walking aside the burly guard as they head towards the bank's staff offices, ignoring the bustle of daily business being conducted around them.

"That's already yesterday's news man, don't you keep up? The police sent a massive raid into the low habs, you should see the pictures! They took the Archangels and the mech units." Elliot continues excitedly, an almost childlike exuberance on his face. "They went in Tobias, first time in decades, story is they went to clear out all the eliXir farms. They never came back, not one of them. Rumour is the military is going in next."

Tobias isn't hugely interested in what happened in the low habitats, no one really liked to talk about them or think about them, they are little more than a festering wasteland, but he raises an eyebrow as he attempts to humour his friend, "I think that's probably unlikely, the police will no doubt arrive back in the mid habs in a few hours and all will be forgotten. Who knows maybe they are taking so long because they are actually achieving some good down there!"

"I dunno Toby, new government, new laws, new damn everything, I wouldn't be surprised if we see-" A loud explosion cuts off Elliot's sentence, replaced only with a blood curdling gurgle as Tobias looks down and sees his friend lying on the floor, grasping his throat, a large shard of rent metal piercing through it.

The chaos unfolds in an instant, a group of men and women charge into the bank as the people inside panic and scream, only adding to the commotion. It takes a few seconds to register the alarm going, no doubt triggered by the explosion. He shakes uncontrollably, fear and panic seizing control of his body, acting on some primal instinct as he drags himself behind a desk for safety and observes his surroundings, every sinew of his body telling him to run, but he can't, the simple motions of a child having escaped him, his legs paralysed in terror. He used to imagine things like this happening, robberies, angry customers, in his mind's eye he would live out heroic fantasies and witty arguments, but now that the loud flashes and bangs were ringing out throughout the bank, he was useless, it was all he could do to watch and cower as another small explosion rings out and brings with it a fresh round of screaming and panic as Tobias ducks his head down impossibly further.

Morbid curiosity gnawing at him, he looks up for a moment, transfixed by the scene unveiling before him, he sees a man whose muscle alone would outweigh him, holding some sort of green glowing gun and wearing a wide grin as he discharges a pistol at the roof, the metal work above him melting instantly and beginning to drip molten slag onto the bank floor as he bellows, "Everybody down, this is a robbery!"

Chapter 2

"Damn, I have always wanted to say that! Keep your heads down like the good little sheep you're designed to be and maybe, just maybe, you can all go back to your meaningless existence!" A ragged looking man, his pale skin making it clear he was from the lower levels, the beard on his face out of control and unkempt, his head shaved to the skin in a weird contrast, sporting tattoos of various colours and designs across most of his heavy form, his face defies his age, looking in his fifties he is likely a lot younger, his attire mixed with his personal hygiene make him look as though he should be scavenging in the recyclers for food. Directly behind him are two other men, neither of them rippling with muscle as their seeming leader, if anything they both look hungry, a glazed look in their eyes. For all their appearances, they are clearly well armed, however, the glow of energy weapons reflecting off the synth-marble floors as they begin to spread around the bank.

The seconds stretch into eternity, in the few moments that have passed almost everyone in the bank is taking a newfound interest in the craftsmanship that went into creating the patterns on the floor. Tobias continues to cower behind the table, the holo-screen flickering from the proximity of the energy weapons, his eyes remain transfixed on Elliot who toils on the floor, clutching at the shard of metal piercing his throat.

"Hayley, get your arse over here." the hulking leader shouts across the bank to someone he previously hadn't noticed, a blonde woman, her clothes cleaner than the rest but certainly a lot less of them, exposing tattoos of naked women and various symbols, notably short, barely coming up to the chest of the larger man. Unlike the rest she appears to be unarmed, no holster around her waist apparent and the glow of energy weapons absent.

"Yes Cesar?" the woman speaks with a tone so gentle it seems like it shouldn't exist in such a bleak surrounding, it cannot be appreciated for long however as the harsh guttural tones of Cesar continue. "Give the lads their treats, I will take one too, it won't be long until the Demons turn up. Then th-" he pauses mid-sentence and turns to looks down at Elliot, still in the last throes of his life, one hand clutched to the metal piercing his throat as gargled guttural noises make their last escape, the other hand reaches out desperately to Tobias. "One sec, I can't concentrate with that noise, some people can be so fucking rude." The large man, Cesar, walks over to Elliot. Hovering over him, a larger than life shadow is cast over the security guards form. Tracing the line from the dying man's outstretched hand to Tobias, Cesar grins as he raises his pistol, never breaking eye contact. Tobias feels the shot, from the heat of the energy dispersal to the distinct hissing of its release. The discharge echoes through his body, causing him to jerk back in fright in the same moment as the body of one of his only friends goes limp, hand still gripped futilely around the twisted metal protruding from his throat.

Tobias curls up in a ball, his mind unable to comprehend what's going on, his body shaking involuntarily. In the distance the beautiful blonde hands over syringes, containing some kind of vibrant yellow fluid to each member of the armed robbery, their eyes fixated and widening at the sight of the vials.

"As I was saying, it won't be long until the Demons turn up, then the real fun starts!" Cesar states, seemingly to himself, his eyes never leaving the vial clutched in his now quivering hand, "Hayley, get to work on the terminals, get whatever credit details you can. You two, start taking whatever credsticks these cattle have on them." The muscular brutes hand shakes uncontrollably for a second as he uses it to annunciate his commands before clenching it into a fist. The desperate looking pair waste no time carrying out their orders, like vultures rushing to a rotting carcass their dirt soaked hands make their way through pockets, bags and implants, retrieving credit chips with ruthless efficiency.

Tobias watches the scenes unfolding, his eyes seeing all, but his mind unable to process the magnitude of the events transpiring. He watches as the girl called Hayley begins typing furiously at one of the banks terminals, any other time he may have observed and appreciated her obscured beauty underneath all the tattoo's, implants and plugins, but he finds it hard to focus in his current state, hypnotically watching as the pool of blood pours inexorably from Elliot's neck, forming an ever expanding puddle, one which shows no sign of slowing and threatening to engulf Tobias.

The sound of sirens breaks the blonde woman's concentration from the terminal, "Shit, is that the Demons already?" her voice breaking noticeably as she speaks.

"Can't be, must just be the local sheriff come to save the day," Cesar replies, a deep raucous laugh breaks his speech as he stares at the vial in his hand. "It is finally time for our fix boys and girls! Time for the world to see what they've shut away!" with that he stabs the syringe of viscous yellow fluid violently into his upper arm which immediately begins pumping its contents into the hulking man's body. The reaction is rapid and the results, spectacular. Tobias's eyes widen, his attention back on current events as the man known only as Cesar begins what appears to be a painful transformation. His body contorts as it expands, doing the seemingly impossible, he grows several feet both in height and width, the cold brutal man lets out an ear piercing scream which is immediately chorused by the hostages in the bank, his face is the definition of agony as his body wretches to reach its new size. Tobias had obviously heard the news casts, seen the documentaries about Russia, but he never truly believed the stories about eliXir, nothing could have prepared him for seeing it first-hand. As if the impossibly huge bulk now contorting and screaming wasn't enough to terrify the occupants of the bank, small plates begin forcing and breaking their way out of his skin, the dark brown protrusions continue to grow and appear to harden, taking on an almost chitinous appearance. After what is only a few seconds, the screaming subsides as the transformation is complete, an augmented voice from outside signals the end of the bizarre conversion.

"This is the police, diffuse your illegal plasma weaponry and exit the bank immediately or you will be terminated."

A laugh so deep and loud that it seems to shake the foundations of the building comes from the monstrous abomination in the middle of the bank. "It's finally time to show them what the low habs are all about," with that Cesar surges towards the door, smashing headlong through the antique looking doors causing them to burst from their hinges, reinforced glass and twisted metal fly in all directions as the form drops from view, the only thing Tobias hears is the chaos from outside, the screams come first, followed closely by the sounds of weapons unleashing torrents of fire.

In the bank, the two meagre thugs follow the example of their leader, their eyes bright with the lust for power as they inject themselves with the same yellow vials as Cesar. Immediately they suffer similar writhing convulsions as their new powers reveal themselves. The first bursts into flames, his skin burning as his screams are drowned out by the chaos from the battle outside, his body adapting as he runs outside, each step leaving a charred black footprint in the synth marble floor of the bank. The other man, scrawny and gaunt with a face only a mother could love, changes before Tobias's eyes, firstly his face becomes an attractive woman, his body changing to match, then he turns into a dark skinned tattooed man with long hair draped down his back, he picks up one of the still glowing weapon discarded on the floor, fluorescent green light highlighting the fear and tears of the other hostages as he charges past them, running to join his comrades.

Tobias manages to draw himself out of the fetal position, his fascination at the powered thieves giving him the courage to move. He looks over at the pretty blonde, her hair covering her face, masking the sweat and panic that projects from her brow, he watches as she tenaciously types things into the bank's computers, trying to ignore the unravelling chaos outside. Tobias draws himself to his knees, like a baby realising he can crawl for the first time as he is drawn inexorably to the sounds outside. Staring at the blonde thief, he slithers ever closer to the door, the sounds of the police trying to contain the dangerous criminals is partially drowned by the scream of the crowd and the distinctive roar of Cesar. The eyes of the other hostages follow Tobias' journey, each of them with their own unspoken demand as he edges within sight of the door, a trail of blood marking his journey. It is in that moment that Tobias believes everything the media ever told him about eliXir, he watches as Cesar throws an armoured police car into a group of civilians as round after round bounce off his new chitin-like shell. A figure stands atop the stairs to the bank, his hands streaming gouts of fire into the police below, tendrils of flame flicker from one person to the next igniting groups of people whose screams fill the air. To Tobias, it appears as though the police are overwhelmed, not outnumbered but certainly outgunned. A loud boom shakes Tobias, drawing his eyes upward as he watches the incoming low flying craft, he had heard about them in newscasts and seen them in documentaries but they are all but a myth to him, the Thronos, a black hover vehicle adorned with police symbols and sirens, four powerful rotating thrusters switch position bringing it to a stop near the bank. Without a doubt, he isn't the only person to have heard the incoming vessel, from his vantage Tobias watches as Cesar picks up a nearby police car, his strength making it appear almost weightless and with a roar he hurls it towards the floating transport. The Thronos moves with startling speed and agility, the thrusters rotating and shunting the vessel backwards, the roar of the engines met by the crash of the car smashing into the building behind, debris cascading into the street below. A guttural cry comes from Cesar directed at his failure and as if in reply an armoured panel on the side of the police flyer opens. The contents are awe-inspiring, multiple winged figures, their body armour made up of interlinked plates of a dark grey metal-like material, clearly branded police insignia are displayed on their chest plate, faces covered with helmets similar to the ones that Hover Racers wear.

"Shit, it was only a matter of time," comes a voice from behind and

Tobias is sharply reminded of where he is as he turns his head to see Hayley has finished whatever it was she was doing on the terminals, clutching the last vial of eliXir in her now quivering hand. She barely seems aware of the situation around her as she plunges the needle into her arm. His attentions torn between curiosity and safety, curiosity wins out as he continues to watch the scene outside, three winged forms leap from the floating ship, strange weapons drawn from holsters as their wings extend, small thrusters on their back slowing their descent as a hiss cuts the air, a barrage of energy is unleashed from their pistol like guns. A blinding blue light explodes as the energy impacts against Cesar's body, Tobias recoils instinctively as he tries to blink away the light in his eyes, when he turns back the three flying police are circling Cesar who appears more infuriated than ever. Tobias watches helplessly as the previously ignored thief unleashes a stream of devastating fire into the sky, unable to react quick enough, one of the police is engulfed in flames and for an instant looks like the phoenix from legend as his wings and body ignite as he plummets from the craft. Crashing to the ground the fiery officer seems unconcerned or panicked by the flames engulfing him, pistols in hand he doesn't hesitate to unleash a fusillade of syringes into Cesar's arm, on reflex the hulk raises his arm to protect himself. Tobias picks up the sound of air been sucked in, like a huge vacuum, flickering his sight through the air it is unclear where the sound is coming from, but visually it becomes quickly obvious as he makes out an Archangel standing behind some kind of tripod mounted cannon, bracing himself against the table he is hiding behind, Tobias readies himself for some devastating impact, but it never comes, instead the cannon launches some kind of thick substance all over the fire starter, it seems to turn into some kind of solid substance and there is no sight of the thief anymore.

Cesar is wobbling now, uncertain of his footing as whatever was in the syringes begins to take effect, the elite officer moves forward, flames slowly dying out around him, his armour intact. Tobias lets out a small sigh as an officer closes in, that this might all over soon, but Cesar isn't finished, lashing out his arm in a wide back handed slap, defiant despite the sedative formula surging through his veins, ignorant that his actions are only serving to take it quicker to his heart. The officer flies backward but this time not of his own volition, crashing in a twist of metal as one of the armored police cars breaks his path. The other officers on the Thronos react instantly, Tobias's flickering eyes watch as two officers shoot their strange guns in synchronisation, launching some kind of harpoons with a net between them, pinning Cesar to the ground where it is only a few seconds before he appears to be snoring loud enough to move some small pebbles in front of his face. It is only then, with the illusion of safety restored does Tobias turn back around expectantly, scouring the room for the other two thieves, Hayley and the other hungry one, he looks everywhere but at the corpse of his best friend, Tobias' eyebrows furrow as he realises that he can't see the other thieves, he looks back at the Archangels as they come closer, his shoulders visibly relax and he allows himself a long sigh.

Chapter 3

"Everybody down on the ground now!" the words boom into the lobby, echoing throughout the large old building. Tobias looks around, clearly confused and anxious as he seeks once more his salvation, the Archangels, the elite police force trained to apprehend people with superpowers. More of them have descended from their powerful hovering craft, Tobias squints through the smoke, he considers running to his would be saviours when another captive crawls next to him, stammering "W-What are they doing?" Tobias stares at the woman next to him, her fancy makeup ruined by the tears still streaming down her face, her hair disheveled, he curiously notices the dirt on her knees, pondering *how did that get there?* It takes a moment in this jumble of nonsense for the words to sink in. *What are who doing?* Panic takes control again, frantically looking around the bank for the missing thieves, he quickly realises he still can't see them. Turning back to the bank entrance it immediately dawns on him what the woman is talking about, the officers are all walking slowly toward the bank in a drawn out line, boots crackling on debris as they keep a wide array of weapons trained on the entrance to the bank. The booming voice fills the bank again "Get down now for your own safety!" Tobias spares one final glance at the approaching heavily armed and armoured forms before he hastens to lie down on the floor, he hears the sobs of the woman next to him begin anew but this time mixed in with the scuffling of a bank full of people desperately trying to get their faces as close to the floor as possible.

He firmly takes in the finery of the tiles once more, Tobias' only sense of happenings is the sound of heavy boots scuffing the polished floor and the weeping of grown men and women whose day has been little more than inconvenienced by the events of the day. It feels like an eternity passes before eventually a calmer voice fills the bank, "This building is now secure, stand up and form orderly lines for a short DNA scan and you will be allowed to go about your business." Tobias forces himself slowly to his feet and watches as a man in an official looking uniform drags away Elliot's body, he feels himself beginning to emotionally break down once more but before he can a loud hiss cuts the air, bringing his attention once more to the steps of the bank where two officers are standing over Cesar's hulking form, a large chunk of brain and chitin splatters against their uniforms and the damaged stairs. His vision lingers on another motionless body from today's events, he isn't sure how long he has been staring before a helmeted officer snaps him out of it with a firm, no-nonsense voice, "Arms out."

Compliant as always Tobias holds out his arms in supplication, the officer hovers a black device over one of them, a long awkward silence follows until the machine makes a mechanical grinding punctuated with a beep. The officer looks down at the machine for a moment before pressing a few buttons grumbling audibly beneath his helmet, "bloody new machines. Incomplete reading, please try and stay very still sir." Tobias looks down at his arms while the officer starts the processing again, it is only now he realises his hands are still shaking from the adrenaline pumping, unspent, through his system.

Before the routine can finish, a loud sharp crack rings in the bank followed in reply by the now inevitable screaming. The officer seems unconcerned as Tobias frantically looks around for the source of the commotion, it doesn't take long, the heavily armored officers at the front of the bank have shot a few extra rounds into Cesar's unmoving body. "Sorry sir, but I am going to have to remind you to stay still, these scanners are very sensitive." Moments later, the scanner makes the same mechanical chorus and the officer places it back in a pouch on the rear of his belt. "Stay here please sir, I think this device is malfunctioning," Tobias allows his arms and shoulders to slump while he waits, it isn't long until the officer returns with another man in tow, this one, however, isn't wearing a helmet, revealing a scruff of short bold ginger hair leading to a trimmed beard, there is a surprising lack of scars on his face and upon seeing Tobias, an exhausted and broken man, the senior officer' head tilts for a moment, a flash of recognition passing across his face before the stern look once again carves it with creases, only his blue eyes betray the coldness in his expression. "Hello Sir, I am Sergeant Russells, I am the senior officer on site, there has been a small problem with the scan I am just going to use a different device, please stay very still." The officer barely looks at the device, watching instead Tobias as he stares intently down at the scanner, his body and mind a quivering, broken mess. As if to punctuate the broken human in front of him, the device makes the familiar mechanical grinding followed by a sharp beep. The Sergeant looks to the officer for a brief instant, Tobias doesn't register the exchange, doesn't notice the officer putting a hand to his sidearm and unfastening to clip. "Sir, I'm afraid you have tested positive for the use of eliXir, put your hands on the ground and stay calm."

Chapter 4

"These orders are bullshit!" The firm words are punctuated by the cracking slap of papers hitting the cheap metal desk. A tense silence hangs in the air for a few moments before the well-built police officer breaks it with a sigh "With all due respect." The police captain's office was large but sparsely decorated, only a single small green fern in the corner provided by the station breaks up the dull functional grey the office has been painted in. The desk in the centre of the room still shakes from the force of the large stack of papers smashed upon it.

Captain Avalos is sitting comfortably at his desk, an old news cast about eliXir plays on his screen, only a solitary raised eyebrow giving any indication he has even noticed the intrusion into his office, his eyes never break from the screen to even acknowledge the presence of the papers slowly spreading over his desk, let alone the person across from him.

Sergeant Russells is of average height, muscular as his job demanded without going over the top, he is used to having the attention of those he addresses, whether through his rugged good looks or pale blue eyes, he commands attention through his manner and force of will. What he lacked, in the eyes of his superiors, was finesse. No one ever doubted his intellect or ability to do the job, but he is morally righteous and has a bad habit of pissing off his partners and bosses. For all his well-trained perceptiveness, he never had quite gleaned that this might be the reason he is still Sergeant.

"What was wrong with how it was before? We bring them in and when the eliXir is out of their system, they can be processed and deported?" he leans on the table, inadvertently shuffling more papers out of the way. The olive skinned Captain lets out a deep sigh, the type that gives away that this is not the first time this conversation has been had, the same sigh Avalos used when his daughter would ask for more sweets after being told no three times.

The Captain managed to keep a semblance of calm in his voice "The problem, Sergeant," with a clear emphasis on the rank, "is that the current system is not working. You may feel like your day to day job here is successful, but there is more eliXir than ever on the streets, do you know Sergeant that we had some of our first cases of kids using the fucking stuff to bully each other?" The further the Captain got into his speech the louder his voice grew, the more anger started to seep through "Don't answer that, of course you fucking know. Repeat offenses are at an all-time high, the sentences have been growing more and more lenient. Oh and let us not forget Mayor Fucking Lewis is going for a second term and wants to show he has bigger balls than Candidate Whogivesafuck. So whilst you may not think it is morally the best decision to bring back capital punishment for this offense, it is above your pay grade. But most important," By now he is waving a single, sausage like digit across the table at Sergeant Russells "Most very importantly, it's none of your fucking concern, dismissed." With seemingly practiced precision the Captain immediately returns to watching the old news cast, almost as if this entire conversation had not even taken place.

"Yes Sir," Russells says dejectedly whilst exiting the office with a defeated slump in his shoulders, he paces towards the armory, his strides long and meaningful despite his disappointment. He storms through the station quickly, eyes following him down every corridor, some are colleagues, eyeing him with jealousy or respect, he rarely notices anymore, some others are criminals, people he had helped bring in, whilst others just glared into space, high off who knows what.

He focuses on his destination as he storms down the corridors, each one as featureless and dull as the last, the flaking grey paint hadn't had a new coat in the time he has been stationed here. He considers what he can do next, he could take the issue to the Captain's superior, but that would just as likely get him reprimanded for breaking the chain of command, the force didn't appreciate it when you bunny hopped their structure. Another turn and another dull corridor, this one at least has windows looking into some of the cells and interrogation rooms, not that the view inside them is any better, people on eliXir come downs, for the most part, clutching their stomachs, huddled over in pain for the need of another hit.

Russells shakes his head disapprovingly as he turns the final corner toward the armory, a military green thick metal door stands before him, yellow crusted paint writing above it simply declaring *Armory*. He holds out his wrist, palm-upwards for the DNA Scanner, a few seconds later and the hiss of inner workings kicks in as the door slides upwards.

The smell, whilst familiar, never fails to fill Russells with a sense of pride and nausea at the same time, the strong stench of blood, sweat and tears. The armory itself is wall to wall with heavy duty lockers, each one with an identical scanner on the door, guaranteed to make sure that no one except the owner is able to gain entry to the expensive and dangerous equipment contained within. As he makes his way to his own locker, a loud debate is taking place across the room, tensions are clearly high in the ranks since the announcement earlier today.

"Rodriguez, you may have no problem adding another notch onto your gun but it ain't right man, I mean sure, sometimes we have no choice, 'iXirs get out of control and we have to put them down. But a blanket execution order on anyone found using it? It's crazy man, crazy." That was Officer Barnard, a tall and wiry man, his thick brown hair is damp with sweat and he's sporting a fresh cut on his lower lip, crusted blood still affixed to his chin, there is little doubt he was at the tail end of a shift.

"If you have a problem shooting 'iXirs, then maybe you signed up for the wrong job, I signed up for one reason, to stop the problem with idiots super juicing up on eliXir and causing mass devastation. It doesn't matter who they are, they inject that shit, they give up their right to further life." 'iXirs had become somewhat of a squad colloquialism, the higher ups don't really approve but don't do much to quash it either. Captain Rodriguez had long been a staunch supporter of any movement towards the killing of eliXir abusers, it always frustrated Russells how flippant Rodriguez is towards human life.

"It's that bloody simple to you isn't it? It doesn't matter if it's a repeat offender or a kid who takes it for the first time. They take it, *they give up their right to further life*. Your scanner plays judge and jury, you get to play executioner. I can't believe it's come to this." Barnard finishes unfastening his boots and tosses them into his locker with a huge clang, the frustration on his face a mirror of Russells' feelings.

"Damn right it's that bloody simple and it's about damn time. You may think it's primitive and brutal, but it's going to lower the rate of eliXir abuse in weeks, then we can finally start dealing with those infested fucking lower habs, ain't that right Sarge'?" Rodriguez sneers while tilting his head towards Russells.

He lets the question linger as he opens his locker, his gear neatly packed within, armor, wrist mounted comm unit, DNA scanner, boots, optical display helmet, all in its rightful place and cleaned. He always believed it was important to respect one's gear, that proper care could result in saving lives.

"You know my opinion already Captain Rodriguez, I believe that everyone has a right to a second chance. Some high up politician wants to get re-elected, improve his chances at making it into the upper-hab's, he doesn't give a shit what happens down here and even less of a shit about what happens in the lower-habs, we are just his pawns to power. Decreasing eliXir use looks good on his resumé and it doesn't matter who gets hurt on the way." He pauses, unhooking his armored vest and securing it to his torso before continuing "We all signed up to make the hab's a safer place, I don't think any of us signed up to be someone else's executioners."

Russells looks around the room as he grabs his heavy duty boots from the locker, he can see the divide within the squad, whilst some look his way, nodding in agreement, just as many others are shaking their heads and giving Rodriguez sideways glances. He finishes up his armor by sliding on his tactical helmet, tapping a button on his wrist brings the heads up display to life, readouts flash by showing the boot up sequence, the usual acknowledgements and updates of ongoing cases and important notices. He dismisses them and looks around the room as the heads up display reacts and provides him information on the officers as he looks at each in turn and ensuring the helmet is calibrated properly. Finally, he checks his wrist mounted unit, a single red pinging light turns solid green indicating his DNAAR is active, the final check always gives him a sense of satisfaction that he's completed everything in order.

"Right!" Barnard chips in "who are we to make the choice of who lives or dies? We are peacekeepers, not some rich bastards death squad." The same people who were nodding before nodded again, but nothing had changed, the divide in the room is still painfully obvious.

"And how exactly are we supposed to keep the 'peace' when 'iXirs get released and go right back to abusing? Sure, we can react quickly and the Archangels even quicker, but never quick enough, there is always a few dead or some other collateral damage. How long until we have another catastrophic event like in Russia huh?" Officer Hartle shakes his head after finishing and the room quickly falls silent, the discussion clearly over for now.

Everyone breaks into their own private conversations as Russells completes his checks on his pistol and begins reading the current reports about the Mayor's new policy. By all accounts he was going to win his second term, the people of the habs were terrified of people from the lowers coming up high on eliXir and causing chaos, it was this terror that inevitably fed into his political popularity.

A door at the back of the armory opens with a rapid whoosh causing everyone to turn, just as the red light above it begins to fill the room with its warm glow. Both could only mean one thing, there is an emergency and as if to confirm the thought the alarms around the room begin to blare.

"Officers, on me, we have a job to do." Captain Rodriguez shouts concisely, jogging toward the newly opened door.

Chapter 5

Alarm bells ring throughout the entire station, not just limited to the armory, departmental procedure dictates that in the event of evident super power use, all officers in the area are to be alerted immediately. Largely that was irrelevant, most of the eliXir users that Russells had to deal with only gained minor powers, different coloured skin, scale growth, tentacles, all fairly standard, but with the random nature of the drug they had to be cautious, for every skin colouration it was just as likely that someone could become atomic or telekinetic which usually resulted in the Archangels been called in, even then losses could be high and civilian casualties higher still. It was this point that bothered Russells the most about the drug, the randomness of it. *How could someone sit back and inject a drug that could literally turn them into a human bomb?* He considers and not for the first time.

The red alarm continues ringing overhead as Russells passes underneath it into the open briefing room, it is a large cross shape with each tip of the cross leading into another squads locker room, the walls are all the same, a drab green olive colour, very military standard green, the centre of the room is slightly more open, allowing multiple squads to stand around the briefing holo table, they are the first squad in but not by much, no sooner have they reached the table than other squads stomp into the room, as they coalesce around the holo table the only sound is that of clanging from the thick boots on the metal mesh floor, the early political talk and idle conversation gone in favour of disciplined silence as they await orders.

He looks over at Rodriguez and quietly whispers, "Captain, you seem to have not only managed to forget your wrist device but one of your boots is undone." He keeps his tone respectful but light, he wasn't trying to embarrass the other officer but he felt it was important to lead by example.

"Christ. I'll get it before we leave if that's okay with you, mom?" he leans down and begins lacing up his boot as the Superintendent enters the room.

Superintendent Carls comes to a stop in front of the active holotable in the centre of the cross, despite some years behind the desk it is clear he still works hard, his muscular physique evident even under his dreary uniform, his face is littered with scars, his years of service on the front lines having taken their toll. As a result, he looked not unlike an angry dog, he is not a good looking man.

"Right Officers, listen up, we have reason to believe some scum from the low hab's have somehow made their way up the VacChutes, cameras have spotted them heading towards the commerce district, they must have already used eliXir once to get up the chute so it stands to reason they may have more on their persons. Sergeant Russells you and your squad will be heading on a direct intercept with the targets, squads Beta, Charlie and Delta will be running a wide perimeter should they deviate from their current path. We are informed from above that the Archangels are already on standby if we need further support. Any questions?"

Russells looks around the room, everyone is transfixed on the holo table which shows the camera footage of lower habitants darting from alley to alley to stay out of sight in the habs. Russells breaks the silence first. "Sir, are our orders to detain these suspects in order to reintegrate them in the Lower Habs?" the question raised some eyebrows as Russells had expected.

"Let's be clear and get this out the way here and now. The Mayor has changed the law on how we deal with eliXir users, we are not politicians here, we are enforcers of the law. As such, eliXir users, past and present are to be dealt with lethal force. If your scanner registers an eliXir user, that person is to receive a death sentence. Good? Great, we are against the clock here people, move out, more information on the suspects will be fed through your HUD's on route. Dismissed." The matter was clearly not up for discussion and Russells can do little else than clench his fists.

With the prompt dismissal, everyone begins filing back through the large metal doors they had only shortly before entered through. No one stops to talk as they exit the locker room, with everyone rushing to grab the last bits of gear and head towards the station's garage, tensions are high, a lot of the officers still have reservations about executing past criminals or anyone not currently hostile, Russells included.

He bustles with the rest of the squad down the stairs towards the station's garage, there are already some officers starting up their cars, mostly black vehicles with occasional blue highlights, the sirens on the roof would soon be deafening the streets as they headed to one of the chutes. Various aerials adorned the vehicle, set to receive signals from all manner of networks to keep them updated on whatever they happened to be attending. The sides of the vehicle were bulky and thick, reinforced plating making the cars look more intimidating than those used by most of the force.

"Ready to go Sarge, or do you need some time to get your delicate sensibilities in order?" Rodriguez smirks, his arms crossed and leaning on the top of one of the squad cars.

"Just get in the car, we have our orders," Russells tries to sound authoritative but can't help the frustration evident in his tone. "Yes Sir!" the reply came with that continued smirk and a mock salute.

Russells takes the passenger seat, as is regulation for an officer in charge, he couldn't well drive, communicate and organise his team after all. As the car hums to life, Russells can feel the vibrations from the plasma-based engine rumbling through his seat before it settles down, various readouts begin their system cycle as he taps the button on the side of his visor "Mission report," he says, instantly his visor is displaying a myriad of information, the status of his squad, the briefing data about the targets and their current known whereabouts. For most people, it would be an overwhelming amount of data to process, but Russells, like the rest of his team, had trained with this gear and is well versed in its usage.

He can tell the other teams are in their cars already, the urgency of their orders not lost on anyone, local surveillance footage shows pictures of the targets but little else, their names and previous offenses not known which is fairly typical when people from the low habs snuck up.

His intercom hisses for a second before a voice bursts through. "Sarge? What's the situation?" Officer Barker requests, Russells gives his readouts a last overview before replying "Surveillance suggests they are currently on route to the bank located here." He looks at the bank on the map, blinking twice in quick succession, the retinal scanner clicks as it takes a screen capture and relays it to his squad, "At this point given their direct line towards it, we can assume it's their destination, squad car's one through three will set up a barricade at the front, cars four and five will take the rear. We will approach this as a hostage situation, Archangels are on standby should it turn hostile."

Rodriguez chuckles and whispers "What? Afraid to handle it yourself? I'm sure the only reason you are in charge here is the higher up's are testing your resolve, see if you have what it takes to follow the hard orders." Russells opens his mouth to reply but has no come back, he is probably right he realises, Rodriguez is his ranked superior and should be in charge of this mission. Why is he running the operation? He doesn't have time to think on that, focus on the here and now and the potential problems he is about to run into, as if in tune with his thoughts, the augmented visor shows a new alert, a red light blinks in the top right of his vision, he looks at it and is automatically updated that the bank they are on route to is now being robbed and hostages have been taken.

He opens the channel to the whole squad, "Officers, we have an update in progress, the bank is now under siege, hostages have been taken and a robbery is in underway. Deployment remains the same, be alert, approaching location in two minutes."

A choir of upbeat pinging noises confirms that all squad cars have received the message and have understood.

Russells takes a second to look over at Rodriguez, he still has that smirk on his face, driving one handed while the other is resting on his pistol. He is looking forward to this, he is one of those officers who joined up for the action and the thrill, no doubt he'd sign up for the Archangels once he had served long enough in his current position. Russells had seen many officers like Rodriguez in the past, they usually ended up dead or reprimanded for taking things too far. The new law on eliXir users actually supports officers like Rodriguez though and that is what worries Russells so much.

His headset flickers again as they take a hard turn around one of the final corners before their destination, the tyres screeching as they fight to keep the car on its course. Russells let out a sigh as he reads the latest notification, *Plasma weapons discharged on site, Archangels on Standby.*

A deep and disturbing chuckle comes from the driver's seat, Russells half wishes to himself that Rodriguez is simply enjoying the drive, but he quickly dispels any such illusion.

"Looks like this alert might have some action after all, it looks like the shit is about to hit the fan. All the fans!" He laughs.

Russells gives the notification a last acknowledgement. *Archangels on Standby.* He rests a hand on his side arm as they pass the final corner and the bank comes into view.

Chapter 6

Their armoured squad car screeches around the final corner from the bank, Rodriguez is careful to avoid civilians as he brings them to a halt front and centre at the banks steps, the building has been around far longer than the more modern fabricated structures surrounding it, fake marble walls reflect the light from the police sirens down onto the stairs below, reinforced windows on either side of a large gothic style door, it looks an odd blend of historical and modern at the same time, flanked by a variety of other shops all with the modern trappings of neon lights, holo's of half-naked women and advertisements for a dozen different products, it only made the bank stand out all the more.

Russells grabs the handset for his vehicles built in loudspeaker as two more squad cars pull up in front and behind, creating a small blockade, it's a well-executed maneuver and performed quickly, like they are trained. He pulls the handset up to his mouth and turns to face his panicked audience, "This is the police, please move calmly away from the bank and return to your habs."

He turns back towards the bank as he taps a button on his wrist mounted computer, it brings up a video feed from the squad cars behind the bank, confident that a perimeter is in place he taps again to open his microphone to the rest of the squad "Barnard and White, you are on crowd control, get those shufflers out of the way of any potential danger. Everyone else, eyes front and centre be alert, remember we do not know the situation inside and do not discharge any weapons until I give the order."

Grasping the loudspeaker microphone to his mouth once more, he doesn't notice as Rodriguez draws his weapon and gestures to some of his comrades to do the same. "This is the police, diffuse your plasma weaponry or you will be terminated."

Seconds that feel like hours pass by and Russells' eyes dart between the feed from the rear position and the bank in front of him. Data feeds from command indicate the Archangels are currently in the district and are in flight.

The large cast iron gothic doors burst outwards, flying from their hinges, dust from the fake marble creates a cloud around the opening, the grinding crunch makes Russells grit his teeth as one of the doors collides with the police cruiser next to his. The force of the impact causes the armored vehicle to slide backwards and a yell pierces out as one of his officers doesn't get out of the way of the screeching wall of metal and is pinned beneath the wreckage. Russell`s maintains his focus on the dusty opening as a bulk of muscle and armored chitin, similar to a beetle, the human head atop the mountain of meat looks oddly small and out of place, but the chitin has formed a sort of helmet around him.

Russell`s brings the loudspeaker too his mouth once more "Cease and des-" before he can finish, a thunderstorm of cracks drown him out as Rodriguez and the officers around him unleash a torrent of gunfire upon the chitinous criminal, he taps a button on his wrist computer, opening a channel to everyone, "Hold your fire! Armoured exo shell, Barker and Hartle switch to sleeper needles." Russell`s spares a moment to look over at the wreckage next to him, Simmons is clearly in pain and can't get himself out from under the tangled mess of metal, with a flurry of buttons a red cross confirmation on his heads up display confirms a med unit is on route.

A loud roar brings everyone's attention back to the door, a light glows behind the hulking mass and what looks like flame given form files in behind him. "Sleeper rounds, NOW!" Russell`s roars into the headset, the other officers respond with practised precision, the custom needled rounds fly at both the powered individuals. Russell`s calls for the rear squads to move in, orders for them to secure hostages and engage any hostiles on sight. He grunts in frustration as the needle rounds prove ineffective against both targets, bouncing off the larger man's chitinous shell and muscle and melting as they close the distance to the fiery humanoid form.

"Brace!" Russell`s commands the officers as he himself dives behind their vehicle. No sooner are they in cover than large slabs of brickwork come crashing around them, the muscled freak kicking and throwing whatever he can towards them. "Hold…" he taps a few more buttons on his wrist pad and begins relaying information, "two hostiles on site, one with strength level 3 including an armored chitin exoskeleton, second hostile is an elemental wraith, fire variety, eta?" before he can hear the response, flames dance from the hands of the fire wraith, they don't travel as expected, like a flame thrower, but instead they snake and warp their way around the cars, like tendrils of pure fire, "Kinetic!" shouts Russells, "Retreat, move back and take cover, Archangels are on route." Breaking position, he sprints towards the next nearest cover as he looks over his shoulder and sees one of the fiery tendrils wrap their way around Hartle, flames enveloping him as smoke fills the area. Rodriguez obviously notices the same and breaks his retreat to re-engage, bullets fly recklessly at the pyro kinetic and achieve nothing, Russells grabs his shoulder and pulls him back. "We can't win this one, let the Archangels take over," as he points overhead.

Dust and debris are kicked up and shake around as the thrusters from the hover vehicle rotate to put it into a full hover as the side doors slide open, Russells can't help but feel a little jealous as he watches them descend, their array of custom weaponry and armour far outstripping anything they get in the department.

Green balls of bright plasma begin discharging from their weaponry and forces Russells and his comrades to avert their eyes, maintaining his cool he barks into the communicator "Check the injured, get the perimeter established and civilians away from the bank entrance, the Angels have this under control now," Rodriguez grunts next to him and is nursing some charred flesh on his arm "Bloody show offs."

The gunfire quickly desists and a voice crackles through Russells' communicator "Officer Russells, this is Archangel Commander Piran, hostiles are down, Archangels will be on standby while your men go about their business, Piran out."

"Right men, let's get inside and see the situation, keep your eyes open and be alert. Scan everyone inside, we don't want anyone slipping through." one of the officers replies quietly over the squad channel "Well, that's the hard part over, time for the routine bit."

Chapter 7

Russells climbs the stairs to the bank, sparing a quick glance at the corpse of the chitinous hulk, the helpless fool is pinned by an electronet, a charged crosshatch pattern burned into his skin from where it discharged, a dozen needles riddle his body and twice that lay broken and useless on the floor around him. A series of plasma rounds have clearly been used to execute him, having burned right through the exoskeleton like it was nothing. He once again finds himself jealous of the weaponry the Archangels have access too.

A crunching sound annunciates every step as he walks into the bank, the glass and marble chips grinding under his heavy boots. The rear squad has entered the bank already and a few of the other officers are telling everyone to remain calm and stay on the ground.

"Collier," Russells whispers, "please get that corpse out of here, these people have seen enough," he gestures to the charred mess on the steps, acrid black smoke slowly rising from the body.

He looks over his shoulder and sees the Archangels regrouping underneath their impressive hover vehicle, they haven't left yet and aren't quite at ease, like a group of stoic statues all staring in his direction. Russells shakes off the feeling he is being watched and judged "Deploy scanners, watch the exits, make sure no one tries to slip out," positioning himself more or less in the middle of the bank's lobby, he doesn't take the time to appreciate the architecture as he watches over proceedings.

A loud bang snaps his attention back to the stairs, two officers, not from his squad, are standing over the corpse of the chitin brute, pistols drawn and taking pot shots at the corpse.

"Fuck sake," he curses under his breath, large strides see him covering the distance from the bank to the officers in moments. "Stow your weapons you god forsaken rookies, you aren't on the firing range or training now, you are lucky the Archangels don't shoot you on the spot for being so damn stupid. Go find your commanding officer, tell him how stupid you both are and demand to be put on latrine duty." After holstering both of their pistols, the two officers walk away with their heads lowered, like two children scolded for some indiscretion.

As he looks around for Officer Collier to equally admonish him for his lapse in duty a voice calls out to him, "Sergeant Russells?" Turning on his heels, he sees the familiar face of one of his officers.

"Barker, everything okay?" he asks, raising an inquisitive eyebrow. "I'm not sure if I'm using this thing right." He shakes the scanner around, "but I'm getting confused readings on one of the civvies." Russells nods in reply, "Let's take a look, lead the way."

Removing his helmet as they approach the civilian in question, the tall man could be easily described as gangly, his wiry frame making his suit look ill fitting. The man seems oblivious to his surroundings, the trauma of current events leaving his eyes hollow and frightened, there is something familiar in them but Russells can't quite place it.

"Hello Sir, I am Sergeant Russell, I am the senior officer on site, there has been a small problem with the scan I am just going to use a different device, please stay very still." Sergeant Russells barely looks at the device, instead watching the broken man before him carefully as he stares down at the scanner. As if to punctuate the poor man's current state, the scanner makes its usual grinding sounds as if something inside the device is alive and upset until it finally stops, making a sharp ping to indicate completion. Russells looks down at the screen, a flashing symbol indicating a positive result, the weary man, broken in front him, had at some point in his life taken eliXir.

The Sergeant looks to the officer for a brief instant and nods, Tobias doesn't register the gesture, doesn't notice the officer putting a hand to his sidearm, unfastening to clip. "Sir, I'm afraid you have tested positive for the use of eliXir, put your hands on the ground and stay calm."

"W-w-what?" Tobias stumbles, he can feel the blood draining from his face as the words and their ramifications ruminate in his mind. "Sir, please, hands on the ground and remain calm, we will take you to the station and get this cleared up." Slumping onto his knees as the other officer draws his pistol, the barrel pointing squarely at him, only serving to send panic coursing through him, instinctively he puts his hands up in surrender, his head skittishly looking around the room for help or somewhere to flee, just anything to get him out of this hell. "Sir, with all due respect, we have our orders," the officer with the gun states, making Tobias feel as if he doesn't exist. "Stand down Barker, we will take him into custody and deal with this at the station, there has been enough blood shed for today." The taller officer, Russells, leans in to place a hand over the top of the pistol but Barker flinches and side steps, the barrel of the gun never straying from the direction of Tobias' head. Barker takes his eyes off Tobias and looks over at the Sergeant, "I'm sorry Sarge, I can't do that." Raising his voice the senior officer speaks once more, but makes no further gesture to disarm his comrade. "Stand down, that is an order, do I need to remi-" the command is cut short as a series of screams and commotion erupt from behind them.

From on his knees, hands trembling as the officers turn around to find the source of the disturbance, he watches as the bank quickly becomes pure chaos once more. Tables and chairs are attacking people, walking around as if they have been given life, using their metal appendages to club and stab at anyone not quick enough to get out of the way. For a brief moment, he forgets the gun pointed as his head before giving it his undivided attention once more.

Russells hastily begins scanning the room, looking for the source of the chaos, it's difficult to make out anything with people running around and the building itself coming to life. He can hear the chaos from outside indicating the effect must be widening outwards, he looks past the tables and chairs, frantically looking for the powered individual, realising the situation will escalate quickly unless controlled.

He sees a downed officer, Collier possibly, struggling on the floor, a blonde lady with long cascading hair covering most of her face, leaving only a menacing toothy grin as she makes clawing gestures in the air with her fingers. The floored officer's body is being tortured by animated office supplies, he recoils in horror as he helplessly watches a stapler repeatedly smashing itself against the unconscious officer's arm, each beat leaving a small metal memento, meanwhile a small army of paper clips stab at his face and neck leaving small blossoming red pin pricks as they go. Without glancing over his shoulder Russells barks loudly, "Officer Barker, engage that woman immediately," with one long arm extended and pointing at the blonde powered woman and the other reaching for his pistol as he begins taking methodical steps to close the gap between himself and the woman.

"Negative Sergeant," Barker takes his eyes from Tobias, his hands still held high and eyes wide, shouting over the commotion at his commanding officer. "He could be one of them, an accomplice," the words are punctuated by the shaking of the gun at Tobias's head.

The bank is a mess of people running around, crashing into each other and trying to avoid the living artifacts threatening to kill them. Russells has his pistol drawn when he hears Barker shout from over his shoulder. He's unable to get a clear shot on the blonde lady in the chaos as he continues to approach, he spares a moment to look over his shoulder back at Officer Barker, regretting taking off his helmet as he has to shout to be heard. "Dammit Barker, not now, engage the threat," acting on his own advice, he turns once more to the scrawny woman with just enough time to acknowledge the chair sailing through the air towards him before it collides with his head, sending him careening across the marbled floor as his world turns black.

Chapter 8

"Dammit Barker, not now, engage the threat," the words seem distant in the whirlwind of sound. Tobias doesn't flinch, doesn't move, as the scene unfolds before him, frozen by a heady concoction of fear and fascination. His eyes move to the entrance of the bank, people fighting one another to be the next in line to get to the front of the crowd only to realise it's blocked, stacks of large tables barring the way, their legs lashing out at whoever tries to escape next. Through widened eyes he watches as a man in a dark navy suit, ruined now with dust and dirt he notes, pulls a lady by the shoulder, dragging her down in his panic driven effort to get to the front of the crowd. The mass of people pulses and groans like one organism as it almost continuously pushes some people back and swallows new people to the front. Like sheep being herded through a single gate, Tobias meanders, his mind transfixed on the spectacle.

"Sarge!" The guttural shout comes from the officer watching over him, the cold black metal of the pistol never wavering from his own head. He looks up the barrel of the gun, the officer at the end of it paying him little mind now, his open hand stretched out in warning, not a warning Tobias quickly realises, a vain gesture at trying to pull someone back who you can't reach.

Tobias doesn't move from his frozen stance as Officer Barker dashes towards his fallen superior, on some level he understands that Barker might execute him, but he knows for certain that if he runs now, he'll be shot for sure. He watches on as Barker rolls over the Sergeant, he appears to be breathing, blood slowly seeps from a nasty gash on his head. Tobias can see Barker's lips moving, the expression on his face one of anger tempered only by uncertainty, his shouts lost in the screams of the injured, confused and dying.

Despite his body feeling petrified, it offers no such practical impenetrability as Tobias is sent crashing, his own world spinning as an unknown assailant presses him onto the unyielding marbled floor. The writhing mess of limbs and the weight of the attacker make it impossible for him to get back to his feet, a screeching in his ear forces his hands to the sides of his head as he attempts to roll to the side, disengaging from what he now realises is a woman who was atop him, she flails wildly, reaching at snake like creatures pricking at her body, it takes a moment for him to realise they are pencils and pens given life, piercing her flesh and forcing their way under her skin. His ears ring from the woman's howl, he slowly rises to his feet just in time to see the wave of flesh coming towards him, a large mass of the people cascading towards him. Disoriented and confused, he wonders for a moment why this group of people seem intent on charging and crushing him. In bemused clarity it clicks, these people aren't rushing to destroy him, they are trying to find another exit after being apparently dissuaded from using the main one, the thought is little comfort as it dawns on him, he is between them and the rear exit and that whilst crushing him might not be their intent, it will be the grim reality.

Tobias's eyes flitter around the room, seeking desperately for help, for someone to tell him what to do or where to go, to find some comfort in order. He sees Barker, still standing over the Sergeant and shouting into his headset, only mere moments having passed, even with the ringing in his ears quickly subsiding he is still no closer to hearing what the man is shouting. The sea of people at the bank's main door is significantly reduced, both by the newly made wave of people rushing toward him and the fact some were now unconscious and littering the floor around the exit. Tobias doesn't need to look over his shoulder, he knew now where the exit was, his familiarity with a place he visited daily affording him some sense of orientation and in that instant, he makes a choice. He could stop and help the woman next to him for surely she would be trampled under the herd of terrified people, he could rush over to Barker, the now questionable safety of order and out of the way of the swarm, or he could seek safety outside of the bank.

He pivots one foot as he pushes with the other, affording himself the maximum amount of momentum as he turns and breaks into a sprint. He is relieved that the way to the rear exit has somehow escaped the super powered woman's notice as his feet pound against the floor, each step bringing him closer to safety and away from the horde inadvertently pursuing him.

There was only one choice, the choice that would lead to continued survival. Flight. He isn't proud of the choice, but without powers or weapons what else can he do, he wonders.

"Stop him! Angel support to the rear exit, NOW!" Are the last words Tobias hears before he bursts out of the back exit, disheartened that as his hearing returns the first thing he hears is the roaring of Officer Barker to apprehend him.

The back alley is everything that the street and bank aren't, the smell of two week old trash bags fused with the aromas of the streets to create something so foul that the rush of it makes Tobias want to retch. Despite the generated sunlight from above, the alley somehow remains in mysterious shadow, head darting left and right, there is no obvious path back to the streets or the front of the bank.

His stomach churns, smells invading his nostrils combined with adrenaline and uncertainty, fused together to brew the perfect storm for panic yet somehow they provide him a sharpness of thought. Options swirl through his head, if he stays, Officer Barker or someone else, will execute him, he doesn't really know why, the police scanners had shown he had used eliXir recently, but he knew he had never taken it, "Shit," he curses to the alleyway floor in between panted breaths. "I wouldn't even know where to get it, let alone take it," Wrestling alternatives in his mind, he doesn't take much notice as the throng of people flood out of the exit behind him, their momentum broken as they breach the alley way and into perceived safety. His mind claws for options but finds no purchase, no alternative to staying and praying.

He feels his hair start to ruffle in the breeze, packs of empty junk food bustle past him and flow towards the nearest VacChute. Over the bleating of the panicked masses, it takes a while for Tobias to hear the whirling blades of the Thronos' multiple turbines, it takes longer still for him to realise what the noise actually is. His stomach finally stops churning its cocktail of terror as he looks up, seeing for the first time in detail the sleek black hover vessel overhead, his adrenaline spikes, offering what little it has left, sending his feet grinding against the loose gravel and tarmac of the back alley, like wheels spinning on a car from the old movie vids, it takes a moment for Tobias' feet to find any traction, his knees buckling from uncertainty before finally he breaks into a sprint down the alley.

His mind is empty as he bounds down a twisting maze of alleys, the bold neon lights from the streets a distant memory. With every turn it feels as if the world is getting darker, smaller, the old brick walls are a tattered brown, masked with layers of thick moss and residue, they seem to close in on either side, the narrowness of the alleys making it difficult for the light to pierce through.

Tobias lunges around another corner, the thumping in his chest a stark reminder of how out of shape he is. So preoccupied with the roaring sound of the Archangels drawing in to take him away that he doesn't notice where the combination of dripping water and years of dirt residue have created a slick pool of ichor upon the otherwise gravelly surface. No sooner do his black work shoes step in the pool, than he slams down hard onto his side, as if sensing life, the liquid grasps to his dust littered suit, soaking him thoroughly in the short amount time he spends sliding through it. Instinctively Tobias reaches for his face, rushing to wipe the rancid slime away from it, fighting back the overwhelming rising rush of vomit from his stomach as his hands are torn between clawing the liquid from his eyes or covering his ears from the deafening engines overhead. Blinking rapidly, his eyes desperate to be clean again as he vainly tries to scrape the liquid from his face. His vision is blurry through stinging eyes but it slowly reveals where he has ended up. A dead end. The end he finds himself in is well lit by glowing signs everywhere, squinting to focus, he realises the signs are a warning of sorts. As more comes into focus he quickly realises where he has found himself, each neighbourhood has a VacChute and he was face to face with one right now.

Authorised Trash Depositors only. One of neon green signs flares in the alley. *DANGER OF DEATH*. A bold yellow pulsing sign above the chute signals. The VacChutes or simply Chutes as they are colloquially called are where most of the trash from the neighbourhood are deposited, launched down into the underground landfills known as the Low Hab's. It is against the law to go to the Low Habitats and on the rare occasions where someone from the Low Hab's used powers to come to the Mid Habs, the punishment was usually a swift execution from the Archangels.

He has to turn back, Tobias realises, the thought blaring through his mind like the warnings in front of him, he would turn back, surrender himself for another scan and everything would be fine this time, he might get a penalty and a telling off for running away from Officer Barker, but in the panic surely that was understandable? The continued pitter-patter of the water from a nearby pipe into the ever expanding puddle of muck made Tobias realise the alley was quietly serene, the only other sound the low buzz of the warning signage over the VacChute. His breathing slowed to normal, for the first time since the chaos in the bank he can finally breathe properly.

He is drawn inexorably to the VacChute, controlled small paces bring him slowly closer, he knows it isn't an option, that he has to turn back and explain himself, but he walks forward all the same, leaning cautiously as the poorly maintained partially rusted doors grind and grate as they slide open. Recoiling back as the smell of months and years of discarded trash rushes up the chute, he strains once more to hold in the churning inside his stomach but it isn't enough, he bends double, face to face once more with the pool on the floor as he adds to its form, emptying his stomach all over the alleyway floor.

"Stop right there!" A distorted voice shouts out, "This is your only warning." Tobias jerks upright, his hands held impossibly high in surrender, saliva dripping down his chin as his body shakes uncontrollably, a single figure stands at the opposite end of the alley way, some kind long barreled rifle he doesn't recognise is trained in his direction, the persons face is covered by a tactical helmet, the front just a reflective black surface that hides their face, the rest of their clothing is equally alien to him, all kinds of pouches and devices cling to various belts and clips. Tobias starts to speak, but only a rasping noise comes out, he coughs and swallows the vile chunk of whatever it is that came up, "I-I didn't do anything...I was just scared, everything happened so fast. Please, you have to help me." his voice cracks as he stutters out the pleading words.

"Down on your knees, now!" the armoured figure shouts, the distorted voice only making it sound more threatening as the rifle in their hands glows to life. Tobias flails his hands in front of him, as if in some vain hope that they will ward off whatever happens next. "Please, don't do this! I-I'm innocent, that machine, it was wrong, PLEASE!" desperation clings onto every word as he shakes his head back and forth, from the corner of his eye he notices once more the glowing signs for the VacChute behind him as the realisation hits him, this figure in front of him is going to kill him, the rifle will discharge and he will die.

With a surge of resolution, he turns and dives towards the open chute, his only thought is the slim chance of survival, but that at least death would be on his own terms. The last sound he hears is that of a pulse round ricocheting off the side of the VacChute, like a snake hissing a final warning before it attacks and then there is nothing. Just the fall and the darkness.

Chapter 9

In an instant Tobias loses all sense of anything, flailing his arms and legs in a vain hope of finding anything to stop his freefall. Panic makes the seconds feel like hours, but as the VacChute changes direction, his body collides with the hard metal, knocking the wind out of his lungs as he gasps and struggles for air amidst his terror. The wall he is sliding down for a moment gives him a sense of direction, he scrapes with his hands against the smooth metal surface, hoping to find anything to slow his descent, but years of detritus have created a film of sludge more slippery than any polished metal could be.

Fighting for air, the chute rotates once more, plunging Tobias into another freefall, tumbling head over feet, over and over, he occasionally catches a glimpse of something below, a light source somewhere below finally breaking the pitch darkness of the chute. Spinning uncontrollably towards the light, he abuses the return of oxygen to his lungs by letting out a terrified scream. He has no thoughts, his mind crippled with fright as the light below grows larger and closer, the end of his descent and life drawing near.

He forces his eyes closed, not wanting to face the inevitability of his situation. Then his world becomes pain, as he crashes into a mountain of wretched waste, his body feels like it is on fire as agony wracks every inch of him, despite no longer in free fall he continues to flail, struggling to find any purchase in the quicksand like rancid mush he finds himself trapped within. Despite the distress, he wades through the rubbish, gasping for breath as he sinks deeper into the heap, occasionally his hands or feet catch onto a particularly firm piece of rubbish and after what is only a couple of minutes he is rolling down the side of the mountain and onto his back, adrenaline spent, breathing rapidly, he mutters "No, no, no," repeatedly as he brings himself shakily to his feet, his legs burning with the effort of bringing him this far.

Looking around for the first time he is disoriented by his surroundings. In almost all directions is darkness, a darkness so complete it makes his eyes burn trying to focus for anything to penetrate it. Looking upward there is no SkyCast here, the roof of the low hab so high it cannot be seen. The VacChute above provides one of the two light sources which make anything visible down here, the exit to the chute still having some functioning warnings and lights that allow Tobias to see himself and the looming trash mountain he so almost lost himself within. The largest light source in the darkness is a large settlement of some kind, Tobias finds it oddly difficult to tell exactly how close or far away the city is, but is fairly sure it must be substantial in size.

He looks at the VacChute longingly, wondering if he could climb back up, back to life he used to have. Even if he could get up the ever growing mound of garbage, he wouldn't be able to reach the chute, not that he could climb it anyway he submits. He watches curiously as a blinking light drops from the chute. Tobias squints to make it out, it could be a drone, perhaps they are looking to rescue him from the low habs and bring him back to his old life. The blinking light quickly descends into the trash and is swallowed entirely, Tobias' shoulders slump as hope fails him once again.

A shockwave sends months of rotten food and broken debris flying in all directions, Tobias covers his eyes, instinctively protecting his face from the garbage based shrapnel as the concussive force launches him backwards, he lands hard on his back as he gets peppered with an assortment of detritus. He slowly drags himself back to his feet, wiping furiously at his clothes in a fruitless effort to return them to their once organised and clean state.

The filth mound no longer reaching such lofty heights he turns towards the lights of the low hab city. Shadows flicker against the horizon and for a moment Tobias rubs his eyes, his vision not used to such an environment. Blinking the last of the filth from his eyes, the silhouettes haven't stopped flickering and appear to be getting bigger, as they draw nearer and their forms become more distinct, Tobias raises his hands as the two figures separate and their human forms become clear.

"Hey Stranger," one of the shadows yells, his voice deep and rough, like something is perpetually caught in his throat. "You must be very lost and confused right now, welcome to the low habs, my name is Mikael." Years of decorum kick in, pushing any fear and anxiety down "Tobias, I'm not supposed to be here, I'm sorry for the intrusion. There was a mistake and I ended up here, c-can you help me get back up?" Tobias stammers, blinking in a desperate effort to make his eyes adapt to the darkness, as Mikael and the stranger draw closer to lights from the VacChute he can finally make out some of their features. Mikael is the larger of the two men, their heights roughly equal, his shoulders broad and arms muscular but enough body fat to stop him looking musclebound, his straw-like greyish hair has almost entirely receded and what little remains floats and wisps carefree. His facial features are as grizzly as his voice, a bulbous nose looks as if it has been broken multiple times and never set back, his eyebrows whilst matching his hair colour are far more bushy and alive, almost touching his temples, they would be cause for a smile if it wasn't for the cold unfeeling look in the man's eyes. "We're getting kind of used to visitors these days!" he lets out a chilling laugh before continuing "Of course we can help you Tobias." The contrast in tone takes Tobias back, the other man's voice is almost melodic by comparison. "Tell us, by what mistake did you end up here? Maybe once we know we can help you better? Oh where are my manners, I'm Samuel but please call me Sam," speaks the man with long auburn hair, pulled slick away from his face and into a ponytail reaching almost to his shoulder blades, some patchy facial hair forms a scraggly beard which only serves to look more displaced on his gaunt form. If these men shared food it was clear who got the lions share Tobias mused. The corners of the man's mouth peak in a small smile, warming and inviting as Tobias stutters to rapidly recall all that has transpired. "I-I was caught in a bank robbery, there were explosions a-and I ran. The police thought I was an eliXir user, I'm not, but their scanner said I was. They were going to kill me, I have to get back, have to explain that I'm not what they say I am. Then I can go back to my life," he shakes his head back and forth as he speaks, anxiety creeping into his mannerisms. Sam's smile only widens as he places a hand on Tobias' shoulder in a comforting gesture, "It's going to be okay friend, we'll get you back to your old life, we should get out of here though in case any of your upper friends come through the chute looking for you, we've had quite enough visitors in the last day or two." Tobias stumbles forward as the man applies a small amount of pressure to his shoulder, just enough to start him on in the direction of the city in the dark.

Each halfhearted step forward kicks up a small cloud of dust behind them as the group lumbers towards the lights in the distance. "You're lucky ya know Tobias." Sam begins, taking a few spritely steps ahead before turning to face him whilst walking backwards, "if you had still been on top of that heap when that grenade went off, there wouldn't be enough left of you to tell apart from the rest of the rubbish. Shit, you're lucky you even survived the fall, you're not the first person to jump down a Chute ya know? Most die from the impacts in the chute or when hitting the bottom."

"Yeah, you got real lucky alright!" Mikael snorts "I'm not sure being down here is lucky, but I guess it beats being dead."

It isn't long before the lights of the shanty city begin to grow and Tobias realises they weren't actually far away. His curiosity gets the better of him as he turns to Sam, wetting his lips with his tongue before coughing, the taste of all the rancid trash he failed to scrape off earlier a grim reminder of his travels, eventually he manages to splutter out "I'm surprised your...erm...homes are so close to the Chute." A heavy hand clamps down on his shoulder and sends him spinning, Tobias is quickly face to face with Mikael's angry eyebrows "We aren't all born into your luxuries Toby, down here...us *Lowers,*" spit splutters from his mouth as he emphasises the word, "We have to make do with what we can grow in this light forsaken place and what you Uppers decide to throw into the Chute. Now stop dragging your feet," Mikael pushes at Tobias' shoulder as he releases it, nudging him to carry on towards the city, "We don't want to be near the Chute if the people upset at you come down here, they won't hesitate to just murder everyone in their way." Shaking slightly from the confrontation with Mikael, Tobias forces his feet forward, praying that each one will bring him one closer to getting home.

Chapter 10

As the group continues to stumble towards the ramshackle city, Tobias' eyes begin to adapt to the darkness and the lights become a little less harsh, details of the city start to make themselves known. The heady tall buildings of the mid habs are completely absent here, almost all of the abodes are one floor, the smooth and clean modern style gone in favour of the scavenged look, no one wall made out of the same material, there are no windows in sight, just holes in the walls which a few houses have built shutters for.

Tobias opens his mouth but the words fail to escape, his sensibilities and etiquette holding back the stream of questions about how they could live down here. *Why would they live down here?* He thought for a moment. There are no street lamps, but the city is surprisingly well illuminated he realises, almost all the buildings having lights on inside or have some wired lights hanging down on the outside. Curiosity finally gets the better of him and Tobias can't hold back another question, "How do you get electricity down here?"

Sam chimes in seemingly unoffended by the question, "Well, as you have probably heard, eliXir use is quite popular here, many years ago, someone ran a cable up to the cave roof, like most things down here, they are gifts from above, we tapped into the power from the VacChute and use it to power our fair city. No one really remembers those times though Toby, most of us were born down here and will die down here." Tobias looks over as Sam seems to lose himself at the end of the sentence, his thin smile lost as his shoulders slump for a moment before he catches himself, "But don't you worry Toby, this place isn't for you, we will get you out of here." Tobias returns his view to the city, they are close now, lots of figures can be seen moving around, silhouettes against the bright lights, but it suddenly hits him just how many people live down here.

Mikael coughs, clearing his throat but it sounds more like a chainsaw being revved "Welcome to the lower habitats Tobias, our homes." As the group walk into town, the environment flips in an instant, Tobias is no longer in the dark walking to the light, but is encased and protected by the lights of the city, looking back over his shoulder the only thing he can make out behind him are the flashing lights and signals on the VacChute. The further they walk in the city the less ramshackle the buildings become, some even resembling the housing units of the middle habs. Tobias feels everyone's eyes on him as they traverse the streets, children stop playing in the street to point and stare, the only person who doesn't stop and gawk doesn't appear to notice him at all, a man in torn and tattered clothing, dried blood visible on what little remains of his outfit and an odd white foam dribbling from his lips makes Tobias shudder.

As they walk past the man, he spares a look over his shoulder but is shunted as Mikael nudges his shoulder and raises his head in the direction of the street corner, the group turn as one and head down another street. It doesn't take long until Tobias notices another person, another man, the same dead look in his eyes, the same look of thirst about his entire body, "eliXir addicted." Sam simply states, "eliXir makes you feel powerful Toby, like you could do anything, like we aren't just stuck in this abyss, but it's temporary, people get addicted to the power, addicted to the freedom, but it isn't free, the drug takes its toll on the body, the body craves more." Tobias doesn't reply, but nods, his mind racing with the surge of new information and surroundings.

At first, the addicts are sporadic, but the deeper they get into the city, the more he sees, men and women all sitting with their backs against walls, arms cradling their knees and a distant blank look in their eyes. It isn't just the addicts that look starved he observes, everyone does.

Tobias' addled mind suddenly realises why people are staring at him, even despite their dirtied nature, he is still exceptionally better dressed than anyone he has met so far, not only that, but whilst he would never consider his build overweight, he is well fed and is in significantly better state of nutrition than the people here. He licks his lips tentatively as he asks the awkward question, "Sam, I'm sorry if this is rude, but how do you all survive down here? How do you grow food?"

Mikael snorts, Tobias can't believe the size of the trenches on his forehead as he frowns, clearly not happy with the question but Sam quickly defuses the situation by placing a hand on Tobias' shoulder and bringing his attention away from Mikael's angry frowns, "Well thankfully we have power from the benevolent mid habs, meaning we can keep UV lights running all year around and grow crops, the only problem we have is keeping the bulbs running, finding unbroken UV bulbs with reasonable life left in them is one of the priorities our 'salvagers' look for."

Mikael chuckles, a rumbling grunt that spooks Tobias. "Salvagers…
you mean shit crawlers," Sam frowns before continuing "Salvagers are
critical to life down here Toby, they venture to the different VacChutes
every day and bring back whatever supplies they can find, without
them our way of life down here would collapse. We aren't savages
down here, no matter what they tell you up there." He points up at the
black void that is the sky, "We have schools, farms, families. It might
not look like much to you, but it's our city, our lives." Tobias was
astounded, savages was exactly what Tobias was told to believe. The
media warned about the inhabitants of the low habitats, that it was
crucial if any ever came up that you were to inform the authorities
immediately. They were dangerous, everyone in the low habitats was
dangerous. As the group continues to venture down the makeshift
streets, seeing the elixir addicts slumped at the roadsides, children
running around, adults busying themselves with various daily chores,
he couldn't help but feel misinformed.

His curiosity biting at his lips combined with Sam being so
welcoming, Tobias can't help but try and break the misinformation.
"We keep passing people, the addicts you called them, but how come
there aren't people everywhere like I saw earlier? Erm...people with
powers I mean? I haven't seen any, not that I want too." the stumbled
mess of a question hangs in the air for a moment as the group pass
another corner, quieter and less crowded, it is thankfully easier for
Tobias to hear the reply.

"Simple. It's expensive and hard to come by, we mostly trade in
goods and services. As you can imagine, an addled and weak drug
addict doesn't have a lot to offer." Tobias nods, some small element
of understanding settling in his brain, "The good news though Toby,
is that we are almost there." Sam's thin stringy arm outstretched to a

single digit points too one of the larger buildings on this street, despite its size, Tobias notes, it doesn't stand out from any of the other buildings, corrugated sheets of metal reinforcing the thick wooden frame making up the large majority, there are no windows or port holes on the building, but where there are cracks and gaps a dull orange light shines out onto the street. Mikael waves a thick trunk of an arm at the two men standing outside the building, similar in build to himself, rough clothes threatening to tear under the bulk of the men's muscles, they nod a greeting almost in unison. "Don't worry." Sam softly reassures with a small smirk rising at the corner of his mouth, "They are just some of Mikael's friends. I think they feel lost when he isn't here."

"Oh, erm... okay." Tobias stammers, "Where are we anyway?"

"It might not look like much, but this is home to one of our most skilled doctors, we don't have many down here and he is well supplied and connected as a result." he nods to the two heavies on the door, "and well protected naturally. If anyone can get you back to your old life it's the Doc." Sam finishes as he moves to open the rickety door that leads into the building. Tobias can tell opening the door wasn't easy and required some force to pull open, the metal scraping against the hard stone floor as it opens outwards.

Sam slinks into the building first and gestures for Tobias to follow him inside, as he takes his first tentative steps into the building the acrid metallic stench of blood assaults him as he takes in the darkened room, a low buzzing light swings from its cable attached to the roof in a room made of the same corrugated sheet metal as the outside structure, cold and unfeeling it sends chills down his spine, the only decorations being scraps of clothes littered around. All of his senses scream at him to leave immediately, he rocks on his foot, attempting to take a step backwards, but clumsily collides with Mikael lurking behind him "Everything okay Tobias?" the hulking giant mumbles, his tone lacking any sense of empathy. He takes a deep breath, fighting back the urge to splutter and spit the taste from his mouth. "I-sorry, yes, everything is fine, I wasn't expecting the smell is all, who are we here to meet?" he musters, Sam has strode ahead and is now at the opposite end of the room, a hand raps against the metal, the sound reverberating through the abode. He turns back to look at Tobias, overshadowed by Mikael's bulk in the doorframe, his familiar smile looks less inviting and more like a horror-vid under the single flickering light.

"I told you before Toby, we are here to visit the Doc. I know this place ain't very inviting, but we don't have access to all your fancy technology from up high to do the cleaning for us." He raps the side of his fist against the metal once more. "We are here to see the boss," Sam shouts at the makeshift door. Despite his trepidations, Tobias steps forward, staring at the floor and placing each foot delicately in front of the other, careful to avoid standing in any of the dark puddles and personal effects. A series of clangs and scrapes come from the other side of the door, a few seconds later it shunts outwards, "Hello friends," the warm greeting comes from the first overweight person he has seen in the Lower Habs and he looks anything but warm, brown drab heavy overalls lined with assorted pockets, each one with a variety of tools poking out, he looks at first glance more mechanic than doctor. His belly guts out and makes the bloodied apron around his waist look close to bursting. Shorter than Tobias, even in the dull flickering light he can make out the man's cold brown eyes, almost a perfect match for the rest of his attire, his head is almost completely bald with the exception of a few fleeting strands struggling to maintain a foothold.

"We have a visitor I see Samuel," a smile faintly traces his lips as his thick moustache wafts outward while he speaks, "Excellent, please do come in friend, Mikael close the door would you?" Tobias spares a fleeting glance over his shoulder, the door grinds to a close as he turns back to the Doctor, who has already turned and is walking away from them, Sam nods at Tobias before making a few quick paces to catch up to the larger man. Despite the pangs of tiredness in his legs, he manages to methodically plunge deeper into the building, following in the path of the other two men. Passing through the angular makeshift door frame, the building doesn't get any more inviting as Tobias follows the men, they are talking amongst themselves, despite straining to try and hear, he can't make out what the men are saying as they turn a corner and begin their way down a corridor lined with doors, it strikes Tobias as oddly familiar, despite the construction materials, it bears a resemblance to the health facilities of the middle habitats, even if it does lack the sense of cleanliness. A firm looking door stands out from the rest at the end of the corridor, less shanty than the rest it has a sturdy straight door frame and hinges, time and care were clearly spent putting it into place.

He tries to glance between cracks in the walls and doors as they proceed down the corridor, his curiosity teasing to know what is going on behind closed doors, disappointingly they all appear to be empty, all save the final one before they reach the end of the corridor, "…It's perfect timing," he hears the Doctor mutter as he peers through the gaps in the wall once more, the room has a large metallic slab in the centre, he can just about see cabinets strewn around the room along with some towels and rags. His eyes fixate on the woman lying on the slab however, despite thick leather restraints on the table, she seems to just be laying there, occasionally tossing and turning, long purple dyed hair is messily draped over her face.

"Tobias, shall we talk about your predicament now?" Snapping back around he sees that Sam and the Doctor have reached the end of the corridor and the door is ajar for him. The small office is the most inviting place he has seen all day and immediately he feels the weight on his shoulders lighten, a layer of deep red carpet lines the floor and despite being made of the same sheet metal as the rest of the building this is the first he has seen which has no cracks or gaps. A clean white fabricated table draws attention to itself in the centre of the room, a couple of fold up chairs look the most out of place, backs to Tobias as they face the larger and more comfortable but imposing looking leather chair. The Doctor walks calmly into the room as Samuel and Tobias follow.

"Please, take a seat," the larger man suggests as he himself slumps into the larger chair, his bulk slinking into the well-worn leather.

"Thank you, erm… Doctor?" The question hangs in the air for a moment as Tobias pulls out a chair to sit on, his hands shaking from a combination of nerves and exhaustion, his eyes flitter around the room, expensive looking equipment adorns the walls, various medical scanners and monitors which Tobias doesn't understand the purpose of.

"Lorenz, Doctor Lorenz. Samuel tells me you came down the Vac Chute from the Middle Habs?" Doctor Lorenz states as he reaches into a drawer on his desk, producing a thick brown cigar and placing it on the table. "What do you know about eliXir Tobias?" he grabs the scalpel off the table and with a rapid strike decapitates the tip of his cigar.

"Well until today, I only knew what the news casts put out, that it is illegal and the consequences of its use, as history has shown, can be catastrophic. I was skeptical until earlier...Today?" he realises mid-sentence he has entirely lost track of time, "Maybe yesterday, my workplace was attacked by some people who took eliXir...and... so many people died...my best friend," he trails off as grief washes over him, staring down at his feet as he runs his fingers through his hair, his shoes are long past office suitable he mentally notes.

The Doctor lets out an intentional, phlegmy cough to bring Tobias back to attention, "Yes, some unruly addicts can cause a lot of destruction to be sure, I suppose in the middle habitats you are blissfully unaware of the realities of production." He pauses and places the cigar in his mouth, picking up a lighter which had sat on the table and clicks it to life. The Doctor takes a few hard puffs to get it started before continuing, not paying Tobias any particular mind, "What most commoners don't realise is, that like most drugs, there is more than one kind of eliXir, there is the pure untainted kind which you'll be surprised to know fetches an insanely high price in the upper habitats." The statement slightly sobers Tobias from his grieving, he looks back up at the Doctor and opens his mouth to interrupt but is silenced by a singular sausage like digit held up in his direction as the man continues with his speech "The second kind is far more common, especially down here, like a drink watered down it becomes less potent, the powers gained from the drug less volatile but no less enjoyable, of course it wasn't as simple as just adding water-" he coughs again, this time less voluntarily, cigar smoke pouring from his mouth in spits and bursts. "My apologies," a deep rumbling chuckle, "these things will kill me one day. Where was I? Yes, the production. As with most things," the large man pushes himself up from his chair with an audible grunt, as Tobias goes to do the same he gestures with a dismissive hand for him to stay seated "- as with most things, the upper habs expect the very best you see, they want the high without the low, so to speak. The addled drug addicts you've almost certainly seen on the way here, they get the lows, they get the eliXir which isn't pure."

"Why are you telling me all this?" Tobias finally plucks up the nerve to ask, shuffling in his seat. "I mean I don't want to seem ungrateful or rude. I don't know much about drugs but I'm not sure what they have to do with me or getting back up to the middle habs?" he rubs his hands together, unsure if it's for warmth or nervousness.

"Well you see my position down here has gained me communication outside of the lower habs themselves, I have contacts in the upper habs. I'm not just a Doctor you see Tobias, I'm also somewhat of a chemist. Making pure eliXir, as I suggested, is actually quite simple, the reason it's not more common place is it requires rather specific and hard to acquire ingredients, I believe this is something you can help me with."

Tobias looks down at himself, his clothes ragged and dirty, he taps the sides of his trousers, not intending to be symbolic but literally checking if anything from his pockets had survived his ordeal, unsurprisingly his keys and wallet were lost, on any other day this would have caused him a great deal of anxiety, but right now it seemed unimportant.

"Nothing so material I'm afraid Tobias." he stubs out his cigar into a crystalline ashtray sitting on the table, only a fraction of it smoked, "the ingredient in question is your adrenal gland, the chemicals and combinations it produces are quite unique."

"What? You want my what?! Why?" Unable to grasp the why of the situation he fruitlessly fumbles for alternatives before self-preservation and selfishness take over "Why not someone else? Why me?"

The corners of Dr. Lorenz's mouth curl in a smile "A fantastic question Tobias. EliXir does many things to the body, whether it's pure or not, most of the effects fade some time after usage, unfortunately the drug seems to mutate the adrenal gland in a way that I at least, do not understand. Meaning that most of the people down here are… shall we say, unsuitable donors. The people most desperate down here cannot offer me the one thing I actually need to continue my operation. Fortunately you can."

Tobias stares at his feet once more, mulling over alternatives and options realising that there are none, he has no currency, no means of communication and an overwhelming desire to get back to his home and normal life. He quickly concludes in his mind that this is his only option and he'd do anything to get back.

"Very well, if it gets me back to my old life, I'll do it." He sighs, shoulders slumping in resignation.

Samuel snorts at the back of the room and Tobias twists his head to look at the man, he'd almost completely forgot that he was in the room, he opens the door and nods at Mikael as the Doctor continues, now facing away from everyone, "Whilst I'm overwhelmed at your generosity, your sacrifice will expand my operations greatly and I am most thankful, but I can't promise your old life back I'm afraid Tobias." He waves in an almost regal fashion at Mikael who enters the room, his hulking feet silenced by the plush carpet on the floor.

"What? Why not? What do you mean sacrifice?" Tobias turns his head furiously, placing his hands on the sides of the seat to bring himself to standing position but is quickly reseated by a large hand on his shoulder.

Dr Lorenz turns his head half over his shoulder looking back at the dirty mess in his office, his smile widening, it would almost be welcoming if not for the situation. "Sorry Tobias. I thought it was obvious, in the mid habs with the correct help and drugs, you might survive without an adrenal gland. But down here in the low habs?" He lets out a single humming chuckle, just enough to make his shoulders jerk before he finishes "The operation will prove to be quite fatal."

Chapter 11

He struggles to open his eyes, his head feeling like his brain has been shook loose and can't stay still. Mere seconds of trying to make himself more alert, end up feeling like hours of helplessness as his body refuses to respond. The sound of crying helps, the only sound he can make out gives him a focus, something for his mind to cling too and stop feeling like a child in deep water. The crying, closer in truth to whimpering, sounds close and if he had to guess he would say only a few feet away, with his new found focus he attempts once more to open his eyes but a bright light instinctively makes him keep them at a wince as he tries to move his hands to cover his face. He can't move his arms, panic begins to set in as he flails against whatever restraints are holding his wrists. His wrists and his ankles he quickly realises are completely bound. "Help! Where am I?! Somebody please… help me!"

A quiet sniff reminds him once more that he isn't alone, he tilts his head in what he believes the direction of the sound to be, squinting open one cautious eye to find the source of the crying, "Hello? I know you are here, where are we? What's going on?"

"It's no use trying to break the restraints." A quivering but feminine voice flatly states, not in a cruel way Tobias notes, but almost matter of factly, devoid of emotion. "Lorenz will be back soon," the voice softly announces.

"Lorenz," Tobias mutters, realisation washing over him like a flood. The Doctor, the low habs, the last thing he could recall was Mikael hovering over him as Doctor Lorenz told him that his life was forfeit. That explains that throbbing at the back of his head he thinks as he slowly widens his eyes, a short woman rocks back and forth on the floor, her knees curled up to her chest and slightly covered by her long purple matted hair, she resumes her whimpering as she continues to rock, her clothes are like a lot of others he's seen so far, similar to the middle habs but tattered and worn past the point of functionality. In his peripheral vision he can make out the bright light which was so blinding when he first woke up, some kind of artificial light has been left on and pointing directly at him.

His head aching, he looks down at his situation, lying flat on a thick slab of metal some makeshift straps have been added to form the basis of his imprisonment, ignoring the woman's warning he strains once more, but despite looking ramshackle the bindings serve their purpose. The archaic table upon which he lays adds to the odd contrast within the room itself, the cabinets and tables around the outside are dirty and the onset of rust has begun, but upon them sits what looks to him like high tech equipment, machinery that wouldn't look out of place in a hospital or dentists in the middle habs but whose purpose is completely lost too him. He looks down once more at the sobbing girl on the floor.

"You have to help me." Tobias pleads, "I shouldn't be here, I just want to get back home, please. I didn't ask for this, I just want to go back up." As the final words leave his lips the woman jerks upright, the snapping motion causes her hair to fall to the sides of her face and for the first time Tobias gets a good look at her, her skin is as pale as any he has ever seen but the majority is dirty save for the streams where her tears have run down. Her eyes are staring at him now, weary and withdrawn, red lines crackle from the centre like a thunderstorm but that doesn't break from the beauty of the light blue found within. Even with the dirt and lack of cleanliness, Tobias can tell she is pretty.

"Up?" She murmurs, her eyes never breaking contact from his, "You are from above?" she lurches awkwardly to her feet, her legs shake and arms tremble at the effort and Tobias can't help but notice that she lacks weight, her frame on the border of thin and gaunt.

"Yes! From the middle habitats." Tobias blurts out "Please, help me out of here. Lorenz is going to kill me, please, I'll do anything, I don't want to die here." He pauses, letting out a large sigh and allowing his body to slump. The feeling of helplessness draining his will once more.

He watches as she suffers some kind of spasm, it starts at her neck and flows down her body in a ripple, it's clearly involuntary and causes the woman some discomfort. "Are… you okay?" he tentatively inquires.

"I'm fine. I think. The shakes are just one of the effects of not getting eliXir, Lorenz says I can't have anymore. Not yet, maybe not ever. I don't know." Her head slumps from exhaustion, her chin just shy of her chest as she whispers "Promise to take me with you? Lorenz says I have nothing left he needs." The tears stream once more down her face and her shoulders jerk as she breaks into weeping. The sound of whimpering adds to the din of the room and leaves Tobias uncertain what to say, but before his social adequacies can take over the woman throws back her head and lunges at the table, her hands slap down hard against it and the snap rings through the room, in an instant her demeanour is one of pure rage "NOTHING!" She screams, Tobias winces and recoils from the woman even though he knows her anger isn't directed at him. She takes a step back and gestures to herself, "Nothing…" she growls, "I'm nothing to him."

"I'm Tobias. Help me out of these restraints and we can leave here together. We can get you help in the Middle Habs." He surprises even himself with how calm and collected the words leave his throat and he is relieved to see that the effort isn't in vain, the attractive but scraggy figure before him collects herself, "I'm Neomi." She smiles at him but her attention quickly moves to the door as it swings open, Tobias awkwardly turns and twists his head, trying to see who has entered the room.

"Off you go little girl," a rough voice reverberates around the room and instantly makes Neomi jump and skitter out like a scolded child. Heavy footsteps thud against the hard floor as the figure approaches and slowly comes into view, the man before him would look almost comedic in any other circumstances, almost as wide shouldered as Mikael and close to as muscle laden, blonde hair shaved to only a millimeter or two from baldness matches the beard contained within some kind of hygiene netting. "Let's see what the boss is working with shall we?" Despite its roughness there is a certain calming influence about his demeanour, probably the ridiculously small apron threatening to burst at any moment Tobias thinks. "Working with? He's going to kill me! I won't survive he said. Please, you seem like a good man, help me out of these restraints." He keeps rocking and turning his head occasionally squinting in the light to try and keep his vision on the man as he walks around the table with a high end scanner in his hand, running it over his body as he goes.

The cackle that follows sends a shudder colder than any metal table down Tobias's back. "Little man, be quiet, I do not care." Tobias opens his mouth to speak, begging and pleading the only thing he can think to do, the only thing that might save his life. The angry look that the apron wearing hulk is brandishing is enough to immediately make him close it again as he slumps fully onto the table, his muscles release from their tension as he gives himself over to the helplessness.

The machine in the man's hand makes three sharp beeps in quick succession. *The second time today a machine has signalled the end of my life,* Tobias thinks in frustration. The man smacks a hairy paw against the side of the device, a few seconds later it beeps three times again. The man grunts and blows out the hair on his upper lip "Fucking shit equipment, you have no idea how good you had it up there." The man clearly isn't waiting for a response however as he turns his back towards the door, shaking the scanner furiously whilst staring at it in confusion.

He storms out of the room in a huff, the straps of his apron fluttering behind him like a tail as he goes. Tobias lies his head back and closes his eyes, torn between the discomfort of constantly twisting his neck and the light shining in his face. There is a certain serene silence in the room now, aside from the low buzz of the light he can't hear anything else, his head still hurts but he could easily pass out from exhaustion he realises. He occasionally tugs at the restraints, unsure if he's even trying to break them or just keep himself awake, aware that he likely only has one more chance to persuade anyone to let him free.

Tobias is almost thankful when Dr. Lorenz and the apron wearing nurse return, something to focus on and keep himself alert, even if the focus is survival.

"Dr. Lorenz, there must be something else we can arrange? I'm not rich but I do have some savings, I can help your organisation down here, I can provide you with things from the middle habs?" Tobias is struck by the ingenuity of his offer and feels a surge of hope when the muscled nurse looks to the Doctor, waiting to see what his boss does next.

"A very generous offer to be sure Tobias, unfortunately you see, my operations here are at somewhat of a critical mass, the demand from the upper habs is more than I can currently fulfill you see and I'm stuck with a deficit of…" he smirks, an evil twinkle in his eyes "ingredients." He takes the scanner from the nurse and proceeds to run it over Tobias' mid-section. After a few seconds he throws back his head and lets out a single emphatic laugh. "Perfect." He affectionately taps him across the face, "My golden goose. Your adrenal gland is quite perfect, freshly drained, perfect for harvesting." The morbid excitement on his face sends chills through Tobias and he clenches his fist and tugs against the restraints, fear driving him to be far away from this place, from this man.

Dr. Lorenz pulls in close to Tobias, yellowed dirty teeth showing in a wide grin, he tries not to gag as the man's putrid cigar fuelled breath wafts in his face. "It's too late for you Tobias, but I promise I'll make it painless, it's the least I can do." He turns to the nurse and hands him the scanner and starts talking about preparations for the procedure, reeling off a long list of chemicals which are meaningless to him. They seem oblivious to the figure standing in the ajar doorway, Tobias can just about make out her upper body from his position, just enough visibility to watch with mouth wide as she slams two needles into her arm, a quick flash of pain rushes over her face as the yellow liquid drains into her before she swats them onto the floor. The needles make a gentle tingle sound as they bounce off the open door before hitting the ground. Doctor Lorenz looks up, his own eyes wide as he takes an apprehensive step back.

Neomi's hands glow with a bold yellow light, one that almost drips from her hands. She looks at the table and the hopeless Tobias and with a confidence he would never have expected from her states "Let's go."

76

Chapter 12

He struggles to open his eyes, head feeling like his brain has been shook loose and can't stay still. Mere seconds of trying to make himself more alert, feel like hours of helplessness as his body refuses to respond. The sound of crying helps, it is the only sound he can make out which gives him a focus, something for his mind to cling too and stop feeling like a child in deep water. A firm voice snaps his attention, as he places his hands down on the hard smooth floor at his sides, "Sarge? Can you hear me Sarge?" The familiar tone of Officer Barker' voice brings him slightly more to his senses as he attempts to sit up, "Stay down please Sergeant, you took a nasty head wound back there," the calm yet commanding voice doesn't meet much resistance and he lays back down, the pounding in the back of his head refusing the subside. "What's the situation Barker?" the question comes out far more gruffly than he intended, but he doesn't move to change it, instead spending his effort on peeling his eyes open. Kneeling next to him is the younger officer, Russells is pleased to note that he no longer has his pistol drawn as he looks over at the source of the other voice, a young man probably in his mid-twenties with some kind of tribal tattoos is packing up medical supplies into a large green box, his attention already shifting from Russells. "The situation is closed,

Captain Avalos has requested a report as soon as possible. The powered users have been executed on the scene and civilians are been treated for injuries, fatalities are within company acceptable limits." *Company acceptable limits,* the phrase always made him sick to his stomach even when he didn't have a head wound, compensations would be paid alongside commendations and bonuses. "Everyone was executed? Barker I gave you an order - " Barker raises a hand and interrupts "One individual escaped, jumped into a Vac Chute to the lower levels, it's doubtful he survived and the Angels are investigating further. Sir, I know you don't want to hear this," he looks down at the floor, clearly not trying to make eye contact, "But I was following orders. My feelings are irrelevant, I did what we signed up to do, protect the public."

Russells considers arguing with the officer, but instead pulls himself up to a seated position as an sharp tutting sound comes from the medic, he looks around at the aftermath in the bank, the structural damage alone is significant, with smashed furniture and massive chunks of masonry scattered all over the floor, there is hardly a single marbled tile that is intact. He tries to count the wounded, but finds it difficult with all the people running around, it is clear by the blood smears and lack of attention that there are more than just wounded people still lying around. "We can discuss it later Barker, help me up, I need to see what the situation is."

"Sergeant, you have a concussion, you shouldn't be walking around." The medic is standing now as he protests, he's surprisingly tall and is now carrying his medic supplies in a carry case one handed, fully prepared to move onto the next job.

"I respect your opinion, but I too have a job to do, thank you," Russells dismisses softly as he takes the hand Barker is offering to get him standing, for an instant he fears that the medic may be right, his legs almost completely collapse from under him and he clinches to Barker's arm for support, thankful that at least his arms haven't betrayed him. Objects in the distance blur in and out of focus, he closes his eyes for a moment hoping they'll adjust somehow. "Officer Barker, do you know where Rodriguez is?"

The officer shakes his head "Sorry Sir, I was making sure you got medical attention, I haven't looked around much elsewhere." It was difficult to be frustrated at the young officer, he should have known better than to sit and babysit another officer when civilians needed support but it was difficult to be subjective when it was his own health and safety in question.

He slaps his hand gently against the other officers arm, "Thank you Barker. Go and see if anyone else needs support."

Losing his walking aid almost causes him to stumble back onto his knees, but he grinds his teeth and forces himself to take a step forward, each step exhausting his will as he heads towards the main entrance of the bank.

The door is just a shambled mess of metal on the floor, it is clear in places where something with extreme heat has been used to force the door open, molten metal now solidified again has formed against the edges of some of the metal. The scene outside is worse than he recollected, one of the squad cars is now a burnt out husk, medic crews are rushing around everywhere, one thing is certain, that even despite the perimeter, civilians outside had been caught in the incident. "Shit," he gently whispers to himself, he spots Rodriguez sitting on the back of an MSU, Medical Support Unit, his arm is wrapped in soothing wraps and slung up. His tanned Latino skin is covered in soot and dirt but it does little to hide the look of anger lining his face. They lock eyes as Russells carefully and slowly navigates his way down the stairs towards the flashing lights of the MSU, Rodriguez raises his good arm and in one snap gesture signals for Russells to join him.

As he draws closer he gets a better sight of the damage, even with the gel on, that charred flesh is going to take some time to heal and will likely need grafts, he was going to be out of action for a little while. Russells knew that was only going to serve to rile him up even more. He was surprised when the other man spoke, calm and flat, very matter of fact "It turned bad quickly, Avalos wants you to report in over radio then return back. How this turned out wasn't on you Russells, but Avalos is pissed. He's going to want heads to roll and from what I understand happened in there, he's going to want to know why you disobeyed orders. The one you wouldn't execute ran into the Vac-Chutes, the Archangel units didn't give pursuit, he could be alive down there, could have died in the fall." He shrugs his shoulders.

"I couldn't just execute him Rodriguez, the scanner was malfunctioning, we needed more time and more tests. You know those things aren't perfect." he quickly changes the subject, "Why didn't the Archangels pursue? They are more than equipped for vertical descent."

The muscular Latino turns to look him dead in the eye "You know why Russells. Orders from above," he points to the sky, or rather the SkyCast "The Angels don't bite the hand that feeds, ya know? It's why no one goes down there, we've all heard about the chop shops and the eliXir problem down there, you think they aren't equipped to stamp it out if they didn't want too?" He'd never seen Rodriguez so emotional about anything before, he was a taken back and doesn't know what to say. "Don't act stupid Russells. I know you have your own moral code you feel like you have to do right by, but don't be naive. You know what happens down there just as much as the rest of us and you know why it's allowed to happen." He swallows his arguments, forces down his own indignation before continuing.

"I'll go radio in with command, you okay here?" He points at the other man's slung up arm, eager to be away from this conversation, "I'll be fine, few weeks off right?" the chuckle was clearly for his benefit, it was obvious Rodriguez wasn't looking forward to the next few weeks.

Using his hands to push himself up, he slinks over towards the nearest squad car that is still on its wheels and slumps inside. He takes a deep breath, the exhale as much a sigh as relief. He grabs the headset from the centre console and places his thumb on the scanner "Captain Avalos," he states. Despite no feedback acknowledgement he hears the call going through on the internal speaker.

"Sergeant Russells. I trust you have a site report." The Captain is being deliberately formal, probably trying to avoid shouting and swearing on a recorded channel, not a good sign, Russells thinks.

"Yes Sir, we encountered powered eliXir users onsite, we engaged immediately but were overwhelmed by a pyrokinetic and strength enhanced individual with an armoured exoskeleton. Archangel support was provided and the situation was believed to be contained. We entered the bank and began routine scans on civilians to look for shifters or anyone with non-physical powers. It was at this time we found ourselves under attack by an unknown numbers of powered individuals, injuries are high," he winces and swallows, "but within company acceptable limits."

"I understand a known eliXir user escaped?" he wasn't probing Russells knew, he had already received reports from a handful of officers by now as well as heads up display feeds, the Captain was seeing if Russells would trip himself up, provide the noose to hang himself.

"Officer Barker scanned an individual on site and came to me after the scanner showed two incomplete readings but potential eliXir use. I came and completed a scan myself and got a similar result. With the scanner not giving a complete reading I decided it would be best to detain the individual until we could get a better reading and be certain," he cringed in anticipation of the scolding barrage to follow.

"Officer Barker was following orders and wanted to execute a known eliXir user on site, but you ordered him not too, then you were knocked unconscious by another powered individual, is that correct?" the Captain's voice was still disturbingly calm, it sent a shiver down his spine and made his stomach flip.

"Yes sir, that is correct. I belie-" the radio crackled with static for a moment "Thank you Sergeant Russells, report to me back at Command immediately."

With that the headset went dead. He gently leans backwards onto the chairs head support, looking up at the roof before closing his eyes. He whispers gently, "Shit."

Chapter 13

The car slowly navigates the streets, its systems set to automatic driving. Russells doesn't feel much like driving right now, he stares out the window of the vehicle, even though the SkyCast is set to a beautiful sunny day, the neon signs are still lit and flashing on almost every storefront he passes, newscasts play relentlessly, already showing the latest feeds from the bank robbery, the images aren't being censored or cut he realises, they are showing the full coverage, corpses been carried out of the building on stretchers, blood everywhere and occasional cuts to the dead body of the armored exoskeleton of one of the thieves. The media is certainly pushing the anti-powers agenda firmly. Perhaps eager to get on side with the new Mayor he wonders.

He looks over at the passenger seat, Officer Barker's scanner loosely rocks, he sighs while staring at it, could his future career all by ruined by a piece of faulty electronics? There is a certain irony he realises, the device is designed to decide the fate of others, to scan their body and determine if their DNA has been altered by the use of eliXir in their past. He had never touched the drug himself and yet still, here he sat, the black box having control over his fate.

He pulls his head back to the view in front, the cars navigation system indicating they are about to arrive, the large stone building stands out amongst the prefabricated apartments surrounding it, if not for the building materials, then the navy blue chipped and old paint looked dated compared the smooth clean finish of the grey habitats. It's deceptive he supposes, the old sturdy looking building belies the level of organisation and technology within. As the patrol car pulls into the parking garage at the rear of the station, the large security door jerks open automatically, it might not look very smooth he appreciates but it's damn near impenetrable. He places a hand on the passenger seat, grabbing the cursed scanner and heading back into the station and destined for the Captains office.

The station is surprisingly calm, relatively anyway, most officers are going about their normal routine. *Is an outbreak of powered individuals and carnage so common place? Are people just ignorant to it when they haven't lived through it?* He shakes off the thoughts and bounds towards the Captain's office. He gives the scanner in his hand a final glance before he knocks on the door

"Come in," the Captain barks, Russells opens the door and isn't surprised to see a lingering cloud of cigarette smoke despite the air filtration unit humming in the corner, "Sergeant Russells." he stands from the table, his chair scraping against the floor and punctuating the gesture "I assume that's Officer Barker's scanner?" He holds out a chunky hand with his palm open, Russells fights back the urge to sigh and holds his head high as he hands it over "Correct Sir, I believe the uni-" the Captain silences him with his usual singular held up thick digit. He begins pressing buttons on the scanner, almost certainly reviewing the scans Russells knew, the captain frowns as he checks the readouts but eventually he places the device calmly on his desk before looking back to the Sergeant.

"I'm no fucking tech expert, but as best I can see this shows three positive scans. So please," He coughs and Russells isn't sure if it's the cigarettes or for some kind of emphasis, "Fucking please, explain to me why you not only ignored orders I explained to you in no uncertain terms this morning but also ordered another fucking officer to do the same?" Every time he swore he ground up his face and bit his lip to emphasise the hard F. The Captain slumps into his chair, his fury seemingly spent in the short flurry, Russells pauses for a moment to ensure it was over before talking, hands behind his back and chin held high "I understand Captain that the reading was displaying as positive and orders are to execute anyone believed to be using or having had used eliXir, but each scan was incomplete, I'm not sure if it was a fault with the unit or something interfering, unfortunately before I could try another scanner things escalated and the individual in question escaped custody by fleeing to the low habs."

The Captain takes a deep drag from the cigarette previously resting in a tray on his desk before he shouts, the effort clearly straining "Let me make this really clear Russells. Next time a scanner shows a positive result, I don't care if it also says the person is a unicorn, that the scan is incomplete or the scanner is on fucking fire. You carry out your sworn god damn duty or I'll shoot you myself! Is that clear enough for you Sergeant? I'd hate to be giving you conflicting or confusing messages."

Russells bites his tongue, he wants to defend his morals, wants to say that this is wrong, but now isn't the time he knows. If I argue now, he'll suspend me and any chance I've got at fighting for a fairer system goes with it. "Understood Sir." he flatly states, putting on the appearance of being deflated to go with it.

"Good," his manner flips on the spot, as if that is all that had to be said on the matter has been said. "As you were in charge of the operation you can go and answer the questions of the horde of reporters that has been practically banging down the front doors since this morning," the Captain turns back to the computer with a huff, sure enough he was dismissed, he was partly relieved, this could have gone worse he reviewed as he turns and leaves the office. Despite his new order he doesn't head directly to the front of the station, he might not be a vain man, but if he didn't look orderly people would assume things were worse than they were, so he walks to the locker room to organise himself and get a change of uniform before heading out. It isn't until he strips down that he realises how messed up his uniform is, caked in blood around the shoulder plates which he assumed was his, it is difficult to even tell the original colour of the uniform in places due to the dirt and dust. He looks in the small mirror inlaid in the locker and places his uniform hat on in a manner which mostly covers the bandage wrapped around his head, he's thankful in a way that it hit him in the back of the head, easier to hide, a quick wash in the bathroom and a change of uniform and Russells finds himself strutting towards the front of the station, it isn't his first time addressing the press, but it was usually on smaller details and incidents, usually with better success. He coughs to clear his throat before pushing open the double doors leading out to the front of the station.

The press outside stand at their well versed ease, a rookie might have considered it odd, them not instantly shouting questions at him, but he knew from experience they stood out here most the day waiting for one officer or another to keep them updated on some minor event, it was a sort of symbiotic relationship Russells supposed.

He always though it funny how some of the press looked like aliens from another world, the amount of technology and recording devices each wore, antenna, microphone, cameras poking out in all directions, often accompanied with substantial backpacks that contained the processing and battery to make each of the people arrayed before him into mobile news hubs.

He nods politely at the assembled group, "Hello, I am Sergeant Russells and I am currently overseeing the incident that happened at Future Plus Bank this morning. I am here to field questions for only a few minutes, so please: one at a time."

A few of the reporters immediately hold up enthusiastic hands, almost as if his invitation had spurred something inside them. Some officers like to field questions from certain reporters, normally the most attractive ones, but Russells simply doesn't care, he points at one at random, a slightly overweight gentleman whose backpack was plumped on the floor next to him spoke at his requested pointing "We have some on the site reports Sergeant, but could you give us an official statement on what happened?"

The obvious question at least came first he thought "This morning me and my team were responding to an alert that the cameras around a VacChute had triggered an alarm for individuals from the lower habs entering the area, there was high risk that these individuals may have been using eliXir. En route we received updates that they had taken hostages in the bank. Upon arrival we were engaged by a powered threat and responded accordingly. With the support of an Archangel unit, we were able to contain the threat with minimal casualties."

Hands shot up immediately into the air again, this time he pointed at a young woman, she looked really eager, youthful exuberance he supposed, "Sergeant Russells. How come no one was brought in alive?"

"As I'm sure you've heard already, the Mayor and the government have added new levels to super powered law enforcement. It is important that everyone knows, that the law now states that if anyone is found to be in use of eliXir they will be dealt with accordingly."

"You mean killed, correct Sergeant? It is important that everyone knows after all." Whilst her face was stern and professional she couldn't hide the smugness in her tone.

He fought back a sigh of frustration, projecting cool professionalism as best as he could muster "Correct. The punishment for use of eliXir is death."

He was thankful this time for the flourishing show of hands, he made a note not to ask the young woman again, this time a tall man with dark skin got the privilege. "Can you report on if the low habs have been abandoned? Do the police have any intention of enforcing these new laws down there, where eliXir usage is believed to be at an all-time high?"

Russells hated using the age old cliché but in this case it was safer for his career, "I cannot comment about that at this time, please keep questions focused around the Future Plus Bank incident only."

Before he could pick another reporter, the dark skin man interjects again "Are the rumours true that a suspect escaped into the low habs this morning? Will the police follow the suspect?"

He grits his teeth, his jaw tensing, he hates how quickly and freely information flows sometimes, "A suspect fled the scene, we don't know if at this time they were involved with the incident at the bank. I cannot comment on the rest at this time as it is still active. Thank you for your patience, I will answer more questions later." He turns dismissively towards the reporters and back towards the sanctity of the station, a voice shouts from behind, he doesn't need to turn to know it's the awkward young lady.

"Why are the police scared of going down there Sergeant? Are you finally admitting that the low habs aren't safe? That they haven't been in years?!"

Chapter 14

Bubbles of green float around the room and for a moment Tobias wonders if he is hallucinating. The bubbles look harmless, like the ones kids would blow out of little plastic circles using watered soap, only with a heavy green tinge.

"Bubbles my dear? Go and play outside and leave me to my work and I'll forget all about the fact you've stolen some of my product." The Doctors body language belittles the confidence in his statement, shying behind the brutish nurse.

Her azure eyes flicker for an instant to one of the bubbles floating over the top of one of tables, with a quiet pop it turns into a small pool of liquid that splashes on the work surface with a hiss, within moments it has melted through to the rock floor below where it continues it's hissing for a few seconds.

Doctor Lorenz's eyes narrow, frustration and anger battling across his features. "I see," he finally seethes as he stands hopelessly while more and more bubbles float from Neomi's hands and fill the room, Tobias' realises that they aren't moving with the wind or with gravity like he would expect, they coalesce and form a sort of loose barrier around the other men, as more and more fill the area there is no possible way they could move without popping one or more of the acidic globes.

"You're making a terrible mistake Neomi. Where do you think you're going to go? How long do you think you'll survive without my eliXir? Foolish girl, stop this immediately."

"Oh, so you know my name now do you Doctor?" She casually strides towards Tobias and places her hands against his restraints, they bubble and hiss before collapsing at his sides. He lunges forward with his arm, slapping the bright light from his face as he jumps to his feet.

"Thank you. Thank you so much, I would be dead if it wasn't for you. We need to leave, Sam and Mikael might still be around and I don't even know who else." He looks pleadingly into her eyes, made even more beautiful by her surge of confidence and standing tall.

"You're right, I could hold them off but I don't know for how long, once they realise I'm using, they will too and this turns into a real shit show " She replies, her tone gentle as she grabs Tobias by the wrist and despite his eagerness to leave, her haste and purposefulness almost pulls him off his feet. After a quick glance down the grim dark corridor of makeshift metal plates, she points for Tobias to lead the way. As he leaves the room he hears a series of pops behind him followed almost immediately by a blood curdling series of screams. He spares a quick glance over his shoulder to see the aproned nurse is on his back, reeling and rocking from side to side while clutching his chest, a plume of thick green smoke rising between his fingertips. He can't see the Doctor properly, but he appears to be hunched in a sort of fetal mixed with kneeling position, the same almost fluorescent smoke rising from his form. He notes there are distinctly less bubbles floating around but

Tobias can't stop to count as he feels Neomi's hands pressing against his back pushing him out of the room and into the dingy metallic corridor.

He doesn't hesitate any further to grasp at his freedom, his curiosity from earlier fading as he keeps his eyes dead centre, no longer wanting to know or caring what is in each side room as he bounds past them at a sprint. As the screams fade into the distance, the pair slow upon reaching a corner ahead, sparing a look at Neomi, her matted purple hair flowing behind as she rushes ahead of him into the corner, she gestures with a waving palm for him to move to one side and let her ahead, a surety on her face which made him feel at ease.

"Come on," she spurts between heavy breaths. She's smiling he realises, *is this thrilling to her or is she just happy to be escaping?* He wonders, running after her down another corridor, suddenly she twists to the left and barges through one of the corrugated doors, Tobias is close enough behind that he hears the surprised gasps beyond as the door almost flies off its rusty hinges, accompanied with the ear piercing scrape that seems to be common place with doors in the low habs.

"Neomi, what are y-" The familiar slithering tones of Sam are cut short as two huge unnatural bubbles warp and form from each of Neomi's hands, two long walls take shape between the door they're hovering by and one at the other end of the room, everything on the other sides of the green hued bubbles look almost comedic, the multitude of henchmen on the other side are all distorted in size and shape by the texture of the newly made bubble tunnel.

"How do you know how to do that?" Tobias gasps, dumbstruck by another amazing display of the powers that eliXir grants but pleased that at least this time people aren't dying.

"I'll explain later, let's go!" she grabs his wrist like a child once more and pulls him through the narrow tunnel she has made, pulling his remaining arm close to his body, terrified he might accidently graze the bubble walls and lose a digit or worse.

"Don't burst my bubble guys and don't follow us!" She shouts behind her as she kicks open the door at the end of the tunnel and within an instant they are back into the barrens of the low habitats.

Chapter 15

Neomi doesn't relent once they break into the open air of the low habitats, only turning briefly to throw out her hands at the opening they just left, hundreds of small acidic bubbles float towards the door and form a cross hatched mesh before stopping still.

"Follow me" she lightly commands, before sprinting down the street seemingly carefree. Tobias chases after her, eager not to be left behind. They bound down street after street and into narrower alley's, Tobias spares little time to take in the sights, but he is glad that for the most part there aren't many people around, no one to report back to Dr. Lorenz where they are heading. He opens his mouth to ask if everyone is asleep but quickly shuts it, partly realising he has no idea what time of day it is down here but also as he struggles to find the breath for questions, his lungs burning for a reprieve.

They pass another corner and he notices that the buildings aren't as makeshift as they started out, that they are more well founded, not dissimilar to the fabricated habitats of the middle level. "Wait…" he pants, unsure if his lungs are going to force him to the ground before or after his aching legs. "…These living spaces…they aren't…"

It seems that the eliXir and powers haven't made Neomi immune to fatigue either, she places her hands on her knees as she bends over to catch her breath, "Aren't shit." Tobias can just about make out a cheeky grin on her face beneath all the hair flowing over it. She throws back her head and flicks it all back over her shoulders, "There is so much you don't know about the lower habitats Toby."

He isn't sure if she's talking about him personally or everyone in the middle habitats, it doesn't matter he supposes. "We should find somewhere to hide. We can't keep running forever Neomi."

She turns on the spot, taking in her surroundings, Tobias is more lost than he can possibly fathom but she seems confident and he focuses on catching his breath instead of panicking. "There," she points to a large building at the far end of the alley way, almost the last before it links back to a larger road. *Roads...* he realises he hasn't seen a single vehicle down here so why are there roads he thinks. "We can hide in there." Neomi reiterates before leading the way at a jog, he doesn't voice any complaint, thankful for even a minute at a slower pace.

The large grey building, despite being dusty and dirty, has a familiarity which should make him feel at ease he realises, but instead it just serves to confuse him. identical to any sort of industrial building that might be seen in the middle habs, small metal framed windows run along all sides of the top half of the building and a sturdy metal roof is still intact, the walls are mostly smooth plaster. As the pair get closer to the building Neomi drops to her knees.

"I...feel so tired..." He crouches down beside her, she's panting heavily and shaking her head. Anxiety lines his bushy eyebrows "Are you okay?" he manages to keep his voice somewhat steady despite the heavy gasps his lungs keep demanding.

"I'm exhausted, you'll have to help me inside, I don't think I can stand up right now," it isn't the time for questions he decides and places her arm around his shoulders, mimicking what he has seen in holo vids before, he forces his own legs past their crying reservations and gets them both to their feet and lumbering towards the entrance of the building. Sparing a wary glance around to ensure no one is watching he shuffles slowly towards the imposing metal door barring their way into the building, he quietly but firmly pushes the door open, never considering for a moment it could be locked. "Dammit. Neomi… can you?" he nods his head towards the lock.

She shakes her head, like someone trying to keep themselves alert when they should be asleep, she holds up her remaining hand, placing it shakily on the door lock, smoke begins to rise from her fingertips and small teardrops of molten metal drip from the bottom of the lock. After a few seconds her arm slumps to her side and threatens to pull both of them back to their knees.

"It's gone." She sighs, her tone resigned, the confidence drained from not only her body but her spirit. "What has gone?" He enquires as he gives the door a sturdy shove, thankful that whatever was melted was sufficient to break the lock. He takes an apprehensive step forward, the door frame not wide enough for both of them as he holds her close to diminish their form.

"The eliXir. The power. They're gone." With the last word she trips over her own feet and this time the strength of his own legs give out and they are sent sprawling all over the tiled floor of the industrial building. He straightens out a leg and gives the door a nudge closed before forcing himself to sit up, massive crates fill up the entire room, they appear to be in some kind of warehouse he thankfully realises. Neomi is shaking, sweat pouring down her face, "I need more, more eliXir, I…so weak. Tired." Tobias feels the dreaded familiarity of uselessness. "I don't have any Neomi. Rest. I'll take a look around," she nods weakly, clenching his hand in hers, without warning her body convulses for a few seconds, no sooner do they start than they end, she rolls over and vomits against the side of a crate. Tobias holds her head and settles her on her side, "Neomi?" he whispers, but there is no response and it's clear that she has passed out, he is thankful that at least her breathing is steady now.

Slouching back against a large crate, he habitually reaches into his pocket for his data slate, he finds himself once more in a state of amazement, that despite all that has happened, the handheld device is still in his pocket and safely protected by his wallet. The blue holoscreen buzzes to light, casting its glow in a small radius around him. No connection. With a tap he attempts to load up the mapping software, only to be completely unsurprised when it shows no known location for his implant. He lets out a sigh and whispers to himself, "Typical." He turns off the display once more as he stands up and warily eyes the office above him, curiosity quickly overcoming any sense of trepidation he has as he slowly but gently makes his way up the metal catwalk stairs and towards the office area, the only light comes from outside, the artificial lighting of other buildings and habs piercing through the grime soaked windows to provide at least some illumination.

He chuckles to himself as he turns the door handle, the realisation that it's the first door handle he has seen in the lower habitats he finds amusing. It creaks as it slides open but Tobias is thankful that for once a door opens without grinding against the floor. The office isn't anything exciting, a table with a computer terminal has a comfortable looking chair next to it and the rest of the room is dominated by a conference table surrounded with chairs. He slumps himself into the chair and his legs immediately reply with a thankful release of tension.

He blows off a surprisingly thin layer of dust before turning on the terminal with a small prayer to the god of electronics. The screen immediately flares to life, even with the brightness set to low it still contrasts harshly against the dark room, the familiar blue glow fills the room and he feels stupid for not noticing the light switch on the wall when he first entered. *Actually I should probably keep it dark*, he thinks as the computer finishes its maintenance cycle.

He places his data slate next to the terminal and after a few taps on the touch screen it overrides any antiquated encryption the old terminal has, the devices are quickly connected and his slate immediately starts chirping and pinging with updates from a dozen applications. He picks it up and with a swipe disregards all the updates, seconds later he is viewing the news feeds, all of them mention the events at the bank and that four people from the low habs attempted a robbery and were all apprehended and executed, each news outlet is keen to let their views on the new power laws and the Mayor known. He quickly rechecks the mapping application, a small flashing notification indicating it knows the location of his subdermal implant, but it's immediately followed by the frustrating message stating it has no maps of the area he is currently in, annoyed with the software Tobias closes it and reverts back to the news. Scouring the outlets for what feels like hours, each one has details on the powers involved, how the police and Archangels dealt with the threats, some quotes from a Sergeant Russells, but not once is his own name mentioned, despite the morass of media coverage, not one of them is displaying his picture or name. A little beacon of hope warms his insides against the biting cold of the lower habitats. If there is no record of me being there, he could return to the middle habs, he clutches to the idea as he turns off the data slate.

He turns off the terminal and rises to his feet, eager to go check on Neomi. He pauses momentarily as he spots the calendar on the wall, "Morpho Girls," the current month is an attractive woman whose body is vastly out of proportion and stretches in impossible but tantalising ways. He frowns as he notices the logo on the calendar, a hollow triangle with a three arrows pointing up and splitting. Pro Life Corp.

Chapter 16

Tobias rushes down the catwalk, any sensibility about being quiet lost in a rush to search the rest of the warehouse. He holds up his data slate and with a single swipe motion increases the illumination it provides, a blue highlight showing the crates in more detail, with the dark banished he can see clearly that each crate is marked with the same symbol as the calendar. He heads to a palette where the metallic boxes are smaller, just below his waist height. He pushes a button and the top of the crate slides open like an old shop front grill. He riffles through the crate, not really sure what he is looking for, but eager to see what the Pro Life Corp could possibly be storing down here.

He pulls out a small statuette of a woman in barely any clothing followed by another of a monkey swinging from a small tree. "Art?" He whispers confusingly. He carefully returns the statues to the crate before closing it and moving onto another, full of smaller containers he opens one to sate his curiosity, but is disappointed as it just contains tacky looking jewelry. He holds his data slate against the side of the crate. "No," he gasps, the address on the side is in the Upper Habitats.

The loud gurgling and a churning in his stomach makes him cringe and place a hand on his stomach, a stark reminder that he hasn't eaten in some time, it suddenly hits Tobias that he has no idea how long has passed, between the lack of daylight and being knocked unconscious it could have been hours or days. As he lazily presses the button on another crate, this time he has something in mind, hoping that the storage container might actually have some food inside, he quickly flashes his attention to his data slate, wincing slightly to stop the brightness blinding him. 7:34pm, no wonder his stomach is rumbling, he thinks, mourning his loss of lunch and now dinner.

A crack and a snap make a short sharp echo in the warehouse as Tobias drops his dataslate onto the solid plasteel floor. His eyes fixated on the crate he just opened, small clear plastic boxes containing row after row of glass vials, their distinct yellow glow lighting his face in the dark. Before today he'd never seen a single vial of eliXir outside of the news casts and now here he was, face to face with dozens. He gently opens a box and holds up one of the vials in front of him, it looks so harmless, even pretty in a way he thinks. A simple vial with an auto injector and small label. A Pro Life Corp label. He can't believe such a little thing can cause so much harm, so much destruction, he shakes his head in disbelief, even a few days ago he wouldn't have believed it but now he is seeing it first-hand.

Lost in his own thoughts he panics when he hears a sudden shuffle and groan from nearby. He stuffs the vial into his pocket and runs back to Neomi. They almost completely crash into each other as he rushes around the corner of a pallet, she is leaning heavily against a large crate and Tobias is pretty sure she would collapse if not for the support, her hair is soaked, he places a hand on her shoulder, clammy and damp, she looks more fatigued than anyone he's ever met. "You should be resting," he offers but she barely notices him, her eyes transfixed over his shoulder.

"Are you okay?" He asks confusedly, she brushes his hand off her shoulder and takes a strained series of steps forward as he moves out of the way.

"Shit. Shit. Shit. Yes! What-" she cuts herself short as she continues towards the crate and the obvious realisation hits Tobias, *the eliXir vials.*

"I've never seen so much before," she exclaims, the yellow glow from the crate revealing a look of pure joy partially hidden by her disheveled hair.

He gently calls to her "Neomi, you shouldn't, I'm not sure it's a good idea in -"

Her head twists quickly and the joy is gone in a flash, replaced with a vicious look which makes Tobias take a single step back. "You don't know what it's like. You don't even know what this is worth do you middler?" He hadn't heard the term before but the tone made it clear it wasn't complimentary. "This isn't the shit you find all over place down here, this isn't cut, muddled, diluted. This is pure eliXir. This is what they were going to make you into," she is speaking quickly, sucking rapid breaths in her excitement. "Selling just one vial of this in the upper habs would mean you would never have to work again in the mid. You get that, right?!" She looks back at the crate holding up one of the plastic boxes with three vials inside.

In an instant she places it back and throws herself back from the crate, slumping on her behind with her hands supporting her back. "This was made by Lorenz, that's the company he works for. His patrols must circulate around here, shit, if anyone finds us here they'll report it back to him. We have to go Toby. Now."

"You can barely stand," he interjects, taking a few cautious steps towards her. He wants to help her up, but can't stop feeling like he is approaching a cornered animal. "I don't know how far we'll get in your condition, you need more rest."

A ringing of metal crashing against metal causes the pair to jump, Neomi is on her feet first, her hand reaching into the crate and grasping one of the boxes. Tobias' flight instinct reacts rapidly and he clasps his hand around one of Neomi's wrists and he whispers hurriedly "Come on!" He pulls her in the opposite direction of the sound, too weak to resist or argue she allows herself to be dragged along by one hand, clutching the box close to her chest with the other.

The pair hasten through the aisles, Tobias straining to support Neomi's weight and maintain a sense of quiet. He can just about make out the sounds of voices coming from behind them, there is definitely more than one person talking, but more than that he can't tell.

"We should go back, get it all Toby." Neomi whispers, her voice strained and weak but he is thankful she at least manages a modicum of quiet.

"We can't, we have to go, if they catch us they'll kill us both," he doesn't stop to entertain her, keeping them moving and hoping to find another exit in the maze of crates.

"They wouldn't stand a chance against me if I used one of these," she looks down at the glowing yellow container clutched to her chest.

"No, you can't, you're in no condition for more and we need to be quiet." He tries to sound authoritative but realises he has no idea what taking another vial would do to her and similarly has no idea how to sound authoritative. He clasps the singular vial in his own pocket, his mind screams for him to throw it away, that it will only lead to suffering, but he clutches it all the same.

They turn another corner and the light at the end of the tunnel makes itself known, a simple blue door with a push lever is all that stands behind them and escape. Neomi bends over double and coughs hard, the sound pierced by a sharp shattering. "NO!" She screams before hacking out a mouthful of curdled blood. "No, no, no , no." She murmurs over and over whilst running her hands through the quickly thinning yellow liquid, the vials she was carrying are shattered all over the warehouse floor, she was completely ignorant to the glass shards shredding her fingers and mixing blood to the tincture.

"We have to go Neomi! Come on!" He begs. "They're coming, we have to go, now!" He looks at the door, a crack of light creeping from the bottom calling too him.

"We can go back! Get more, fuck them Toby, let's go back." She looks at him with wide eyes and clenched teeth, a volatile mix of desperation and fury.

He swallows firmly and deliberately, grabbing her arms and pulling her upwards before turning towards the door at a run. He ignores her cries and her furious swearing, straining as she flails at his arm with her remaining hand, his focus solely on the door and freedom, vowing to save her as she did him.

His resolution for freedom stronger than ever, he raises a foot and kicks the bar to send the door sprawling open. The cold wind bites against his skin but he is thankful for the second wind it brings with it. Neomi's flailing subsides and he spares a look back at her before they pour out into the street, tears stream down her face, her eyes drooped with exhaustion.

Remembering the alley ways of the mid habs and how their

labyrinthine ways saved him once so far so he places his trust in them again as the pair plunge further. Leaving behind the main road and hopefully their pursuers, he rolls the vial in his pocket between his fingertips and decides it best not to tell Neomi. Not now.

Chapter 17

They bound from alley to alley until they reach a junction which appears to break out onto some sort of street, Neomi collapses immediately against the wall and it's clear to Tobias that she won't be going any further for a little while. The throbbing in his legs remind him that he isn't sure he has much left in him either, he finds it amazing that Neomi managed it this far after the state she was in.

He slides his hands into his pockets as he turns to his side, eager to avoid the glares coming from the panting woman opposite him. He is surprised at the amount of people walking up and down the road, their clothes dusty but in relatively good condition, the smell of food wafting from somewhere sends his stomach into cramps and he clenches his jaw in a futile effort to stymie the hunger. His legs quiver from the exhaustion, but he shuffles himself slightly closer to the corner of the junction.

He frowns as he looks left and right, not quite able to fully comprehend exactly what he's seeing. Like the warehouse, the buildings here aren't hand built ramshackle rooms like some favela, but instead they are plain concrete squares, each one almost identical to the next. *They're identical to the houses in the mid habs,* he realises.

"Those housing units," he points and Neomi slowly raises her head from where her chin was slumping on her chest as he continues, "These are identical to the middle habs, Samuel said most of the things down here were made from things abandoned from above, but there is no way these were built like that." He quickly withdraws his hand so as to not attract any attention from passersby.

Neomi gives a weak smile that only touches one side of her mouth and certainly doesn't reach her eyes. "Samuel talks a lot of shit." She hacks violently and Tobias reaches to see if she's okay but she waves him aside "It's not all like that down here, it's a big place, what you saw were the slums, where the low habs have expanded outwards and most people don't want to go there. You'd probably find most of life down here is pretty similar to what you know Toby. People own shops, they trade, they live. They are just as scared of eliXir as you are. It's why Lorenz does what he does outside of the main housing, if he did it here he'd be driven out. We don't have your private police or fancy Archangels, but the people here aren't beyond driving someone out into the dark beyond. It's why Lorenz surrounds himself with muscled idiots, he needs the protection." She lets out a light laugh and at least this one warms her blue eyes, she purses her lower lip and looks at him like someone would a child who just got an obvious question wrong. "You really have no idea what it's like down here do you? Is everyone so clueless about down here?" for a moment, incredulity straightens his back before it fades as quickly as it arose and he avoids eyes contact, feeling like a child who has been scolded, "You are right. We don't really know what it's like down here. The news casts tell us down here is an eliXir fueled storm of chaos and destruction. That soon the Archangels and the military will come and put an end to it all. We are told that if we suspect we've seen someone from the lower habs that we report it to the authorities immediately. It isn't just me Neomi, no one I've ever met has a clue what it's like down here. How could they?" The question lingers, neither of them having a suitable answer.

"There is some good news." Tobias leans forward excitedly, his smile cracking the dirt on his face. "While you were recovering in the warehouse, I found a connection and checked the newscasts from home, the reports don't have any pictures of me or mention me by name, there is no record of me being at the incident. Once we get up to the mid habs we should be fine. So…" he shuffles awkwardly "How do we get up there?" he points upwards as if gesturing to the sky.

Neomi shrugs "I don't know. The reason no one from-" she mimics his pointing with a cheeky smile "-from up there polices down here is because it doesn't really matter does it? We can't get up, therefore it doesn't matter what we do down here. Ignorance is bliss."

"But the bank robbers from earlier, the reason why I'm down here, they got up there somehow right? They were from down here and got up." he asks, Neomi unexpectedly moves to takes his hand in hers, he releases the vial he forgot he was clutching and takes her hand.

"Promise me Toby, promise me you'll take me up with you." All the earlier frustration and fury is lost from her eyes and is replaced with sad desperation, but she doesn't let go of his hand

Without pausing he calmly replies "I promise." A tear runs down her cheek as she smiles at him, despite the physical exertion marring her features there is no doubt about her beauty and he feels like in this moment he would promise her anything.

The smile from her face slowly fades and she withdraws her hand "Have you even for a moment thought about what it would be like? To have powers?" She looks down at the floor avoiding eye contact, trying to avoid any potential judgement that might be in his eyes.

Tobias is taken back by the question and sudden change in topic. "I… I don't. Well, we're all shown the newscasts, what happened in Russia. How could anyone want that?" The words come out more harshly than he intended and he immediately wishes he'd phrased it differently.

"How could anyone want it?" In an instant the fury is back in her features and if he wasn't leaning against the wall, Tobias was fairly sure he'd have been pushed back.

"Want what?" Neomi spits in anger, "The power to take back your life? You never been bullied by someone stronger than you? Someone who has the power. Can you look me in the eye and say you've never once wished that for once the tables were turned? That you could have the power?!"

He shies away from her for an instant and looks out into the street, people are looking in their direction but none of them seem particularly bothered. He turns back to her, her purple hair matted with dirt, clothes torn and muddied, whilst he imagines he doesn't exactly look much better right now it made his reply escape from his lips before he could rein it in "Do I wish I could have power? Maybe. Maybe on a dark day I've wondered, what it would be like. But look at you, where has having power gotten you?" His heart isn't in the rebuttal and he feels like a hypocrite as he rolls the vial around in his pocket, the smooth glass rocking between his fingers as he lets his mind wonder what it must feel like to be in control.

Chapter 18

"We don't all have the luxury of fucking choosing." The fire in her eyes threatens to burn through Tobias's skull and he finds himself straining to find a semblance of words that might make things better, but it's futile and Neomi shows no sign of relenting, "Not everyone has a nice easy job and government stipend, some of us down here are offered one choice. Take a hit and see what you get and hope that what you get can be used to help someone else for money. Dealers like Lorenz are more than happy to help you for a while, get you addicted like this." She holds out a quivering hand, "Addicted to the power. No one down here can afford the pure stuff, so of course we get hooked."

She rises to her feet and for a moment he flinches, worried that he might be about to get struck but instead she surprises him by offering an open hand, some of her strength having seemingly returned.

"Let's move. We've stayed here long enough, besides, we need to get up to your cosy middle habitats right?" She offers a small smile but despite it feeling warm and genuine, he declines, despite wanting to take it, he places his hands behind him and forces himself up from the wall. "Tell me about your life up there Toby. What's it like?"

Awkwardness washes over Tobias as the pair now casually walk down the street together, he finds it hard not to be amazed by the similarities between here and the middle habs, the construction style, the infrastructure. The frivolities are gone, there aren't neon lights advertising a thousand different products with half naked people, but there are masses of small shops and residential buildings. "Toby?" Neomi looks over at him with genuine concern.

"Sorry, I was thinking about something else. My life in the middle? Well I have a job that is quite menial but pays well, the bank that was robbed I mentioned earlier, that was where I worked. Work." He stumbles to correct himself before continuing "I live in a government provided house but I have spent some credits on small comforts. You'll like it there, we will tell the government you've moved from another district, they'll help set you up with work and a place to live. You can always live with me whilst we wait for administration," he almost trips over his own feet and he is glad his face is dirtied to hide his glowering red complexion, embarrassed by what he's offered, and not sure if it's because of where she's from or because of how pretty she is. He's almost thankful when she seemingly doesn't notice his awkwardness.

"What about friends and family?" They turn a corner down a street and Tobias finds himself hoping Neomi has a destination in mind as he's lost in a way that would make almost anyone feel nervous and uncomfortable.

He shrugs his shoulders before replying, he tries putting on a brave face of nonchalance as he recalls what normally makes people uncomfortable, but recent events make it more difficult than he's used too, "No family, my parents died when I was a young teenager, some kind of transport accident, I don't really know all the details, I didn't want to know back then and as time passed it just became less relevant. I was an only child and not really social before they died and I shielded myself even more as I got older." He found himself surprised at the openness and willingness to open up right now, but given the frequency of near death experiences in the last god knows how many hours, keeping things to himself seemed pointless. "I had a friend from work, Elliot. He was a good guy, we would sometimes meet up if he wasn't busy with his family." He chokes back the feeling in his throat, the feeling that he just wants to collapse on to his knees and cry, the pain is written all over his face however and Neomi can't help but notice it.

"What happened to him?" she gently asks.

"He died this morning during the robbery at the bank. At least I think it was this morning." He reaches into his pocket for his dataslate to check the time, frustrated at himself for forgetting so soon his best friend's death, but Neomi places a hand on his wrists "Not here, data slates aren't that common, you'd draw attention." She removes her hand and coyly adds, "Sorry."

Eager to change the topic, Neomi continues, "Our experiences of the government are so different. To you they seem like a supportive big brother, someone who looks after you and makes sure you're okay. Down here, we don't know them, they've long ago abandoned us, we feel the remnants of their establishment, we live in them. But apart from the occasional raid from above all we know of them is that they make sure we stay here, that for whatever reason they want us here and we can't change that. Sam was saying that some guy up there is threatening to come down and sort out all the drug users."

Tobias gently nods, "The laws have recently changed. Anyone found to be using or having used eliXir is to be immediately put to death as a danger to all life." He rotes off almost directly some information from the reminders the government has been putting out.

"Do you think that applies to the upper habs?" She chuckles, almost tauntingly and Tobias realises he had never once considered it, the government had said this was a new law and that it would be enforced, he just assumed it would be country wide. *Hell*, he thinks, *until this morning I didn't even know there two types of eliXir.*

She laughs again, "You look cute when you're having revelations and culture shocks." With that the inevitable flares of embarrassment light up once more and he's convinced he must be visible from anywhere in the low habs.

He smiles for what feels like the first time in days and at least a small amount of fatigue fades with it. Emboldened and eager to dispel the sensation of aimless wandering he asks "So, what is the plan exactly? You seem confident you know where you are going."

She runs her fingers through her hair, the gesture sending a small cloud of dust behind them but giving her an air of confidence that Tobias wishes he could project. A wry smile lines her face and she looks as mischievous as anyone he's ever met. "It's simple Toby, we are going to take the lift."

Chapter 19

"Wait," he asks, placing a hand on her upper arm, her skin surprisingly soft despite the dirt that seemed to be everywhere in the lower habs, "What do you mean, 'Take the lift'? There is a lift to the middle habs all along!?" He struggles to contain his anticipation and excitement at a potential route back to his normal life.

The pair seem almost brazen now, a new urgency providing fuel for their fire, even Neomi seems to have shaken off her fatigue and is walking with haste down the progressively busier streets. "Sure, how do you think the people that built this place got out? How do you think Lorenz and the other chop shop runners get their pure eliXir to the upper habs? This isn't the only city in the low habs either, ya know? For every sector you have up in the middle habs there are one or more cities like this one." She talks with her head to the side as Tobias struggles to keep pace.

"I guess…I never really gave it any thought, I haven't had a lot of time for thinking things through as of late," he walks quickly but with his hands in his pockets, shoulders withdrawn to try and avoid bringing any attention to himself. "So if these lifts are common knowledge why don't more people use them?" even to Tobias it seemed obvious there had to be a catch, some reason that floods of people from the lower habs didn't use them.

As they turn another corner in the street, he notices this one has a shop selling repaired and renewed electrical products, but his breath is taken away when he sees the tall metallic shaft whose top disappears into the darkness above. He gently shakes his head in disbelief as Neomi points at the structure, "The lift, the one in this section anyway, is controlled by Lorenz and his thugs, there is always a couple of his people making sure no one goes near the lift without him present and those guards always have eliXir on them. In all the time I've been here no one has even attempted to use the lift." Tobias is amazed at how flippant she sounds, he feels once more like a child asking obvious questions and completely out of his depth of understanding.

"Are the guards that threatening?" he rubs his eyes to try but is instantly reminded of the state of his hands as eyes sting in protest.

"Not entirely." she shrugs, "But think about it Tobias, what is your destination? The middle habs, so when those lift doors open what do you think we're going to see? It won't be an exciting lightshow, it will be police with DNA Scanners and orders to arrest anyone on site."

"Actually the Mayor announced new laws under immediate effect, anyone who scans positive for eliXir use is to be terminated." The correctional reminder causes an awkward silence for a minute as the pair walk side by side without a word passing. Tobias lets his eyes and mind wander, still completely bemused that there aren't advertisements broadcast everywhere, that the constant barrage of lights and sound are completely absent here. He'd never even considered that down here there wouldn't be a need for an implant to direct them. "Wait. So if Lorenz controls the lift from here and the police are at the exits, how does he get his drugs out at all?"

"Bribes mostly. Most of the police on the lift are there either because they are the bottom of the food chain or because they're corrupt as fuck. Lorenz pays them well to look the other way when he's making a shipment. It's all one big shit trickle." She laughs at her own profanity, "Lorenz pays from the bottom up, he pays the grunts to look the other way. But the uppers, they pay downwards, the commissioners, politicians, police, they're all paid to ignore the bribes, ignore the drug mules. That's my understanding anyway." She shrugs her shoulders, acknowledging that this is the natural order of things.

His views on authority being cracked away, he can't help his curiosity being piqued as he keeps probing for more information "How does he pay for the bribes? No offense, but it doesn't look like there is much wealth down here," he winces at the end and watches Neomi warily, she smiles at him, her eyes warm, but he can't help but feel like she's looking down on him.

"The eliXir you saw me using earlier, it's not pure. It lacks," she pauses and pokes him playfully in the stomach, but he can't bring himself to smile given the implications "the human component. What I was using, it's mixed and blended with a host of other stuff. Gives a shorter hit and some nasty side effects. The pure stuff back in the warehouse, that wouldn't have side effects and the powers could last for a longer duration. Just one vial is worth millions, that one little box could have set us up for life in the middle Toby." Her smile quickly fades and her eyes look vacantly into the distance, almost as if someone just flicked a switch and turned her off.

"That's why Lorenz got so excited by me I guess, he kept saying how perfect I was. Why me though? Surely there are plenty of people down here who would make an easier target?"

"Hardly anyone down here is pure, everyone has taken a hit at some point or is born of someone who has. The further down in generations we go the harder it is to find someone. I hear rumours occasionally that someone from the mid habs is kidnapped and bought down here and… well, ya know? The people at the top don't care who dies to make their drug, hell they probably just see the middle habs as a biological farm." Once again Tobias finds himself alarmed by how nonchalant Neomi seems about all of this.

"I'm sure if that was the case someone would say something or do something. My home isn't just a breeding ground for drug farms." He scoffs at the idea and Neomi looks at him sideways before continuing, "Check your data slate then, has anyone said anything or done anything to come and find you?" The demand hits him hard, the only people who might be looking for him are the Archangels, he's ashamed that he has no friends or family who will come looking for him and ashamed to admit she's right, even if he had someone who cared, no one would come down here to look for him.

"Fine. You're right." He begrudgingly states as they march closer and closer towards the spire in the distance.

"Ignorance is bliss Toby. As long as it's only a few people, no one in the middle habs complains. As long as the eliXir flows down here and no one meddles with us, no one complains down here and as long as pure eliXir keeps making its way to the upper habs, no one complains up there. A nice cycle of corruption and compliant non-interference." He feels his blood boiling, not so much at having his views shaken or being wrong, but at the frustration of being powerless and insignificant. He rolls the vial in his pocket around between his fingers once more and can't help but feel tempted to lash out, he pauses as they walk past an open yard area, kids all playing on makeshift playground equipment. The sight stops him dead in his steps, a sight so normal, so innocent.

"We have schools and kids down here as well ya know?" She nudges him with her elbow trying to break his sudden stupor. "It's not much further now Toby, come on."

Chapter 20

"Fucking reporters," he curses under his breath as he stomps through the station hallways, his heavy formal boots announcing each step as a mass of other officers are talking to civilians, filing reports and generally going about their business.

Russells reaches the end of the main hub of the station, internally debating whether to go back to the bank or not. On the one hand he knows he should get back there, support his squad and get things back to normal as soon as possible, but the nagging voice at the back of the mind, it's all too familiar and it has gotten him into trouble more times than he can count. The voice of doing what he feels is right.

He curls his right hand into a fist, partially to keep the fatigue at bay and stop his head from pounding at his sanity, but mostly in frustration at himself. He proceeds purposefully and quickly through the corridors of the station until he's eventually in a long thin corridor with a dozen closed doors on each side. It's quieter here, the civilians and chaos of the main precinct now behind him, he is thankful for the calm. He continues until he reaches a door simply labelled "Tech" and thrusts it open.

He hides his satisfaction and smile at making the single technician inside almost throw everything across the table in the process of nearly falling out of her chair.

"Fuck. You scared the shit out of me Sergeant." A scruffy woman spins around in her chair, her hair is a chestnut mess, there is no order to the woman at all that Russells could make out, her clothes are a mishmashed mess of colour and logos, one of her eyes had a twinkle in it which Russells knew well enough was an expensive tech implant, what its purpose was he wasn't sure, technology was never really his forté

"Sorry Mel, I can't help myself. Someone has to come along and remind you there is a world outside this room every so often." He smiled, Melissa had been in this precinct when he was assigned here and despite rarely leaving her room, he always made an effort to visit every so often to check in.

"Was that a joke Sergeant? Did your recent engagement at the bank shake the stick out of your ass?" She laughed loudly at her own joke but quickly turned pink with embarrassment when she let out a snort. "Erm.. anyway, I see more of the world that you could imagine Russells." She swivels back around in her chair to turn her attention back to vast array of screens and holo read outs. "Is this a social visit or is there something I can do for you?"

He knew she didn't mean it in a blunt manner, that it was just her way, he supposed he was pleased someone didn't sugar coat anything and cut right to the chase. "A little of both if I'm honest. I don't know what you've picked up so far but earlier during the engagement at Future Plus Bank, the scanner Officer Barker had, it was acting up, I'm just wondering if you've ever heard about anything similar." Russells wished he'd thought this through, he should have brought the scanner with him, it would have been difficult to persuade the Captain but it would have been better to have it here for Melissa to check over.

She half turns in her chair and talks over her shoulder at him "What do you mean, acting up? I know you lot aren't the most tech savvy but do you have anything more to go on than 'acting up'?" She has a smirk on her face, anyone else might have thought she was being rude but Russells had known Mel long enough to know she was just poking fun at him.

"Well. It scanned a man at the bank as positive three times, but it kept showing incomplete scan." He was frustrated that this was the best account he could give, but it would have to do for now.

"That certainly doesn't sound right Sergeant. Do you have the unit? I could take a look at it now if you want, it shouldn't be possible for a scanner to show as incomplete and still give a positive." Her eyebrows were curled in concern but there was an inquisitive look in her eyes.

"Regrettably, I don't, if I can get it off the Captain do you think you could take a look? As a personal favour." He didn't like adding the last bit, he wasn't a fan of owing people favours, but it wouldn't be right to deceive Mel into thinking this was an official request.

"It's hard to say no to you with your head all bashed up like that!" a cheeky smile flashed across her face before she returns to facing the monitors. "Wait a minute." The words almost slurred into one, "This guy?"

She points towards a screen and one of the larger monitors flickers to a camera feed from the bank, he could clearly see himself and Officer Barker standing next to the lanky man from the bank.

"That's the one, we were scanning him just before everything started going wrong. Well before things went from bad to worse at any rate." He begrudgingly admits. A series of light tuts come from the woman as she flicks her tongue against the roof of her mouth.

Another monitor twitches to a feed from a darkened warehouse. "The Captain came in earlier, asked me to cross check any data I could scrub from the low habs with recognition software. No reason, no explanation, gave me the profile of…" she doesn't adjust her body to look at a different screen and he understands that means she is using her internal implant, "Tobias Barton, 32 years old, Future Plus Bank employee." She spins her chair to face him, her optics making her eye faintly glow blue, "Currently missing in the low habs."

Russells frowned, *why would the Captain bring this personally to Mel and not tell me as the officer in charge.* It bothered him far more than he would like. Mel interrupts his chain of thought to continue, "This feed from the warehouse is the last data I could find from the lower habs at the moment. It's not like there is a lot of tech left down there and it's a miracle any of it functions and broadcasts up here. Actually, that said, the feed is surprisingly good quality."

"Tobias Barton, that name sounds so familiar, do you think you could play back what you have for me Mel?" He leans forward, inspecting the footage as it rewinds and plays. He watches as Tobias rustles around the warehouse, he goes out of sight a lot and there isn't much really to see, but he realises that Mel is right, the feed is exceptional quality given the location. "Could you zoom in on a crate? See what those markings are?" she nods softly and a few seconds later the feed pauses and zooms in on one of the metal containers. He jerks in surprise "That's the Pro Life branding, do they all have that?" The feed snaps to different crates, each one labelled the same.

"What the fuck. Why would there be a load of Pro Life containers down in the low habs? Stolen maybe?" Mel looks to him for answers, but he doesn't have one that makes sense right now.

"Not likely, a shipment of that size missing from here would be noticed and reported for sure." He stands tall and for a split second dizziness wobbles his feet, he grabs the top of Mel's chair and reassuringly states "I'm going to see the Captain about this, thank you for your help Mel, I'll see you soon with that faulty scanner."

"Take care Sergeant," she mocks a military salute and laughs as she turns back to her own business.

He closes the door gently behind him, not wanting to make the poor girl jump twice in one visit. His mind is a mess of ideas and theories about what is going on, but nothing seems to make much sense right now. With his thoughts a whirlwind of confusion, his head spinning in the mix he is surprised to see he has absent mindedly walked into the locker room, he collapses onto a bench, his head clangs against the front of a locker sending a wave of pain through his head alongside the instant regret, he closes his eyes as he tries to make sense of what he has seen today.

"Sarge?" the voice rings in the distance as he feels a gentle tapping slap against his cheek. "You okay?" He groggily opens his eyes and realises what has happened, jumping up with urgency as the young officer in front of him bounces backwards in surprise.

"Shit," he mutters, cursing the loss of time combined with the lack of dignity and bad role modelling he's displayed. There was no time to think on that, he taps the officer on the shoulder, he doesn't know the man's name, not part of his unit, but nevertheless he's thankful someone thought to wake him up. "I'm fine officer, thank you," with that he surges out of the locker room with renewed vigour.

He knows the captain is still going to be furious with him and now isn't a good time to be demanding information, but he grunts as he knows there is no alternative, he needs to know what is going on with someone involved with his case.

It isn't long before he's standing for the third time today in front of the Captains office, he wraps his knuckles on the door and waits for the deep chesty "Come in," before entering his superiors office.

The Captain is still plumply sat behind his desk, the scanner hasn't moved since he was in here a little while ago. "I was hoping not to be seeing you again so soon Sergeant," it was rude and disrespectful but he ignored it, now wasn't the time to rise to his pettiness.

"Sir," he nodded respectfully, hoping that by ignoring the obvious goading it might frustrate the Captain at least a little. "I would like to know why I wasn't informed that a person of interest was still alive from First Plus Bank and that you are having him tracked." It was as formal as he could manage and he tried his best to keep the accusatory tone out of his voice.

The Captain sighed and growled, to a lower ranking noobie it might sound intimidating but Russells stood his ground. "I was asked from the higher up's to keep a track on the man, I wasn't told why, just told to keep an eye on him and keep the uppers informed of any news. Now let it go." He waved dismissively.

"There are crates in the lower habs with Pro Life Corp markings on, do you know that? Is that who is asking for this information?" He catches himself and stands back to attention, the frustration boiling within and threatening to spill out.

"Of course I know, who do you think is asking me to make sure that warehouse is safe?" he stammers and shifts in his chair.

"We aren't their personal army. Captain." He quickly adds the rank at the end, trying to keep the man on the defensive and not feed him an excuse to admonish him.

"You must have heard the old fucking phrase, 'Don't bite the hand that feeds' Sergeant? The police force was privatised years ago, you might not bloody like it, you might not agree with it, but all that fancy tech and weaponry you've got, who do you think pays for it? Who do you think pays YOU?" He points a fat finger levelled at Russells chest. He wasn't ignorant to the level of Pro Life Corp's involvement with the police, that his argument about being a personal army was naive and wistful.

Before he can reply the Captain kicks out the chair in front of Russells, it scrapes against the floor before stopping in front of him. "Sit down you moron, it's not like it matters now anyway. The robbery at First Plus is exactly the catalyst that the Mayor was looking for. The military with support from the Archangels will be going down to the lower habitats later today."

Russells slumps into the seat, the statement hitting him in the chest like a brick. "What? All for one man? That makes no sense. Why are they going down there Captain?" any frustration or fury was lost from his tone, replaced with concern and uncertainty.

The Captain curls his upper lip into a nasty smirk, "The Mayor in his infinite wisdom has decided that it's good politics to reboot the lower habitat in this sector.

The word hung in the air, the implications wild and unbelievable. *Reboot.*

Chapter 21

"What does that even mean Captain? Reboot?!" Russells hands firmly grip the cold metal arms of the chair, his knuckles white with the pressure.

"You aren't that stupid Sergeant. Over 50% of the people in the lower habitats are or have been users of eliXir. The Mayor has decided to no longer ignore this and with immediate effect implement the new law down there for the wellbeing of everyone in this sector." he looks almost bored by the conversation, Russells is astounded at the man's nonchalance about what is essentially a massive scale extermination

"The law? When have the laws here ever been enforced down there? This isn't some minor exercise Captain, you're talking about mass murder, thousands of people being killed without trial, without rights. How can you sit back and be okay with this?!" He is well aware he's on the brink of shouting, on the very edge of losing his temper.

"Yes Sergeant," he spits back, "The law. The laws you are sworn as an officer to enforce and obey. If you don't like it you can tender your resignation right here and I'll gladly accept it," his yellow teeth are bared in a part snarl and part smirk, Russells wants nothing more than to punch him right in the face.

"Whose laws Captain? The laws of the people?! Have the people decided they want to see thousands of dead so they can feel safer? I know I must have missed that fucking vote." He usually tries harder to avoid swearing, especially to his superior officer, but his anger is spilling over and it is the best he could do to contain it to just this. "I'm sure Pro Life Corp are *very* eager to see their investments protected, cleaning their own tracks at the sake of thousands of lives." The smile drops in an instant from the Captains face, his jaw clenches and eyes widen, Russells knew the look all too well. "I wonder how *the people* would react if they found out that Pro Life Corp was still actively using the Lower Habs? What's in that warehouse Captain?" he pushes, partially from frustration but hoping for answers.

"Listen here." the other man growls, his hands balled into fists resting on the table, "What do you want me to do here Russells? Go against the government? Against Pro Life Corp? So you've seen that Pro Life hasn't abandoned the lower habs, so what? Who the fuck even cares? But how do you expect this to go exactly Sergeant? You're pissed at me for not standing up, but if I do I'll be down in the lower habitats quicker than you can blink and no one will bat an eyelid, go on, why don't you do something? There are plenty of vultures on the front doorstep, they'll lap this story up like they always do. See where you end up by the close of the day." The tirade was over and the challenge laid bare right there in front of him.

Russells felt ripped in two, he knew the Captain was right. If he went and spoke to the assembled press outside he'd lose his job and would be missing by the end of the day. He'd heard about it happening in the past, officers sent on lift duty or too another sector, never to be heard from again. *Damn, there were probably half the men in his own squad who wouldn't hesitate to act on the order if it was given.* The futility shook him to the core, it was the right thing to do, what other choice did he have? His police instincts weigh in heavily, he has no evidence of any of this. He can't just go out there and accuse the biggest corporation in the world of… of what? He realises. Legally they haven't done anything wrong and he has no evidence of anything going on in the lower habitats.

The rift he was feeling inside himself must have been clear and he lost sense of how many seconds had passed since the Captain finished speaking. "Sergeant. I know this must be difficult for you. It isn't easy for me either. The military are already on their way. They'll be leading operations below and creating cordons and road blocks up here in case anyone tries to escape via the chutes. You want to do something good? The only bloody thing you can do now is head to the lift or the chutes, try and minimise the collateral damage, because believe me Sergeant, when this starts there will be plenty." With that he pulled out a packet from his pocket and took out a half smoked stick, placing it in his mouth before lighting it, puffing smoke through his nostrils out onto the table. "Whatever you decide Sergeant. I suggest you do it quickly," with the dismissal he leans back in his chair, there was clearly no moral debate raging inside him and it made Russells so incredibly disappointed.

Russells pushes himself up from the chair without a word, it might be the last time he sees his superior officer, but he has nothing left to say to him, not a kind parting word. He resolutely heads back to the changing room, methodically replacing the formal parts of his uniform with tactical pieces, after replacing his headset and display he heads to the armoury and replenishes his magazines with little fuss. He storms through the station like a whirlwind of pure authority, buffeting the door to the Tech office once more, there is no smile or banter when Melissa jolts in her chair.

Rotating the chair to face him the look on his face is sufficient for her to know that this isn't a social visit. "What is it Sergeant? What did the Captain say?" Her questions fire out in quick measure and there is a sense of worry in her tone.

"Nothing good, I need you to be my eyes and ears Mel, there is about to be a lot of activity in the low habs and the exits. I need you to keep me up to date with the situations where I can't be. Can you do that?"

"Most the tech down there is ravaged Sarge." She stammers for an excuse before acknowledging the stern look on his face. "I'll do my best. What the hell is going on? I've got data feeds of a large military presence in the sector and that the Mayor is going to be making an announcement shortly?" Worry creases her face and makes her look younger, like a terrified child. He feels the urge pulling at him to stop and explain, to ease her fears, it pains him that he cannot, that he simply doesn't have time.

"Your best is all I can ask Mel, thank you," he nods curtly and she closes her eyes and returns the gesture.

"I'll keep an eye out for you," she smirks and taps the side of her temple and one of hers lets out a twinkle as her implant activates. "Where are you going anyway?"

He grits his teeth and turns to leave. "I'm going to be on the damned front line of a war."

Chapter 22

"It's really amazing, I had no idea such a thing existed, never even contemplated it." Tobias whispers, his neck craned as he peers up at the spire leading into the darkness. Now that they are closer he is surprised at how large it is. "It's not just tall, look how wide it is, you could fit a huge amount of people and equipment in there."

Neomi sighs as she rustles her hands through her hair, trying to dust off the grime and dirt she's accumulated during the day "How do you think half of this stuff got down here Toby? They didn't just dig a hole and then drop it all down here, there has always been access down here, just no one up there has been allowed to use it for generations." she shakes her body vigorously and Tobias has to stymie a cough as a cloud of dust envelopes them. "Right, off I go then." she takes a confident step forward and Tobias quickly grabs her wrist and pulls her back around the corner they were hiding

"Wait. What are you doing?" he peaks around the corner quickly, the large plated door looks intimidating enough with the cameras and sensors attached to it, even more so with the four large brutes formed up beside it, two are leaning against the door whilst the other two are clearly smoking something, occasional blooms of smoke rising from their forms. "You can't just stroll over there, what are you going to say? What are you going to do? We need a plan or something." he spurts out the questions one after another, whilst he has been mostly happy for Neomi to lead the way and guide him, he still can't shake the frustration of feeling powerless.

"I have a plan. By now we must have lost the people following us and have a good lead, they'll have to check the area slowly and will probably think we're hiding somewhere. Also, I doubt anything about us has made it this far yet, so I'm going to go over there, flirt a little and tell those guys we've got orders from Lorenz to go up and receive some a new erm…" she looked at him, his blood turned cold and he knew completely what she meant. Someone from the middle habs. Someone kidnapped, desperate or deceived who was going to be sent down here and used as a component in a drug. It sickens him more than anything he could imagine. "Erm…yeah, a person." she continues, knowing he understands and obviously not wanting to elaborate, "Hopefully that'll work."

"What about me? Why would I be doing with you?" His tone wasn't desperate but he wanted to make sure he wasn't going to be left behind, although he almost immediately realises she can't very well do much in the middle habs without him. He hoped.

Neomi hums and pauses for a few seconds before replying, the improvisational nature of her plan not doing anything to ease Tobias' nerves. She looks him up and down "No, you can't be my bodyguard." she smirks at her own humour but he can't help but feel at least a little offended. "Maybe," she continues "You can my motivator," she nods seemingly happy with her plan.

"Your what? Motivator? How would that make any sense Neomi.

You're going to tell those four muscle freaks that I'm here to keep you motivated and happy? That's more insane than me being your bodyguard," he chuckles at the ridiculousness of the suggestion before she fires back.

"Like Samuel. Muscles and Motivators. That's what Lorenz calls them. If one fails the other always works," she tilts her head and arches an eyebrow. "Their job. You're job. Is to ease people's minds, to make them feel more comfortable about being down here. Make them feel like everything is going to be fine. That the situation they are in is going to work out for them and that you're going to help them. Ready?" She peers around the corner and gives herself a final shake.

He feels sick to his stomach. He was so easily manipulated, easily led and that wasn't even the part that made him feel so angry, it was planned. Not his arrival, but that Lorenz and his crew were prepared for manipulating people to walk to their own death for his own profits. There wasn't much time for self-pity and frustration however and he whispers a curse as he realises Neomi is already walking towards the lift entrance. He quickly stumbles up onto his feet and falls in behind her, changing his gait to match what in his mind confident people walk like.

He keeps a few steps behind Neomi, choosing to let her lead. As one of the men notices them approach he says something Tobias can't hear and the whole pack turn almost as one to face them. "Neomi. You're a long way from the surgery, you lost darlin'?" the apparent leader of the pack speaks with a deep husky voice, his brown hair is in a rough side parting and the strong wind here bustling it around. Tribal tattoos run down his exposed arms, only a simple black vest top protecting him from the elements.

Like the other men, Tobias' eyes are drawn to Neomi, he hadn't really stopped to admire her figure before, but she was certainly nice to look at and the other men seemed to be enjoying the view, like a pack of wolves eyeing their next meal. He can't understand how she can stand so confidently, that she doesn't immediately turn and run from their predatory eyes, her hair is blowing in the wind and as if by some kind of supernatural power it manages to avoid covering her face, giving her an almost otherworldly appearance.

"Not lost Spuds," the other man's face goes from a creepy grin to an angry scowl in an instant and Tobias is almost certain this isn't the man's name. "I have a job from the Doctor, me and my motivator Toby here are going to go up and collect a donor." She is trying her best to be a blend of cute and seductive but Tobias can't help but think she'd ruined it already with the nickname.

"Uh uh," the man growls, "Not today. Some idiots went up and tried attacking some people so the lift is out of order. You know I don't like it when you call me Spuds little girl." He took a step forward and he towers over Neomi. Tobias was glad that thus far the men had barely paid him a second thought.

"Sorry," she smirks, not backing a step down, he can't help but admire her courage. She places a hand on his chest, "I didn't mean anything by it, surely you can do me a favour and let us up? You know how frustrated the Doctor gets if he doesn't get what he wants." The other three men look to one another as she finishes, none of them seemingly confident in their position. But the tattooed man, Spuds, slaps her hand away.

"You don't get it do you girl, you're out of credit. Out of favours. You owe too much already." This time she takes a step back and

Tobias wishes for an instant he was armed, not that he would stand a chance in a fight but it would make him feel better. "There ain't a chance I'm doing you a favour." He jabs a finger at her shoulder and she stumbles back another step. Tobias starts to panic, four men are all that stand between them and the lift, between him and his normal life.

"Don't be an ass Spuds-" she never gets to finish the sentence, as the man pushes her to the floor, his next words roar like a deranged animal.

"I said don't call me that. You really have no fucking clue. Little girl has built up so much debt, you're pretty little face has got you in so deep that no one would give a damn if you disappeared. If I killed you right now." Tobias starts to take a step forward to intervene but pauses as the other three men look at him, he manages to rustle up the courage to speak at least, "She's an idiot and she's sorry, but there is no need for that. We are just doing what the Doctor asked. We didn't mean to cause any hassle." He hoped he managed to feign come confidence and pictures Samuels slimy face as he speaks, "I'm certain we can talk this through?"

"Fuck off creep," it wasn't the leader this time but the shortest of the three men at the back. He was an odd shape, wide and bulky but the shortness combined with his bald head gave the man an almost alien look. "Don't interrupt Spuds again," the man's own eyes widened as he realises his mistake and he is too slow to block as a backhanded slap catches him across the jaw. The tall tattooed man returns his attention to Neomi as she starts to bring herself to her feet, he scrapes a thick boot against the floor as dust flies at her as she falls back on her palms. He laughs as he slaps his arm and it sends a shudder down Tobias' spine, "Who knows Neomi, tomorrow it could be you I'm injecting," the three other bruisers start cackling and he re-evaluates his earlier assessment, not wolves, hyenas.

The man pulls an amber glowing vial out the leather pouch at his belt as he takes another step towards the defenceless woman, "You'd love this right now I bet? This isn't the dirty shit you normally use either. This is PURE." The emphasis firmly on the final word as he injects it into his arm. The other men start hollering and whooping like a rabid pack of adolescents.

The man groans, seemingly in a moment of pain as black protrusions starts piercing out from the skin on his arms, they grow longer and longer, thin dark tendrils like oily snakes writhe and wriggle in the air.

Tobias looks around rapidly, seeking for help. Neomi is frozen in place, staring up at Spuds with eyes widened by fear, the man flexes his arms and the tendrils move with them, their tips form into sharp points and with a tensing extension they snap out and form solid spikes at the end of the fist, despite all he had seen so far, this made every inch of his body want to run in terror. Even the rest of his pack had backed away slightly and the bald alien was reaching into a pouch of his own at the back of his waist.

Taking a step back Tobias reaches into his own pocket, hand clasped around the vial he stole earlier. No one was paying him any measure and he realises that if he wanted, he could walk away right now and they wouldn't notice. They move to surround Neomi and she looks to Tobias, her eyes hold the same desperate pleading that he had seen in Elliot's before he died. He pushes down his fear, an unfamiliar feeling of courage and power surging up from below as he pushes the vial against his arm and presses the small button on the side, a short hiss announces the needleless injector releasing the payload into his blood.

He drops the vial to the floor and drops to his knees, his arms start shaking as it makes its way to the rest of his body, he slumps his head forward and he suppresses the urge to scream, his blood feels burning hot for a few seconds but then not moments later he shudders as if about to freeze. The only constant is the searing pain in his stomach, so strong that he almost wants to plunge his own hand through his skin and tear out the pain.

"Spuds!" a voice shouts from somewhere in front of him.

"What?! Can't you see I'm about to have a whole world of fun here?" he recognises at least, the tattooed behemoth. "Woah," the man exclaims, "we have a first timer here. You wanting to join in the fun eh little man?"

"Toby… what ha-" her voice cuts off with a heard but not seen blow, a loud thud and a whimper all Tobias can make out. He tries to force himself to his feet. *This was meant to help, meant to make me powerful,* he thinks frustratedly. He starts panicking, feeling like the pain is going to make him pass out as the immolation inside his body moves into his head. A conflagration feels as if it is going to take his body but in an instant it all fades, as if swallowed, the shaking stops and the pain is gone but something is left behind. He can feel it, like another sense he should have had all along, so natural and part of him. He never understood how people could inject eliXir and immediately control their powers, but now he knew.

He brings himself to his feet and reaches out with both his hands and throws them to the side towards the lift. The tendril covered brute goes sprawling through the air, his limbs and ebony vines seek desperately to find a purchase but are found lacking as his body crashes into the lift. The sound of his spine smashing against the metallic shaft causes pause in the rest of the hyenas, as they watch their alphas body drop twenty feet to the hard clay floor below.

The other men begin to back away, one of them breaks rank and begins running towards the nearest alley but Tobias holds a single hand out and firmly clenches it into a fist. The fleeing man trips and lands flat on his face with a loud grunt, tangled with an invisible bola, he holds his hands to his nose as blood trickles between his fingertips.

"He's a fucking TK," the imp growls as he reaches to the pouch at his back, an elbow pushing his apprehensive friend forward as he quickly injects himself with the syringe he produces. "Get 'im." He commands, sparing a quick look over his shoulder at Spuds, his body slumped against the bottom of the lift.

Tobias holds his palms out open in front him and raises them slowly as the man charges towards him. The man's long scruffy black hair flows behind him, eyes widening as his feet rise from the floor, running on the spot for a few seconds like some kind of animated character. Tobias smiles, feeling the power of the eliXir flowing through him, extending from him. He twists his right hand and the flailing figure starts spinning as if caught in a hurricane, his hair whipping him in the face as he whirls around.

"Toby, you're going to kill him." A spluttering voice comes from somewhere to the side, he turns to look at Neomi, a line of blood is quickly drying on her chin.

His voice deep and full of rage he glowers. "Why shouldn't I kill him? They were going to kill you and probably me without any hesitation." he bring his attention back to the so called guards, dropping his hand to his side the spinning man falls to the ground with a thud and holds his hands to the side of his head, rocking back and forth. The final man has all of Tobias' attention, the short imp is showing the effects of the eliXir hit, his arms are somehow wider than before but still all muscle, but at the end of them are ferocious metallic claws, he bounds forward on all fours and his feet create trenches in the dirt as they are replaced with similar talons.

Tobias only scowls at him as the rabid man approaches, his speed massively enhanced by the power manifestation, he waits, confidently, the other man howls as he leaps to get closer, claws extended outwards at Tobias' chest. Tobias raises a single open palm at the imps torso and he stops dead in the air, no sense of momentum, no flailing or reaching, simply frozen in the air. His arms and legs snap to their full length in an X shape and he slowly floats the last few feet until the two men are face to face.

"All my life I've been powerless," Tobias states with a menacingly calm tone, the frozen man purses his lips and tries to spit in his face, but it forms a neat little globe in midair for a few seconds before dropping onto the floor with a quiet tap. "Never again!" he shouts. He feels like a different person, it's not just confidence, it's a sense of being higher on the food chain. Slamming his hand palm down to his waist, the frozen man lets out a brief whelp before it gets cut off by his face crashing down into the floor. It isn't just gravity, the unseen force controlled by Tobias forces him into the ground. He lifts his hand and the man raises several feet off the floor, droplets of blood dripping downwards.

"Please, let me go, I'm sorry, I won't-" he never gets to finish talking as he gets forced once more into the hard floor, again and again. There is no more pleading, the pool of blood growing larger with each collision.

Tobias releases the imp as he notices the dizzy man slowly recovering to his feet. The imp twitches in a pool of his own blood and rolls onto his side, moaning in unconsciousness. He strides forward, quickly closing the gap between them, whatever Neomi whimpers behind him he doesn't hear. The man is struggling to stay on his feet, stumbling around like a child after playing some kind of spinning game. Tobias throws out a punch with his right hand, he's still quite some distance away and his fist finds nothing but empty air, but in his mind he imagines that fist being larger than life, being solid. The stunned man is pulled from his feet with the distinct sound of snapping bone, flying a short distance before slamming onto his back, his long hair covering some of his face he reels around, his arms hugging his chest and ribs in agony.

Tobias looks to his left and right, eagerly looking for someone else to attack, anyone else who could be shown his power, but all he can see and hear is the groaning and crying of the weak.

Chapter 23

"Tobias, you have to calm down," Neomi pleads as she places her hand on his arm. He jerks it away and looks down at her, his eyes glazed with rage "I know what you're going through Toby, the power you're feeling."

"You don't know anything, I've been ignored and downtrodden my entire life!" he snarls, his vision flickering around at the now mostly still bodies arrayed around the area, he doesn't know if they are dead or alive and is dismayed that he doesn't really care.

"I know exactly how that feels!" she spits back, "This is what eliXir feels like Toby, it isn't going to last forever and we shouldn't be here when it wears off, please, come with me. The power. It isn't you, this isn't you." Tears stream down her cheeks and get diluted as they hit the blood on her chin.

He pauses for a moment as the words sink in, but as he turns his head towards the lift shaft, the draw of his old life tugs at him. He feels Neomi's hands clasp around his arm, pulling him back, but with a flick of his hand her arms pull away. The middle habs, just beyond this door, he imagines he is standing on discs of air and with his mind pushes them forward.

Neomi's eyes widen as Tobias flies towards the dirtied metallic lift, it isn't the first time she's seen someone fly but it never fails to be an amazing sight.

The distance between him and the door shrinks in a moment and Tobias pries his hands apart as if he were physically touching the lift. The sounds of screeching metal rends the air, there are no mechanisms in place or rails for the doors to follow as they are pulled outwards from their hinges. In perfect synchronisation, the metal protrusions that were the doors stretch wide enough to make a hole just large enough for Tobias to fly through.

He realises as he bursts through, that the lift isn't here, he looks up and can see the occasional maintenance light but the lift goes so high he can't see the lift cab itself. He squats slightly and pushes himself upwards, the discs from before forgotten he instead imagines himself surrounded in a bubble, a cushion or buffer of invisible force around him, he propels it upwards and rockets skyward. The feeling is unbelievable, the speed he's moving, and how natural it feels. In his mind it makes little sense, he always thought the powers would need practice and training but it just feels intuitive, as if he'd had these powers his entire life and they were his to command.

It doesn't feel like a leap or a jump, there is no sense that he's going to reach a zenith and come crashing back down, lights flicker past faster and after a few seconds pass he finally sees the bottom side of the lift cab, sensors and clamps keeping it firmly in place. He punches upwards and the bubble around him expands, forming a cylinder from his fist and punctures a perfect hole in the bottom of the metallic box.

The lift is nothing special, more sensors and a bio-reader of some kind are all that really make up the dimly lit cubicle. The most important feature in the entirety of his world however, is the door ahead of him. The door between him and the middle habitats. He leaves himself hovering in the centre of the lift, his eyes intent on the door as if looking at it could make it disappear, although he realises with the eliXir running through him he probably could. It isn't the power or the door that halts his path however.

He looks down at his own open palms in front of him and lets out an exhausted sigh, his body slumping in midair as he grasps his own situation. Everything he has seen down in the low habs, both the good and the bad, the suffering that people like Neomi are going through but also the mundanity of most people's lives down there. Could he turn his back on helping them? On flying back down the shaft and helping Neomi to survive and to fight back against those who kidnap and abuse the weak and vulnerable.

He shakes his head in disappointment at himself as a single tear runs down his nose, he hates himself for not pushing forward and it's nothing to do with being brave and helping those below. He's tainted. The second he opens that door, the police and whoever else on the other side will know, they'll scan him again and this time they'll execute him on the spot. Maybe they'd shoot him as soon as the doors open. He's done the one thing he can't return from, he has used eliXir and is now a criminal.

As his head slumps into his chest his powers mimic the action and he slowly descends down the lift shaft. He clenches his fists in frustration at coming so close to getting back his old life, but now all of it is lost, his entire future cast into uncertainty over the decision to save a life.

His feet land softly back on the ground and before him is the rent metal hole that he left behind, like a messy portrait he can see Neomi's face beyond the metal aperture, he is surprised that she doesn't look angry or hurt, but instead her face is sad, tears running freely down her cheeks as he carefully steps through the makeshift doorway. No sooner has he stepped out of the elevator than she darts the last few steps towards him and embraces him in her arms. "I'm so sorry Toby. It's all my fault. If I'd been more careful. I'm sorry." He could feel her tears dampening against his shirt as she struggles to find any semblance of words that could express how sorry she is.

He raises his hands, placing one on the back of her head and one around her back and holds her close, taking comfort in holding her, knowing that there was at least one person in this forsaken place that he cares about. "If it wasn't for me you'd be free." the words splutter out between sobs and he finds it difficult seeing her so vulnerable after everything else he has witnessed from her.

"If it wasn't for you, I would have died on Lorenz's operating table. You didn't do anything wrong Neomi, heck you are the only person I've met down here who actually wanted to help." With an effort he pulls her back, his mucky hands resting atop her thin but equally dirty arms, he looks into her bloodshot blue eyes with more confidence than he feels, "It wasn't your fault."

"I've cost you everything Toby. You'll never be able to return to your home," he knew the truth of it, but hearing it from her was like being stabbed again. He was corrupted, the drug coursing through him meant he could never again have a normal life. "I was never going to be able to come with you, but I wanted this for you, to get you out of this, you didn't deserve it."

He tilts his head inquisitively "What do you mean? This was your plan? I thought we were going to go to middle habs together."

"Don't be silly. You know as well as I do that I could never join you, even if we made it up the lifts I could never have lasted without getting scanned eventually." She lowers her head to look at his feet, shame hanging over her like a veil.

"So why help me?" Tobias asked, confusion wrought all over his face "If you knew there was no chance for you, why risk all this. You could have died back there at Lorenz's or in the warehouse or right here."

"For hope." She mutters, "My life here was over, it still is I suppose. Spuds wasn't wrong. I had nothing left to offer here, I was probably due on the table not long after you. This way I got to live a little longer and for a while I could believe, more than anything, that there might be a way out of this nightmarish loop I was stuck in. The cycle that was certainly going to consume my life sooner or later," her composure breaks once more before she finally manages to stutter "The cycle you're now stuck in," and collapses into his chest once more.

He's taken back, he has never had anyone consider him hope before, to look and see much of anything. It bolsters him almost as much as the power coursing through him. He looks around at the carnage he contributed to not minutes ago, four bodies in various states of pain and disarray. With no hope of going back to his normal life he suggests the most normal thing he can imagine "Let's go get a cup of coffee, we have two lives to plan!"

Chapter 24

The desolate pair wander the unmarked streets, Tobias finds it odd that no one pays them any mind, but then it isn't that much different to the middle habs. People shuffle to their destination and don't give much thought to those around them, he was like that he supposes. People moving hurriedly from one destination to another, it's feels at times like a thriving hub.

He looks up the black void that is the sky here, he never felt particularly strongly one way or another about the SkyCast in the middle habs, but compared to this he finds he misses it. He couldn't tell in truth if the roof of the low habitats was merely meters away or hundreds of meters, the black depths stealing his perception. It frustrates him slightly that he can't figure out how many people are actually down here, each small fabricated housing unit could comfortably fit a couple of families without feeling cramped, and he had probably ran past at least a hundred of them during his time here.

"There." Neomi points. It's a very different venue to what he would have anticipated from his own experiences, there aren't bright signs advertising the cafe itself or a myriad of promotion casts ready to view in an instant. It was plain, the same style as the other fabricated housing only this one had been modified, a long but short window cast along one side allowed you to look in, to see that it was a cafe, without the window he would have walked past the building without a care, it could have been just another set of housing. "It'll be quiet in there, we should be able to get a drink at least.

He nods before pointing at her face. "Won't they think that's suspicious?" Her eye was swollen and red and she still had dried blood on her chin. He wasn't sure how his face looked but he felt tired and if his clothes were any indication he looked like he'd rolled around in dirt and mud for hours.

"It's fine, it's not the first time I've turned up looking like this, besides, people tend not to pry too much where Lorenz is concerned." Tobias' lip curls baring teeth at the mention of the doctor, the name filling him with anger. Neomi leads the way into the cafe, holding the wooden framed door open for him as he follows.

The cafe is surprisingly pleasant inside, despite all outward appearances. Tobias finds it feels almost homely, the hardened earth from outside replaced with some form of tiles, whoever owns the place keeps it exceptionally clean and he immediately feels guilty dragging in the dirt from outside but Neomi seems unfazed as she slinks into one of the chairs against a wall, a lot of the chairs don't match, but at this point Tobias is just happy to rest and he practically falls into one opposite her.

"Do we go and order?" he asks flatly, nodding his head towards a table and counter that are blocking access to a back room, the kitchen he presumes.

"We can do in a bit if you want, I'm sure Shirl will come out and see us anyway. I don't think my legs are willing to get back up right now." She smiles and it drowns out the world, even with one of her eyes slightly squinted and dirt and blood marring her features, he could lose himself in that smile. He realises he is staring and quickly tries to re-engage the conversation, "Erm... yeah I know what you mean, my legs feel like noodles right now, I don't think they could support me another step."

"That will be the eliXir running out," she breaks his sight and stares at the small round table as if the circular stains are the most important things in the world right now. "You'll feel really tired and fatigued, you shouldn't be feeling any cravings though, what you took was pure eliXir."

He ignores the comment, trying to focus on what to do next, "What do you think we should do next Neomi? How will we survive? Lorenz is going to be looking for us right?"

She looks up as a slightly chubby older woman comes out from the kitchen area, her black hair in a high ponytail. Shirl's clothes are tight, struggling to contain her as she slowly strides over to the two of them. "Neomi…you look like shit, who's this?" she doesn't look over at Tobias as she closes the last few feet towards the table.

"Just a friend, any chance we can get a drink?" she smiles again and Tobias doesn't interrupt to introduce himself realising that giving his name is probably a bad idea at the moment.

"Sure, we got some tea, energy drinks or water. What you want?" her voice is gentle but it feels wrong compared to her body language and posture, as if she's expecting to run or fight any moment. *Is that what life is down here? Constant fear,* he wonders, life without the proper governance or authority he can't begin to grasp how that must play out over the generations.

"Tea would be great, he's paying." Neomi nods at him with a smile. He can't tell if she's joking or not but doesn't say anything with Shirl standing over them.

As the lady strides back to the kitchen he turns back to Neomi, she's still trying to pat the dirt out of her hair and return it to its pretty purple hue, but it's useless, it's far too matted with muck. "I can't use my data slate, I don't have any money Neomi, do you even use money down here?" he quickly realises it sounds rude, especially given that down here was now his home too.

"It's a mix, most people will trade services and goods with each other, or just favours. It might not look like it but almost everyone down here has to learn or do something, if you want to eat and live you have to pay your way. At the same time we do have a working currency system down here, it's the same as up there," she does the pointing at the roof that he's quickly becoming accustomed too.

The cogs of Tobias' mind start whirling as he wrestles with trying to understand how they could use the same currency as the middle habitats. "So you have banks here? A central store for money? Surely someone like Lorenz would raid it with his heavies...although then I suppose it would be useless to him if he had it all."

"There are no banks down here Toby, our money is all stored up there. It's all connected, we aren't as separate as you might believe. I wasn't joking about you paying, whilst a nice fancy data-slate like yours isn't common here," she points at his lower body through the table and he instinctively places a hand against his trouser pocket feeling for the device, it was still there thankfully, "It will draw attention but it will still work and you can access your funds just fine somewhere like here. We mostly use older biometric readers or really ancient model data slates."

He nods repeatedly like a child as his mind is distracted "But wait, that means the mid hab banks know all about what life is like down here? How do you set up accounts?" The minutiae of his own experience and job seep through as he tries to get to grips with what he is being told.

"Does it matter Toby?" she slumps back further in her chair with a sigh, not so much frustrated at him, but from the exhaustion of the day's events. "I don't think Lorenz is smart enough to track you with it anyway, so we should be fine."

"What do we do next Neomi? Find somewhere away from Lorenz and live a quiet life? How would I earn money down here? Is there another city we can go to?" His mind wouldn't settle on one question, he feels bad for bombarding her with questions but at the same time he needs some stability, some answers.

"Lorenz won't stop hunting us, you're too valuable. Sorry. As for the rest, I'm not sure. If you stand on the borders of the city you'll see lights in the distance, we assume there are other cities like this one, people have been exiled or chose to go to them before, but no one has ever returned. They don't show up on any networks so we can't communicate with them anyway." She shrugs as Shirl returns with two cups of steaming liquid. It doesn't look like any kind of tea that Tobias has drank before but he accepts it with a smile and pulls out the data slate from his pocket, the woman's eyes go wide as she sees the device but she scans it all the same, "You should keep this one around Neomi," she chuckles whilst nudging her with an elbow.

"I don't think I have much choice," Neomi laughs, at least this time he is sure she is joking as he pulls the cup to his lips, thankful for some refreshment.

"At least this sort of tastes like tea. I think." The earthy flavour of the liquid bolsters him and as Neomi reaches for a small container of sweetener tablets he can't resist the urge to flick his fingers and the container jumps into his hand as he smirks at her. Neomi chuckles as she looks to make sure Shirl isn't watching, "Very funny Toby, those powers should be starting to fade soon. You will feel a bit of a come down when it leaves your system, you won't feel all the cravings but you'll feel really tired and drained."

"Can't wait," he flippantly states, but he can't help but wish they didn't have to leave, that the power he never knew he wanted would stay a little longer. He feels like he can do anything. That if he wants, he can change the world.

Chapter 25

Tobias swirls around the last dregs of the tea, silently wondering what the hell the bits are floating amongst the bottom. Breaking the growing silence, Neomi asks "So you ready to go back to the quiet life?" She is trying her best to put on a brave and uplifting expression, he appreciates the effort.

"I guess. I'm not sure how long this will last," he slaps his pocket containing his data pad. "I'm surprised the bank hasn't blocked my funds already. Normally they are pretty quick at making sure a dead or missing persons assets are frozen or tracked. What kind of job do you think I should get?" he isn't trying to just make conversation, he is fully self-aware that his skill set doesn't necessarily lend itself to the environment he is currently in.

"Muscle for one of the entertainment centres?" she chuckles, "Well what can you do?" she offers and it suddenly feels to Tobias as if he's back in some career centre as a child trying to decide what to spend your entire life doing. It feels as ridiculous now as it did then.

"I don't know. I used to work with numbers and talk to people about their accounts all day. This just feels all so wrong Neomi. I want to help you, you saved my life and have risked everything and I can't do anything to repay you." He feels pathetic and the powers in his system surge to fight back.

"It's fine, we saved each other. If you hadn't turned up when you did and beg for my help, Lorenz would have killed me in a day or two. I'd be in one of those vials." She looks into his eyes with her own lightning blue piercing him. "You don't owe me anything. Now let's look at your hands."

He frowns in utter confusion but offers them up, suddenly concerned that his hands might be some way of knowing that the eliXir is affecting him in some way. Her hands are dainty but her skin tough and worn, yet still the human touch sends goosebumps up his arms.

"Yup, these hands are fine, you'll be able to work the agri-habs with no problems at all. There, you have a job now, you're officially a farmer." She laughs and withdraws her hands.

He doesn't pause to think and blurts out "What do you mean my hands are fine and have no problems? What kind of problems might there be with them for farming?" This only makes her laugh harder and Shirl pokes her head out from the kitchen and smiles herself.

"There is nothing wrong with your hands Toby, I was joking. I mean, you could work the agri-habs if you want, it doesn't take skill to nurture and harvest the fruit and vegetables we grow here," she tilts her head as if measuring whether he could be a farmer or not.

"No." he coughs and clenches his fists in the middle of the table. "I mean, thank you for the suggestion, but no. This isn't right. Not me, not you. Nothing here is right. It's not that I'm hard done by or that I've had some bad luck. This is fundamentally wrong and no one knows or cares," he wants to stand, his body wants to stand tall to match his tone and stance. "I don't want to live in the low habs. Not because it's shit or because it's not what I'm used to. I don't want to live here in fear, no one should live here not knowing if they are going to be kidnapped during the night. Scared every living moment that they could be killed. For what? Survival? No. Killed to fund some habit and power trip of some rich person that doesn't give a fuck that people are dying to literally feed their habit," he raises and pounds one of his fists on the table, it shakes the cups and the liquid that was beginning to settle clouds once more. "I'm not going through the rest of my life scraping by, I don't want wealth or riches. I'm just not going to be just a cog in someone else's machine." He doesn't even realise he's raised himself up and is leaning onto the table.

"Toby, calm down. It's the eliXir speaking. The power is giving you lusts for dreams that you can't live out. I've been there, you feel like it's an out. Like you can do anything. But it's a trap, the power will either destroy you or the addiction will. Trust me." Neomi was sat up herself, no longer slouching in the chair to rest but almost ready to pounce herself, as if threatened.

"Then it will destroy me, I'm not going to stand by and live the rest of my life in fear Neomi. First I'm going to take down Lorenz and all his muscle, I'll show him that he can't do this, he can't have a stranglehold on people and not suffer the consequences of his actions." He stands to his full lanky height.

"First?" she asks with a raised eyebrow.

"The world is messed up. I'll do whatever I can to change it." As the resolutions flow from his tongue the eliXir in his bloodstream responds as if sensing his mental state, he can feel the power in his veins, he knows that if he wanted he could fly right now, that he could pull down an entire hab with the force of his will.

"We're just two people Toby, I'm useless and it won't be long until…" she trails off noticing Shirl is watching from the kitchen, but turns back and whispers "until the powers wear off. There are more chop shops and dealers than just the one where Lorenz was. We'd never get them all. Shit I don't even know if we could get one. The downer from the eliXir would certainly get us before we destroy more than two or three," she states matter of factly but it still warms Tobias to know that she at least is standing by him, that despite his insane crusade he has one person who is willing to help him.

He pushes back his chair firmly and strides towards the door, turning back as he pulls it open and gesturing with a tug of his head for her to follow before commanding, "We will just have to find others who can help us."

Chapter 26

"Where are you going?!" Neomi calls as Tobias strides purposefully into the streets, he feels like it should be lighter and that the dark belittles the mood he's feeling.

"There must be others right?" he starts, "People like you, who have been pushed to the brink, who want to see change in the low habs," he has his arms spread wide and open, gesturing to the entire habitats.

"I don't know many people Toby. Even if I did, everyone understands and is…" she pauses trying to describe the feeling of the people, "content. No one wants to risk going against the people with power, people who could burn the habs to the ground, so they keep their heads down. They go about their lives. People down here don't know what life could be like or should be like, we know about as much of up there as you do about down here."

He walks backwards down the street whilst now raising his voice, he's not shouting or angry, but it's passionate and loud, "I was like that Neomi. Keeping my head down, avoiding trouble. Trouble only comes to those that make it for themselves right? Well I was wrong, everyone here has the right to know, the right to be better. If they don't have the power, then let's give them the power."

Neomi frowns, a deeply worried expression lining her features "What do you mean? Give them the power?" She skips a couple of paces to close the distance between them, hoping that if she's closer he won't shout as loudly.

"I'll start this myself Neomi. I'll go back and get more of Lorenz's eliXir and I'll distribute it to everyone. They can take back their lives, take back what he and anyone else thinks they can take away from them." His long legs take him quickly through the streets and Neomi has to walk quickly to keep up with him.

"Wait...this is crazy, you can't be serious? Lorenz will kill you. Slow down, do you even know where you are going?!" the words fire out in quick succession but they're enough to stop him in the street.

"No. I don't, it all looks so similar and I don't have any navigation systems. But you do, don't you?" He turns to face her and his body screams action, eyes full of purpose. "You can do more than just survive here Neomi, you can make a difference. I don't know why you first took eliXir or how much trouble it has got you in, but there can be an end, you said you felt hope for a while. We can spread that hope to everyone here, just show me the way to the warehouse and we can change this place forever."

Her thoughts are wracked with indecision, the addiction in her body was aching to follow him, to get her hands on the pure eliXir in the warehouse, not only that but it was the right thing to do, if they could rally others to join them then they could really destroy Lorenz's operation permanently. The pull to follow Tobias was strong but so too was the deep rooted fear of Lorenz and his men, not to mention the risk involved with a large group of people all taking eliXir for the first time, it had the potential to save the low habs or tear them apart.

He holds out an open hand for her to take, the resolution in his eyes is piercing and dominating. "Please Neomi, we've come this far and I can't do this without you." She can't believe this is the same man she rescued screaming and begging for his life not hours ago, he was standing tall and proud which gave him a magnetism she couldn't resist but to follow, she places her hand in his and nods gently.

"Fine, you're going to get us both killed, but I'll follow you." there was a weak smile on her face and Tobias returns the gesture.

"I appreciate it," he lets out a small chuckle, "but I need you to lead, I have no idea where I am going." He reluctantly releases her hand and gestures with a small bow and open arm for her to lead the way, he feels a sense of relief as she smiles and steps ahead. As she passes by he clenches his fist as can feel the power inside respond to his call, no lesser or weakened than when he first used them.

"We should probably hurry, pure eliXir might give you powers for longer, but you're going to be pushing the limit of how long you'll get if we don't get there soon." She breaks into a jog and Tobias is astounded that she can manage it, his own battered body is tired, with the rest at Shirls cafe only serving to make his body think it was time to stop for the day. He sighs and pushes himself to keep up with her, thankfully his long legs make it relatively easy to keep up. They pass people in the street and draw their stares but Tobias doesn't care, he isn't hiding anymore, he isn't going to crawl away and give up.

The smaller habitats start to become less frequent and it seems clear to him that they are breaking into the outer area of the lower habs. It certainly isn't a coincidence that there are less people on the streets now and the few that are look addled and gaunt.

Neomi slows to a walk and leads him into a wide alley and turns to him "Are you sure you want to do this? We're almost there, you still have your TK?" she looks predatory now, the indecision and fear gone and the lust for power and excitement clear in her body language.

He tenses his arm and reaches out at the hard dirt rock floor before balling his hand in a fist and slowly raising it, the ground crumbles and a fist sized ball of stone raises from the floor, the power is exhilarating, the limits of what he can do seems beyond his imagination. "Yes, I most definitely do."

She turns to dart down another alley but pauses to say over her shoulder, "You got lucky, ya know? Not only did you not explode or turn into some deformed mess, you actually got one of most powerful abilities. Telekinesis is one of the rarest but most potent."

He can't resist a little smirk as he shrugs, "Lucky me I guess. Shall we?"

Without replying she starts navigating down the quickly tightening alley ways until it suddenly breaks open in front of a familiar building, the metal door firmly closed once more. He places his open hand against her upper arm with a gentle smile, "Probably best if I go first."

She presses her back against the wall to allow him to pass and watches as he approaches the door confidently, he holds out a hand and twists it, with a short snap and a thud the handle drops to the floor. With the door open, the pair rush through without hesitating, it doesn't feel like long has passed since they were last here and they quickly retrace their steps toward the middle of the warehouse. The crate from before has been hastily closed, Tobias doesn't bother with subtlety as he raises a hand and sends the top of the crate flying with a splintered crash.

"TOBY!" Neomi yells from behind him and he turns immediately to see her hiding behind a crate. He can see the cause for her alarm however, from the shadows men approach from all directions, every one of them is carrying a firearm, from pistols to more high tech looking things he doesn't recognise. The banging of heavy shoes against the railings above indicates they are well and truly surrounded.

A familiar voice booms from above, "The good Doctor says if possible to bring you back alive, but that the bitch can be killed." In the dim light of the warehouse Tobias can just barely distinguish the man's features, the bushy eyebrows and badly disjointed nose.

"Mikael. Why bother doing this? You know what is in that crate right? What we could change with that in our hands."

The deep laugh that follows echoes through the building, "Idiot. Lorenz is gonna make us all rich, we're gonna live like fucking kings in the upper habs from the credits that the eliXir is gonna sell for. Fuck this shit hole." He draws a pistol of his own and levels it towards Tobias.

He steps back until he hits the crate of eliXir behind him, he isn't retreating however or looking for an escape, just improving his lines of sight as the roar of gunfire fills the room. It comes from all angles and echoes through the room like a cacophony of thunderbolts. He clutches a hand to his chest and imagines a bubble around himself, he can feel the impacts of each bullet against the shell he has created as he holds out his other hand.

Neomi looks up from her hidden vantage and her eyes bulge, a handful of rounds float in the air, their tips all pointing towards her but suspended in the air. "How did you…" she breathlessly exclaims.

"KEEP FIRING!" The words bellow from above, Tobias releases

the sheathes he had imagined around the other bullets and they drop harmlessly to the floor. With a gesture he pulls the crates in front of Neomi, protecting her from the gunfire as he spends a moment looking around as muzzle flashes decorate the room and provide all the light he needs.

With a snap of his wrist a thug from atop the balcony launches through the air, head over feet again and again before he crashes out of sight. Mikael watches with frustration as he reloads his pistol. The snapping of wood can barely be heard over the orchestra of spent ammunition, but it is certainly felt as planks of wood from all the crates crash into a pair of the armed figures lurking in the shadows, like men attacked with a handful of bats they collapse to the floor in heaps, roiling in pain and unsure where to nurse first.

Tobias flinches as the lights in the warehouse suddenly go bright before sizzling out with a pop. The gunshots have stopped but the warehouse is still brightly lit, he turns to face a blinding sight, at the end of the row of crates is a man with a smouldering head, his hair burned away as his body flickers with electrical energy.

The man channels the lightning in his arms and throws out his hands, a streak of electrical energy flies towards Tobias. It barely misses and crashes behind him with a loud bang. He quickly reaches out with his telekinesis and grabs the first thing he sees, a large crate falls from atop its shelving directly overhead of the lightning powered man. A crackling arm lifts instinctively to stop the crate, the lightning expands around his arm like a large shield of blinding light and energy, the crate ignites and disintegrates upon collapsing into the flickering wall.

With his spare hand the man lunges at Tobias and another line of lightning forks for him. He imagines his body surrounded in a suit of telekinetic armour, he feels it envelop him merely an instant before the bolt strikes against it. *I can do anything I think of but I can't think faster than lightning,* he thinks as the lightning fails to cease, it grasps around his armour like a lasso and throws him against the ceiling. He impacts the corrugated roof hard, causing a wave of force to ripple outwards. He is thankful for his armour preventing him from feeling much of the impact. He watches helplessly, arms wiggling but clasped to his sides, as Mikael flees from the side exit of the warehouse while using an old dataslate. Tobias grunts in frustration, cursing being stuck like this, his own armour thankfully shows no sign of weakness but without warning he finds himself plummeting towards the floor as the lightning binding is released.

He naturally holds his hands out in front of his face and as his mind panics at the fall, he manages to rein it in and exert his will to stop himself instantly in the air, hovering horizontally a few feet from the smooth floor of the warehouse. He levels himself out with a concentrated effort but he is allowed no time to recover as bolt after bolt hit his body, somewhere in his mind he knows they can't hurt him, but he is forced to close his eyes or risk being blinded by the cascading lights.

"TOBY! TOBY!" the repeated cries are only barely audible over the roar of the constant barrage of electric power. Each bolt knocking him further and further back. He covers his eyes as best he can as he hunts the source of the sound, completely unable to see his own attacker, his only sense of direction being the opposite of the one he is being pushed.

He sees Neomi, still in the same place, her mouth screaming something he cannot hear as lightning flickers past her every few seconds, it isn't honed or aimed, but it is unrelenting. He follows the line of her hand as she furiously stabs out a pointing finger. A crate of eliXir is upended on the floor and he immediately understands, sparing one of his hands for a moment he flicks his palm and a vial from the crate rolls along the floor to within her reach.

What feels like minutes pass as he fights against the force impacting his armour, an unpowered person would be nothing but ash at this point, the thought makes him panic, worrying what would happen if his powers ran out right now.

Refusing death or failure he pushes back, forcing his telekinetic shell forward against the tide. Just as he feels like he is making progress the bolts stop. He almost sends himself flying across the warehouse as the barrage ends, he blinks repeatedly, trying desperately to restore his vision.

Lightning still lashes below, Tobias looks down and sees the cause of the distraction, Neomi's form is lumbering towards the lightning thug, no longer the colourful beauty her skin is now stone, smoothed over like a pebble but no less hard. Balls of lightning crash against her chest and dissipate but she shows no sign of stopping, a slow inevitable push.

He rubs his eyes as he hears a roar of defiance from below. Neomi is tangled, multiple tendrils of electricity are wrapped around her wrists and ankles, slowing her approach to an almost stop. The lightning man looks laboured, sweat hissing on his face from the exertion. Tobias acts without hesitation, he focuses his mind and holds out his hand, a nail draws itself from one of the crates, he flings it with all the force of a round from a rifle. It silently wisps through the air but the thug notices, releasing the vines from Neomi and raising his hand instinctively, but it's too late, the nail is already within his guard and passes through the front of his skull without resistance.

The man drops instantly, slumping in a pile and devoid of life as the lightning in his arms ceases, exposing blackened but otherwise normal flesh. Toby grimaces at the sight, dismayed at his own actions. Neomi looks up at him as he slowly floats down to the ground, "Damn Toby." Her voice sounds gravelly, like someone deeply ill.

"We should get out of here before more come back, they'll all have eliXir with them next time and they won't try guns first," she nudges him with her elbow and it sends a shock up his body and he feels like he's been punched by a person three times his size.

"Ouch," he exclaims, regretting letting his armour go when he landed. "I shouldn't have killed him Neomi. I just wanted to help you, but he didn't deserve it. He's just another person having his life controlled by Lorenz," he forces himself to look away from the man with a bloodied hole in the centre of his forehead.

"You did what needed to be done Toby, I know you might not like it and you don't need to, but we have the eliXir now. We can help the people put an end to Lorenz and anyone else like him."

He nods solemnly, reaching out with his hand and levitating three boxes of eliXir off the ground, each is roughly the size of a vid screen and could easily contain fifty vials. "Let's go," he flatly states as he walks towards the exit, the three containers float in close proximity behind him. He doesn't need to look over his shoulder to see if she's following, the loud thuds and crunch of the tiles beneath her stone feet make it clear she's following.

Her grinding voice adds, "Are you sure you don't want to bring a few more?" this time he can tell by her tone that she's smiling, but he knows she isn't joking.

Chapter 27

He storms out of the warehouse, crates hovering behind him eerily, he can feel the supports he is creating for them but to anyone else they would appear to be floating from an invisible force.

"Neomi come on, we aren't having this conversation again."

"Just a few extra, you know how much this stuff is worth Toby, what it can do?" Her voice sounds harsh but the pleading is no less desperate.

"You said yourself, you don't know how much longer my powers will last, I'm carrying what I know we can manage by hand if our powers run out, otherwise we'd have to abandon it god knows where," he doesn't slow his pace and hopes that she will follow. The resounding thuds as her heavy rocky feet impact the ground ease his mind.

"They're watching Toby. Look," she calls from behind him. He sweeps his head around, the housing here is not as compact as deeper in and are slightly further apart but there is no mistaking that the engagement at the warehouse has drawn attention. People lurk at the edges of the street and watch from small windows as the odd looking couple stride confidently down the street. Parents hold their children close but do not stop them from watching.

Tobias continues onwards, wanting to have the biggest impact but is pleased that they have gathered a small following, some of the people who were nearest the warehouse are following them at a distance, morbidly curious to see what might happen next he supposed. They continue backtracking in the direction of Shirl's Cafe.

"Where are we going Toby?" Neomi mutters quietly from behind, "There are more and more people following, they want to know what is going on, I've never seen this many people in one place down here before."

Satisfied that the housing is more dense here, that he can maximise his message, he lowers the crates onto the ground gently before turning to face Neomi, and with a nod he raises himself into the air, there is an element of awe in the crowd as they watch wide eyed as they witness a man levitating twenty feet above them, but not as much as he himself would have displayed a week ago.

He raises his voice as loud as he can manage without coughing and spluttering, but in his mind he imagines waves of energy rippling around him, carrying his voice in waves through the area.

"People of the Low Habs. I'm not from here, I was cast down from above for a criminal offense I never committed and no sooner did I arrive here than I was hunted and told I would be used to make that," he points at the eliXir boxes on the floor. He prays his powers hold for a few more minutes for him to finish this. "It is wrong. I've seen first-hand how afraid you all are, and rightly so! The people that make this care nothing for you or your lives and they wield all the power. I am here to change that. You shouldn't have to live here in fear of some men in the dark coming for you when you sleep, you shouldn't have to fear that your children will become addicted to power or worse. With what I have right here, taken from Lorenz's own facilities, we can take control of our own lives and take control of this city."

People are muttering amongst themselves and pointing at the crates, the crowd is growing and there is no doubt his message is being heard.

"We will return later with this eliXir, we will take as much as we need to destroy Lorenz and his operations, find your courage citizens and fight for the lower habitats and for your lives."

Feeling more confident than he has ever felt and feeling his power ready inside him and burning to be used, he reaches out for Neomi and the crates and pulls them towards him and pushes all of them away from the area.

The group soar through the air and fabricated housing rushes past them below, he doesn't look back to see the reactions of the crowd and he can't help but smile as he hears Neomi laughing and screaming in equal measure behind him.

The housing breaks apart and it's clear they are well away from the main centre of the lower hab city. Lowering them down into an alleyway Neomi looks a little disappointed the flight has come to an end.

"That was so much fun Toby, I've taken plenty of eliXir but I've never had any variant of flight before. You got real lucky with the T.K." Her normally beautiful smile just looks funny with her stony complexion.

"Do you think anyone will show up tomorrow?" He asks worriedly, his confidence tempered by the magnitude of what they are attempting.

The pair sit down with their backs against a housing unit, the crates resting in between them. "Honestly? I don't know. The people here normally keep to themselves, they don't take risks, don't draw attention. They'll do their jobs to pay for food or whatever luxuries there are. We rely on each other in a carefully balanced system, we depend on the farmers and pickers but we equally rely on people to keep the UV systems and irrigation systems functioning who in turn rely on scavengers to go through the Vac Chute waste to find replacement parts. No one wants to disrupt what works here as they would be putting everyone at risk." Her argument makes perfect sense he realises and he finds himself frustratingly relating to keeping his head down and going about his business.

"However, at the same time," Neomi continues and Toby can't help but be transfixed by how her hair now looks like stone dreadlocks "I have never seen that many people in one place, that many people listening to a speech. It might not have been long or seemed like much, but you had their attention, they heard what you had to say. It may be enough to convince them to make a change. Particularly anyone who has lost a family member to the drug gangs."

He nods, it was about the best he could expect he supposed. "We should probably find somewhere to spend… well rest, I have no idea what time it is or if it even matters here."

She looks up at the building "It's fine Toby, I'm sure you didn't mean it but these habs are nearer the outskirts, we should be able to find an empty room without any problems." She stands up and grabs one of the crates of eliXir to carry, he eyes her wearily behind her back but doesn't say anything. The pair moves around to the front of the building and Neomi nudges the door with the back of her fist, it groans open and inside is just a tight hallway, some doors and a staircase going up to another level. He follows her as she walks down the corridor and gently pushes each door to see if any give. "No wonder no one feels safe if this is how you live? No locks or anything?" he shakes his head in dismay.

"People pick where they live, their kids move out when they think they can. We don't have a housing list or guide. Tell me Toby, would a lock stop you or me right now?" she sounds light hearted but her expression is anything but. They venture upstairs as all the doors fail to give way in any apparently satisfactory manner. Upstairs is much of the same, one of the doors has a light glowing from underneath and Neomi doesn't push it, eventually one of the standard housing doors pushes open and admits them to an empty room. Not just empty of people Tobias notes, but empty of anything, no furniture, no technology, no amenities. Just empty space.

"Are there lots of empty habs like this?" Tobias asks while looking around the room, there doesn't appear to be anything to indicate running water or electricity.

Neomi shrugs in response as she carefully lays down a crate on the floor, "Yeah there are quite a few especially here on the outskirts, and every building probably has more empty habs than occupied. The habs this far out are mostly just used by scavengers to rest or store stuff for taking to the centre. Most families tend to stick together and live in one building, support each other you know?" He nods in reply as he gently lowers the other two boxes on top of the other one, making a waist high tower of drugs worth a fortune.

They slump down against the wall, fatigue wracks his limbs and he suddenly wishes his power somehow involved quicker recovery. "I'm glad we have some time to rest, I'm so tired."

"What will we do next Toby? Let's say people show up tomorrow and we take down Lorenz and destroy his operations. As unlikely as it all sounds, what will we do next?" she looks at him with a reassuring smile, her blue eyes the only part of her body not coated in a rock layer.

"Honestly, I don't know. I guess we either settle into normal life here and live out our days scavenging and integrating, or we could try and spread the word of how the low habs are alive and in need of aid." He chuckles jokingly at the futility of the latter suggestion.

"Yeah the eliXir strategy probably wouldn't work so well up there huh?" Her body shudders and looks over at the boxes in the middle of the room then back to Tobias. "I don't get it. You've been on the same eliXir high for ages and mine is fading already. It isn't always the same but still yours has lasted longer than I expected even for a first time user."

"I'm sure they'll run out soon. Thanks back there by the way, your help in the warehouse really turned it around. The telekinesis is so powerful but I just didn't know what to do." he runs a hand through his hair and almost chokes on the amount of dust that fills the air. "Damn, I would love a shower about now." he laughs, leaning his head back against the wall.

"Yeah, the dirt and dust down here never lets up, luckily we aren't complete savages, we do have showers and running water, it just isn't piped into every habitat all the time. Once...I... erm look a little more normal I can ask around our new neighbours if you want?" She shakes her hands in the air as if the fact she doesn't look her normal self somehow needs further explanation causes him to chuckle.

"It's fine, I'm sure we'll just end up dirty again anyway. It's probably better we keep our heads down for now anyway. You should get some sleep, your… transition might be smoother if you're asleep maybe?" He treads carefully around the topic of her coming down, having witnessed first-hand how difficult it could be for her.

Her eyes flicker to the crate, "We have enough that I could just take another one when this wears out? Keep going until later." She shuffles, easing up to move closer to the crates. Tobias waves an open hand and they grind against the floor as he pushes them further away. "Probably best if we just rest. Even if as you said the come downs on pure eliXir are a lot lighter and different, I've never had one before I might need your help." He eases the conversation away from her needs and hopes for the best.

"You're probably right," she resigns, leaning back against the wall once more, her arm twitches and Tobias assumes it means her powers are going to run dry soon. It would make sense he thinks, if the more you use it the less time it lasts, especially the addictive stuff, it has been designed that way.

"You must have seen your fair share of useless or funny looking powers while you're down here. Why don't you tell me some?" He sways the subject and she laughs immediately, obviously remembering some past event, after she regains her composure she begins.

"The saddest power I can remember, is a guy who once got the power of stench. He could create a gas that wasn't deadly or dangerous, it just smelled really really bad. I don't know how much he paid for that hit but what a disappointment that must have been." they laugh together for a little while before she continues, "Let's see, there was a girl who for three hours could change her skin any colour she wanted.

Not much power to be had with that one, she couldn't camouflage or anything like that, just pink skin, green skin, blue skin, lame. Then there was Mr. Snuffles, he took eliXir and grew a thick layer of hair and a tail, like a humanoid dog." She raises a hand before he can interrupt "nothing else, no heightened senses or talking to animals, just a grown man dog hybrid."

"Wow, it really is quite random, does anyone ever get the same power twice?" he tilts his head inquisitively, it was an honest enough question but he also was curious to know if he was likely to feel this power again.

"Not to my knowledge. The creepiest shit I've ever seen was a man who took eliXir and duplicated. Just a small cloud and bang, when the smoke cleared there were two of him right there. Saw him having sex with himself that same day, there's a fucking sight you cannot unsee Toby. One of him killed the other a few days later."

"Wait. A few days? I thought it lasted hours or minutes?" he wondered with hope if this meant he might still have these powers after he fell asleep. He never would have imagined wanting such a thing, let alone wanting to keep it, but it had changed him, he could feel and do things he never would have been able to do before. In a way, he doesn't want it to ever end.

"Yeah, it's weird and not very common, but sometimes, the repercussions of a power don't fade quickly. Extra limbs for example sometimes stick around for a day or two before dropping off harmlessly. It's normally the more physical stuff.

"I see." he pauses, "Right, get some sleep. I'll take first watch and wake you up in erm…" he pulls out his dataslate to get some bearing of time, "I'll wake you up in 4 hours."

She sighs "Urgh, you're annoying sometimes, because you've been nice so far, I suppose I can try." she lies on her back and rolls around awkwardly, her rock like skin grating and grinding against the floor.

"Here. Let me help." He reaches out and levitates her off the ground, it might not be as good as a bed, but it was definitely more comfortable than the floor. "A floating bed for you."

"Very sweet of you," she states as she rolls onto her side, floating on a cushion of his will, "You realise when your powers run out I'm gonna hit the floor right?" she laughed and he was glad in that moment she wasn't facing him, his eyes went wide and he blossomed red, he had not thought of that at all.

Chapter 28

A scream rings out in the distance causing Tobias to jerk upright as he scans the room in a state of anxiety. Neomi is sulking in the corner, during the night he'd decided to put a shield around the eliXir during his watch and she hadn't been able to take any, she is now upset at him as a result but he does his best to ignore it. "What was that? Did you hear something?" Everything is blurry, his eyes struggling with the darkness combined with exhaustion, rubbing them doesn't seem to be achieving much.

"Yes. I'm not deaf Tobias, I heard it. It happens every few days, Lorenz probably needed more supplies with us gone." She doesn't look at him, her arms are wrapped around her knees drawing them up to her chest. The way she so callously refers to people's lives as supplies makes him want to scream or cry, it must be so normal down here that it just doesn't register anymore. It's insane and Tobias can't understand how anyone can live in a state of constant fear.

It does help stir him to action however, forcing himself up from the floor his body aches in resistance, he is glad at least his mind feels somewhat sharp because his muscles feel tense and ready to curl into a ball for a few days. He doesn't consider himself out of shape, but the events of the last twenty odd hours have certainly taken a toll on him.

"Come on Neomi. I know you're pissed off at me," he holds out a hand for her and puts on a cheesy but hopefully warming smile, "but let's go save the habs and put Lorenz in his place," he reaches out for three boxes, he can still feel the power in his body, his blood surges and he feels a warmth flowing through him as the crates of eliXir rise from the ground. As good as it feels he almost immediately realises how inconsiderate he is being, given Neomi's non powered state, she certainly doesn't fail to pick up on it.

"You're just fucking showing off now." Neomi complains as she takes the offered hand and raises herself up, he can't see her well in the dark but he can still tell her powers have faded, that her skin is back to normal. "You're powers have lasted like twelve hours or something. That's bullshit." she slumps her shoulders like an upset teenager and the petulance doesn't suit her.

He struggles to keep a straight face as she sounds like an upset child, but he is at least glad she is standing up. They stumble together out of the small housing unit, the dim light from outside just enough to show them the door. The crates float eerily behind as they make their way back out onto the streets.

His stomach lurches in hunger and Neomi laughs "We should have gotten you some food at Shirl's yesterday, it's easy to not realise how hungry you are when you're using. I'm not sure your delicate middle hab taste buds will enjoy the food down here." She continues to laugh at her own jokes, he instinctively places a hand on his stomach trying to quench the hunger and more so the embarrassing sounds.

"When this is over I'll let you take me out for a meal at Shirl's," he quips, trying to hide his blanched face.

"What like a date? How very forward of you Toby," she giggles once more at her own humour and Tobias is glad they are back out on the street so he can see her better, he is astounded by her beauty and how she looks when she laughs is positively infectious, he can't help but laugh along with her.

"Well we did tell everyone we were coming back soon, perhaps if no one turns up we can get some food instead," he jokes, although a part of him is concerned that everyone will be too scared to fight for themselves, for their society. It takes bravery and the screams in the night might have served as a stark reminder of why they should be scared. *Is it a coincidence?* Not much he can do different either way he supposes as they continue through the streets.

"It was a lot bloody quicker when we flew, you sure you don't want to make a grand entrance and save my feet some time?" she points down at her feet as if for some reason he might need reminding where they were. His own feet feel raw, his work shoes are ill suited for any kind of exertion let alone what he has been doing, with each step a little shudder of pain shoots up into his shins, he can't deny that he is severely tempted just to fly.

"You're probably right, I guess the only difference is that yesterday I didn't need to know where I was going, just away from Shirl's and towards the edges, now I actually need to find somewhere, I mean I don't even know where I am now, I'm relying on good ol' navigator Neomi." It is a poor excuse he knows, especially as flying doesn't cost him anything, "Plus what if I run out of power midair? Splat." he claps his hands together comically, but she looks unamused.

"Let's take a chance Toby, come on. You have power. More power than Lorenz could ever have or wish for, let's show the people what power looks like!" She looks at him with those light blue eyes and he feels more powerless than he can explain to her.

"Fine. We'll be going slower though, I need to be able to hear you saying where to go," he sighs resignedly as she lets out an almost chirping sound in excitement.

He raises them off the ground, they don't look particularly impressive he reflects, they look more like they are levitating instead of flying. He fidgets as he pushes them in the direction that Neomi is pointing, trying to figure out if there is a way he can fly and look more imposing or impressive. The old holo vids of people with superpowers fighting in arenas or in war made them look so much larger than life, with their costumes and heroic names. He doesn't feel heroic or worth following, even with all the power coursing through him.

At least the journey is quick, his feet are thankful for the rest. Neomi is pointing down now, she'd quickly moved to pointing after having to shout to be heard proved frustrating for both of them. He lowers them down and is damned if he can figure out how she knows this is the spot, it looks the same to him and he wonders if the middle habs look as confusing to an outsider.

As they softly land outside of Shirl's cafe, he is disappointed to see no crowd amassed, in fact there are no more or less people around than there were yesterday. He has failed, no one wants to follow him in his mission. Sensing his disappointment Neomi nudges his elbow "Look again, but not at the streets." she whispers.

He scans the buildings and rooftops and quickly realises what she means, there are people standing atop the rooftop balconies, and watching from windows or doorways, he was so preoccupied with landing safely he hadn't noticed them before. They are afraid, but they are more than just curious he realises, they want to do something, they want someone to help them help themselves, but they are still terrified. *They need someone to lead them or push them,* he thinks.

He considers raising himself from the ground again but instead just raises his voice and hopes it carries. Neomi takes his hand in hers and he almost panics and pulls it away, not expecting the gesture. He doesn't let go however and is thankful for the support, it helps him bolster himself before he begins.

"I'm sure many of you heard the screams in the night. Another one of you taken to fuel the drug industry of the rich or to exploit the poor." he decides to fight fear with fear, "It could be you or your children tomorrow. Look at these crates," he points at them for emphasis "these aren't just vials of a drug, these were people. People like you and me who never asked for trouble, never stepped a foot wrong but were convenient for someone else to take advantage of! Make a stand right now! Make a stand today with me. If you've ever lost someone to this drug, then take a vial now. Take one and hold their life in your hand. Turn that loss into power, turn their sacrifice into a better future for everyone!" He hadn't planned a speech, he had given it a little thought while Neomi slept, but now he was here it seems to roll naturally from his tongue and there was no denying the passion in his words.

There's lots shuffling and movement, people passing on the message to others who are out of earshot he realises. He wishes his powers would allow him to spread the message himself, for the passion he feels to be passed on with each message.

A man slowly exits one of the habs and moves towards him, like a domino effect another and another begin to gather. He feels an ease in his shoulders, he hasn't thought about how many he might need to fight against Lorenz's people and their labs, but even the five or six that were gathering in front of him were going to help immensely and he allows himself a smile in satisfaction.

He feels Neomi's hand tense in his own and his smile quickly fades.

The man front and centre of the group is one Tobias recognises, Samuel, he stands tall above the rest, his ponytail hanging down his back, he looks confident flanked by his group of muscle men. "You don't really think a few fucking speeches and a crate of eliXir is going to change anything down here do you Toby? You don't get it do you 'mid hab'?" The small group doesn't move any closer, keeping a distance, Tobias mentally shuffles the crates behind him so he is in the middle and it certainly doesn't evade Samuel's notice.

A smug grin widens on the other man's face as he lowers his voice, "Don't worry Toby, we don't need your little stash, we came prepared," he opens his arms wide like an emperor addressing an audience and his voice is louder than anything Tobias has ever heard, from this distance it is difficult to resist putting his hands over his ears as he winces.

"Dear friends and fellow low hab citizens. I know you are no doubt excited about the events earlier, but allow me to explain, this man before you is a criminal, both above and below, he has stolen from our beloved Dr. Lorenz. He is a liar and a fool, we have been sent to ensure your safety and that this man is dealt with. So please, return to your homes and rest knowing Dr. Lorenz has all of your interests at heart."

Samuel takes a step forward toward them and Neomi shifts behind him, probably to be closer to the eliXir more than wanting his protection he assumes.

"Come on now." his face is a picture of arrogance as his ponytail flicks in the wind, there is a soft plink as the other men drop empty vials against the ground, each one rolling or bouncing for a moment in the near silence before coming to a stop, Samuel tilts his head with a sideways smirk, "this doesn't have to be a confrontation Toby, give us the eliXir crates and the Doctor has given his word he'll secure you transport to the middle habs, your old life, you can pretend this was all a bad dream."

Chapter 29

"You're right," Tobias starts, his fists clenched at his side, feeling the power coursing through him and refusing to be intimidated by anyone, especially not the snake in front of him. "This doesn't have to be a confrontation. I did believe I could make a difference Samuel. Not at first, when I arrived here I was lost and scared." he lowers his head, looking at the hard packed earth below him, it already felt familiar and somehow right to have it beneath his feet. "I just didn't want to see anyone else be threatened with death or be scared for their lives." He can hear the shuffle of feet in front of him, the group dissipating to form a wider semi-circle. "The low levels aren't my home, I wasn't born here. I don't belong here." He feels Neomi grab his wrist from behind, she tugs gently as if trying to get him to face her but he stands firm. "It isn't my home." he unclenches a fist and holds out his hand, palm up and open at waist height, he raises his head to look Samuel in the eyes as he continues, "It is theirs," he pronounces firmly, as vials of lightly glowing eliXir begin to fly through the air at great speed, each heading directly for windows, balconies and bystanders in the street, where he can see someone he stops a vial directly in front of them, hovering inside their reach.

Samuel watches with his jaw dropped wide, for once lost for words, his men look in an equal state of disbelief, they quickly turn back to Tobias, all except one, who goes careening through the air and crashes into the wall of one of the fabricated houses, Tobias can't help but feel a small amount of satisfaction as the smile drops from Samuel's face. The satisfaction is short lived however as chaos breaks loose.

With four men left in front of him including Samuel it is difficult for Tobias not to feel intimidated, but with the power of telekinesis at his fingertips he finds the will to fight. Two of the men strike at the same time, a beam of purple energy blasts towards him from the side as the other man lunges with a pedestrian punch.

Tobias forms a protective barrier around himself as he is quickly becoming accustomed to doing, the energy deflects off him and Tobias realises he has no control over it as the beam singes the air and cuts into one of the habitats in the distance which almost immediately catches fire. With no time to react as the fist of the other man impacts Tobias' shield sending him crashing onto his back several meters away.

He strains to cough, to force air into his lungs as the blow leaves him winded, his head spinning from crashing and rolling against the ground, there is a short scream clearly from a woman which gets cut short and rallies him back to his feet. The final man of the four is standing over Neomi, she's lying on the floor hair covering most of her face as she's slumped on her side.

Another blow crashes into him and sends him once more flying through the lower hab air, his journey cut short as he crashes into the wall of a housing unit, his vision swims with the power of the impact even with his barrier active.

The man who punched him across the habs is standing there

smiling, thick black hair in a centre parting ruffled down his face, his smile revealing a distinct lack of a front tooth. Tobias can't be sure, but he looks more muscular and larger than when the group first arrived.

Samuel is clapping his hands, the confident grin once more across his face, he looks down at Neomi's slumped form and raises her arm with the tip of his foot before letting it crash back down, seemingly happy she isn't conscious, "She's had this long overdue Toby, she's in more debt with the Doctor than she can ever repay, for what it's worth, I am sorry." He laughs as the man with the purple energy blasts follows suit, his thick almost chest length beard flapping with his jowls as he does.

Tobias slowly raises himself back to his feet, careful not to take his eyes off the pack in front of him, especially as he still has no idea what powers the dark skinned man standing over Neomi's unconscious form has.

"Just give up Toby, we've lived here our whole lives and there's more of us, we're just better at this than you," Samuel quips, he's not sure if the man is trying to goad him or get him to give up, but he refuses to give the ponytailed idiot the satisfaction either way he decides.

He strikes out with both hands, one open in a pushing gesture and the other in a fist. The effects whilst invisible are no less devastating. The man lauding over Neomi gets buffeted by a wall of force, it takes almost all his concentration to shape it to avoid blowing Neomi away with him, the man is sent flying up into the air in a series of backward somersaults that looks almost disorienting to watch as it must be to experience. As his fist extends outwards, so too does the ball of energy released from it and the toothless but otherwise handsome man slumps over backwards hard with a gasp cut short, the crunch of the man's ribs can be heard from a distance and Tobias wonders if he may have been too hard, he didn't want to kill the man.

With two of his men down already Samuel decides to step in, he opens his mouth and screams. The sound is so loud and focused it immediately brings Tobias to his knees, hands over his ears and internally begging it for stop whilst his own screams are completely drowned out, the pain wracks his head and he feels like something is going to give any moment, his brain or his ears. He finds himself praying for the latter whilst rolling on the ground.

In an instant the screaming stops, at least he thinks so, the ringing in his ears is so distinct and loud but at least it's more distant. He raises his head from his near foetal position on the ground and see's Samuel breathing deep for another breath, for another shattering blast of screaming.

In his dazed state it is all Tobias can do to flick out a finger, a small burst of force hits Samuel in the side of the head. He knows it isn't enough, little more than a quick distraction, that it won't take long for the man to recover but it's all he can manage.

The man with the impressively long beard takes advantage of the lull in the screaming and unleashes another barrage of energy against the pathetic looking Tobias, but to the man's surprise it still refracts off an unseen barrier, the deflected blast goes almost directly upwards, harmlessly into the darkness above. It casts a light through the area and through blurred vision Tobias weakly holds out a cupped hand in Samuel's direction and watches as the man tries to bang at his own face, punching at an unseen bubble around his own head, even in pain as he is, he manages to take some small measure of satisfaction as the man who served him up to Lorenz chokes for air.

As Tobias delicately raises himself back up to his feet there is a measure of reversal as the man opposite him falls to knees and then collapses on his side, the air in his lungs spent. Tobias walks towards the fallen man as another stream of energy reaches towards him, the bright violet energy lighting up the lower habs, this time he holds an open palm, creating an angled wall between the two of them and the energy once more stretches out into the darkness above.

Tobias gasps as a lightning bolt flies from a rooftop ahead of him and flies over his head. A painful scream rings out somewhere behind him, spinning on the spot and searching for the target, he sees a figure plummeting from the sky behind him, the dark skinned man he'd previously sent flying must have had some kind of flight of his own and had been closing behind him, only now he is plummeting to the ground, his body wracked by lightning.

The sizzle of another stream of energy being released snaps his attention back to the bearded thug but is surprised when nothing impacts his force shell. The blast has impacted the balcony of a habitat where the lightning had come from. Before Tobias can do anything however, the bearded man stumbles as if punched in the stomach, doubling over and gasping for air as another blow catches him in the head and sends him onto his side. There are groans of pain as the thug is hit again and again.

"FUCK YOU!" someone says in furious anger, "The low habs belong to us," he hears from in front of him and it quickly clicks, someone has gained the power of invisibility and has taken the bearded man down with ease. His mind wanders for a moment about whether or not he could create an illusionary person, invisible but able to interact like a person, he snaps out of his delusions and turns his attention to the scene at hand.

Looking to the final thug, the strong one he smashed with a ball of force. He was still down and two people he didn't recognise were quickly binding him with ropes and some kind of plastic ties, it looks most uncomfortable he thinks. He darts over to Neomi and no sooner is he crouched at her side than another woman squats awkwardly beside him.

"Shirl, is she okay?" He has no medical knowledge whatsoever, he could see she was breathing and that was about as far as it extended. He looked at Shirl with pleading and desperate eyes, he would hate if he had let her come this far alongside him only to fall now.

"She's fine, but watch this skinny," she laughs, deep and hoarse as she places a hand on Neomi's face. The cut above her eye closes and the crimson swelling and purple bruises acquired over the last day quickly return to their normal colour. Tobias finds himself in awe, for all his power and Neomi telling him how rare it was, here he was in the presence of someone who had the power of healing, just imagining what power like that could do amazed him, the lives that could be saved.

He thanks Shirl as Neomi opens her eyes, she looks well rested, even the bags under her eyes have gone. "Damn. How long was I out for? I saw a man flying towards me then bam, lights out. I feel like I've been asleep for days. What happened?" She sounded so full of energy and excited, it was more than Tobias could have hoped for and he offers a hand to help her up before explaining.

"I did what we came to do Neomi, I gave the people power, Shirl here healed you, all your cuts, bruises, everything. That's probably why you feel refreshed I guess. Some other person shot lightning and helped me, it was amazing and terrifying at the same time. We've got it under control but we have to make the most of this, we have to go find Lorenz now and put an end to this."

Neomi points to Shirl's cafe, he is thankful that the energy blasts missed it and it's still intact. "Let's go to Shirl's, we'll gather everyone who wants to help and plan our attack," as she says attack a vicious tone washes over her face. Tobias finds it intimidating but doesn't say anything, instead he goes and checks on the crates of eliXir. Two of the crates are still unopened but the one on top is spent, should still be plenty for the attacks on Lorenz's facilities, he hopes.

Chapter 30

The lights of the city are as bright as ever, people dart out of the roads as they hear the sirens blaring, Russell' is thankful at least that the sirens drown out the sound of the constant advertisements, some deal somewhere meant whilst they couldn't be displayed in the car there was nothing to stop them been directed to officers implants. *Just another example of how the corporations from above control everything,* he bemoans.

He forces down the negative thoughts, thinking on whether or not he's safe to be driving and what is he even planning to do once he arrives at the cordon. Struggling to come to grips with everything that is quickly growing out of control, at least the drive gives him something to focus on, to channel his concentration. The navigation pings an update on the quickest route, he knows it isn't going to be a long drive, but with his mind racing it feels like everything is slowed down.

A loud series of beeps indicates a critical incoming message, he presses a button on the steering wheel so as to have it play over the in car systems as his helmet still sits on the passenger seat. "Sarge, it's Mel. I've got an update for you, it includes visual though and the readout here says you don't have your helmet on?"

Dammit, he curses to himself, "Got it Mel, hang on, I'm gonna have to stop." In his own rush he has ended up costing himself time he frustratingly reflects as he taps a button on the dashboard, the sirens immediately cut out and he pulls the police cruiser over to the side of the road.

He turns his attention to the vid screen in the middle console "Go ahead Mel, I'm watching,"

He hears a girly giggle in the background "I know. I'm watching too!"

He sighs "Mel, you remember how I explained there is a massacre about to commence? Let's focus." She's probably nervous, he regrets the order coming out more harshly than he had intended, but he could imagine her silly mock salute as the reply comes through light-heartedly, "Yes Sir!" the console vid screen lights up and footage from the low habs begins to play, the location appears to be one of the old delivery lifts, rarely used anymore but still heavily guarded, some considered the rotation a punishment, but there was no doubt of its importance. The quality wasn't great but there was no mistaking Mr. Barton, even in the grainy footage his clothing stood out from the low hab citizens, he was being assailed by some thugs from the low habs and then it happens.

"I'm sorry Sarge, that place down there, it eats people alive. It looks like your man is now one of them." Russells clenches his jaw as he watches Tobias inject himself with a vial and start single handedly taking down an entire group of thugs.

"He became a TK on his first hit, he got lucky there at least, the poor son of a bitch." he aired the thought to himself mostly but was aware Mel was still on the line. He continues watching as Tobias tears open the lift door. "Wait… how old is this footage Mel? Is he…here now!?" the alarm in his voice is clear but he immediately realises the foolishness of his question.

"Do you think we'd be quietly having this conversation if he was? Nah, keep watching," she jibes. Tobias climbs into the lift and the footage switches to a camera at the top of the lift, the footage is far better quality from inside the lift and the flying scruffy man just floats there, staring at the door.

"Why didn't he come through? He's just floating there, I don't get it Sarge," Mel questions, but Russells gets it. Tobias isn't stupid, he knows right there in that very moment that he cannot go through.

"It's the impact Mel, he knows what he's done, that he is now guilty of the very crime he was accused of in the first place, the accusation which led to all of this. It's the pain of realising he can't return home," the footage ends with Tobias slowly floating back into the darkness. "Thanks for showing me this, it's a shame what has happened to him but it doesn't change that I need to get to the chutes-"

"Not so fast." she quickly interrupts "Before you go, there's actually more footage, you know the warehouse we saw him in before? Well, him and his lady friend went back."

The console lights up once more and the familiar dark warehouse is difficult to see in the contrast of the lights and brightness of the middle habs. "What am I looking at Mel?" he asks somewhat impatiently.

"Just wait." she says, doing nothing to hide the excitement in her voice. He watches as Tobias and his friend enter the warehouse and begin helping themselves to crates of drugs. "Oh fuck." he whispers realising exactly how much eliXir that actually is, but he finds himself even more taken back at the scenes that follow as a group of individuals enter and powered hell breaks loose, it feels all too fresh and familiar from the scenes at the bank, only at least with less innocent people caught in the mix.

"You can see the footage better than me Mel, how clear is it that those crates with the drugs in are from the Pro Life Corp?" he turns off the console and starts the car back on the road but keeps the sirens off for now.

"With a little gamma enhancement, just fine, why? What're you thinking?" the excitement isn't there anymore, she's curious for sure but apprehensive as well.

"I'm thinking this could be what we need to show their true face to the rest of the world, if we can put the spotlight on them, maybe we can stop this bloody culling of the poor people in the low habs. Where do these crates go? Upper habs I bet. You're going to have to trawl through past footage, see what you can dig up?"

"Are you fucking insane?" Mel whispers over the comms, as if somehow whispering hides their conspiring, "We can't go after Pro Life Corp. We just can't, it's just us Sarge, we can't make a difference in all this!"

He grunts "Now you sound like the bloody Captain, it doesn't matter if we can make a difference Mel, we have to try, we can't just stand by and let innocent people die." The resolution in his own voice surprises even himself, but the confidence makes him feel more certain about what he's doing.

"That guy, Tobias Barton, he's not innocent Sarge, you saw him take eliXir, if that was up here, he'd be executed. Let's just drop it before we both end up dead."

"I can't. He might have taken eliXir, but he's not guilty, he had no choice, we put him in that situation Mel. Even if we can't help him, we have to help the others like him."

The intercom cuts off, he isn't sure whether he pushed her too hard or whether she's still on his side, he'll have to hope for the best. He once more pokes the button for the sirens and pushes down hard on the accelerator, he has to get to that lift and he has to get there now.

Chapter 31

Striding into the cafe with crates of super powered drugs floating behind him, the only person who makes sure she gets in before him is Shirl, who had made it very clear she was going in first. Quickly the room begins to fill, people grabbing the limited seating whilst others stand around the edges of the room, capitalising on the opportunity, Shirl is quick to offer drinks to everyone and find herself rushing back and forth to the kitchen. It quickly becomes obvious that the cafe isn't going to hold everyone, with people stood around the door and outside from the best that Tobias can see.

At least this time he was sure that whatever he said next would be passed along the chain to everyone else. As confident as he feels about his plans he can't help but feel a little awkward having everyone in the room focusing on him and Neomi, every set of eyes watching him in anticipation. Every practised instinct inside him was screaming at him to run, to curl up and hide from the attention but he forces them down and stands tall, having Neomi looking healthy and well beside him helps, even if he can't tell her right now.

Forty eight hours ago, this room would have terrified him, not just because of the size of the crowd and the attention but the fact that it was clearly visibly that at least a quarter of the occupants were currently on eliXir, there was a woman in the corner whose hair appeared molten and was smouldering, everyone keeping a small bubble of freedom around here, there was the man next to the kitchen door whose proportions were all wrong, like someone had stretched him out, his head craned against the roof of the cafe. The idea of being in a room of powered individuals should have sent him running, especially after the events at the bank that led to all of this. Instead he felt comforted, these people have chosen to be here, have chosen to listen to him and what he has to say and to fight for their own homes and safety. Now they were looking to him and he couldn't allow himself to disappoint them now.

He coughs to clear his throat but it proves largely ineffective, the thickness of the air and the coating of dust on everything outside were taking their toll. "Thank you everyone," he begins, the murmuring in the room quickly dropping to silence, only the pacing steps of Shirl any competition for his voice in the room. "Thank you for your help out there and for standing up for yourselves and the lower habs. If you are here in this room with me right now it's because you want to stand up against the evil acts of Lorenz and people like him. You don't want to live in fear of what might happen when you close your eyes, what might happen to your children. Today we end all that, we have right here the tools we need to put a stop to all of it, for you to regain control of the lower habs." He places his hands on the crates for emphasis. "Neomi tells me you all know each other, that the community down here is close despite how it looks to me. Find your friends, grab your family and go together. Me and Neomi are going to go directly to the head himself, we will attack Lorenz's facility and put an end to it. The rest of you go in small groups and take a vial each, destroy his facilities on the outskirts, he's made no effort to hide them, no effort to disguise what he does. When it's done, we will all meet at the former head of Lorenz's operations and celebrate the end of fear and the end of tyranny these drugs have brought upon you."

There is no big cheer when he finishes, he didn't know what he had expected really when he'd finished his speech, he hadn't planned it or really thought much about it and had just let the moment take him. It wasn't like the holo vids where groups of people start cheering and pumping their fists in the air, when it was clear he had finished they started mumbling amongst themselves, some started to move into groups which was a promising sign he hoped.

He looks over at Neomi and sees she has a vial in her hand, it shouldn't have surprised him but he didn't see her take it or even open the crate. She stands on a chair and holds the vial up above her head, the distinct glow giving a small light in the room.

"Friends, most of you know me, the scavengers here most certainly do. This man," she gestures at him, not pointing or accusingly but with an open palm, "isn't one of us and he didn't choose to be here, but that hasn't changed what he's been through and what he has seen. He is willing to fight for us and we shouldn't be willing to do any less." In a stylish flourish she kicks one of the crates and it flicks open on its hinge, revealing to all the vials of eliXir contained within.

"Groups of five, take a small container each and go forth, take the power that is rightfully yours, take in your hand the friends and family you've lost and channel it into a wave of destruction that will set us free!"

This time there were cheers and people clapping, he felt a little bit jealous that her speech was so much better received than his but he can't fault the outcome, people were coming forward in their small groups and taking the semi-transparent containers with eliXir inside. Neomi looks at him with a heart-warming smile, he finds it comforting that she is on his side and he returns the gesture, glad to have her help.

She hops down from the table and lands clumsily in front of him, vial still clutched in her hands. "You ready to do this? To be a hero?" considering what they were about to face, her cheerful manner seemed bizarre to him, he leans in and takes a vial for himself, it feels warm in his hand and knowing what it can do gives the small container a sense of awe. Her words made him mentally stumble, he'd never for a moment considered himself a hero, he'd seen the vid casts of so called heroes from when he was younger, people with powers fighting in the military or helping others. Everyone had seen the vid casts of Russia, what could happen when two groups of super powered people in costumes engaged in war. That was the reason powers were outlawed and he couldn't think of himself as a hero.

"I'm no hero," his smile drops and his confident facade falters, "I just want to be able to live without fear, to regain a normal life. I'm not selfless or compassionate." His voice is low but he manages to keep his head held high.

"No heroes then, we don't need a hero anyway." She hasn't stopped smiling and takes his hand into hers and looks him in the eyes, she's stunning and it's all he can do to stay standing as his body loses stability and threatens to betray him. "What we need is someone to follow, someone who can lead us against Lorenz. You can do that Toby, I know you can." The statement bolsters him and he makes his way through the crowd with her following close behind hand in hand, thankfully people have already started leaving the cafe so it's easy to get out onto the streets. The people are already starting to disperse, in small groups in separate directions, the plans now firmly set in motion.

With his spare hand he points it palm down towards the earth, the two of them rise slowly into the air and Tobias shouts "Let this be the end of fear in the low habs!" he doesn't wait for a reaction or see if there is one, instead slowly flying away with Neomi next to him, in another place at another time this would have been incredibly romantic he realises, quickly dismissing the thought as he realises once again that he doesn't know where he is going.

"So, erm... yet again I am relying on you for navigation," he chuckles awkwardly.

"You would be so lost without me," she laughs and points off into the distance, near one of the borders of the city. He knows technically he doesn't need to hold her hand to make them both fly, he wonders if she realises that but is glad for comfort of being close to her.

"Do you think there are enough people to take down all of Lorenz's operations?" he has to raise his voice to be heard but at least not too a shout as they aren't flying nearly as fast this time.

"A lot of those people will be first timers Toby, the power will come naturally as you now know and their powers will last longer as a result, I think each group could easily deal with one of Lorenz's chop shops, there aren't all that many. I just hope they strike quickly and hard before any of the bouncers get chance to power up, I'm sure each of his little slimy facilities has a personal stash for just such reasons."

It hadn't occurred to him in earnest that the facilities they were about to destroy would be well guarded, let alone by people with powers as well, everyone who was educated saw the vids growing up, what happens when two large groups of powered people fight each other, it didn't end well for anyone, particularly not innocent bystanders. "Well, hopefully after all that has happened over the last twenty four hours Lorenz has consolidated his people at his main," he cringes at the final word, "surgery."

"Wouldn't that be really bad for us?" she raises an eyebrow quizzically as she looks over to him.

"Sure, but we can handle it. You broke us out on your own, imagine what two of us can do?" he tries to make a reassuring smile, but the vial of eliXir in her hand was probably more of a comfort than he could hope to be.

Minutes pass as they fly slowly forward, he could certainly fly them faster, but nerves were holding him back. He doesn't mention it out loud but he is terrified of heading back to the place where he almost died, one of the destinations on the spiral of him losing control of his life.

"Look," Neomi breaks his sombre concentration and he looks back to see where she is pointing, somewhere behind them there is a fire, he can't make out what exactly or how big, but it's glow casts high in the lower habitats and he takes it to be a sign of reassurance.

"It looks like we are running late," he quips as he turns back towards the direction of Lorenz's surgery, he lets go of Neomi's hand and surges them both forward, this time with speed and purpose.

Despite a few course changes, it doesn't take long to find their destination and it makes him realise why his legs were so exhausted after fleeing not a day ago, it was further than he'd realised and adrenaline had carried them far. They are here now however, the streets are almost completely empty and he supposes most of the prefab houses around here are probably empty. The only people he can see are the small group standing directly outside of the surgery, they weren't there coincidentally, that much was obvious to him as one of the group points up at them, their light silhouette standing out even against the consuming darkness above.

Neomi doesn't hesitate, whether scared of being caught off guard again or from her lust for the drug, she injects her vial as they descend towards the surgery. A barely audible gasp comes from next to him as the eliXir enters her bloodstream and what follows is the most terrifying, blood curdling scream he has ever heard in his life.

He slams them down harder than expected, the sound causing him to panic, the look in the eyes of the men and women assembled opposite him tell him there is cause to be worried, he turns to Neomi but she is gone, replaced with a muscular tall animal human hybrid.

He looks up at her, she towers over him easily and his instincts are screaming for him to run away, it takes all of his will to remember that it is Neomi in there and he prays she remembers him. Thick dark blue hair covers her form, her arms ending in sharp glistening claws and her feet look almost webbed as she roars once more at the thugs opposite, her mouth is a mass of dagger like small teeth and he realises he can't pin down exactly what she has become.

She turns to him and her face draws closer, the chimeric creature has her blue eyes and he tries to stand his ground and resist the growing urge to flee, the creature winks at him and lets out a smirk which is almost as intimidating as the roaring. In an instant she leaps forward and the last Tobias sees of her is the animalistic form crashing headlong into one of the thugs, their two bodies disappearing into the surgery, the metallic crash of the door smashing inwards drowned out by the agonising scream of the man she has forced through it.

Tobias' recovers before everyone else and doesn't hold back, he has seen how out of control things can get if this turns into a brawl between powered people, thrusting out with his hands the entire group in front of him slams into the walls of the building, one goes straight through the metal sheets with a loud crash. A rapid pull of his hands and the two remaining thugs are pulled from the wall only to be viciously slammed against them once more. He releases them from the coils of his will and they both collapse to the floor, their bodies rattled and broken.

Satisfied he has neutralised the immediate threat he darts towards the surgery, it is a mess inside and the door that flew inwards has left huge trenches in the floor which are now full of blood, the source of which he can't see. The sides of this supposed lobby are largely untouched, Neomi hadn't stopped to look around and had charged headlong into the corridor. Screams can be heard from deeper in the building and Tobias hopes it comes to a swift end and feels sorry for anyone Neomi comes into contact with, well almost anyone he thinks.

Not wanting to risk running recklessly into danger including a bestial Neomi, he treads slowly and carefully through the second smashed door and into the all too familiar corridors of the facility. Some of the corrugated sheets that make up walls have been pushed outwards or dented, presumably where the rampaging beast that was his friend had careened through like a wrecking ball. The side rooms still all appear to be closed from what little he can see, it appears she is making a direct line for Lorenz and cares about little else.

Tobias' hatred for this place encourages him to be more thorough and he throws his hands outwards and a bubble of force expands from out of him. It pushes against the walls and doors, they resist at first but they are no match for his power, for his will. The screeching of metal buckling and grinding as the very walls and doors of the building are forced outwards is deafening but he doesn't relent. He keeps the dome cantered on him as he walks forward through the corridor, the building rippling and breaking in a morass around him. He barely notices and takes no joy in its destruction, it is simply something he wants to see gone.

As a section of wall collapses he watches as a brown skinned man charges towards him, his hands are missing and instead they've become elongated bladed weapons, he looks like something out of a horror vid. His charge falters as he impacts against the dome surrounding Tobias, his attack ending well over a meter away from him. The man takes a moment to realise what has happened and slashes rapidly and wildly at the bubble of force in front him. Tobias grits his teeth and focuses his mind into a point, thrusting like a spear from his own body, he can feel it in the air and knows it to be real but the man opposing him sees nothing, not even as the spear pierces through his leg, pinning him to the floor. The man wails in pain as blood trickles down the invisible spike, it looks most unnatural, like a small blood waterfall he supposes and in the dark Tobias almost feels sorry for the man, slashing with sword-like protrusions at something he can't see to try and free himself. He pays him no mind and continues towards Lorenz's office, remembering all too well every step along the way.

As he draws nearer he shrinks the dome and ceases the destruction of the building and its equipment. Turning a corner into the wake of not his own demolishing but he presumes Neomi's, the fancy door that was the entry to Lorenz's office is in ruins and it suddenly dawns on Tobias that in her rage and animalistic form she may have just killed him on site. Not that he particularly wanted the satisfaction, it hadn't really occurred to him what he was going to do once he got this far, he doesn't consider himself a killer and isn't sure he has it in him to kill the man despite what he is doing down here.

"Please, don't kill me! I don't want to die!" Come the shouting pleas from up ahead, the voice has a distorted familiarity, he knew it to be Lorenz's but it sounded impossibly more phlegmy and hoarse than it had last time. The shout spurs Tobias to hurry the last few steps into the office, the chairs and table are in ruins and Neomi is hunched over due to being too tall for the room, it is obvious seeing her here how the structure took so much damage as she rampaged through it.

"You don't deserve to live," the growling voice was a long distance from her usual soft tones and Tobias is taken back as he didn't realise she could even still talk in this form.

"It's you!" Lorenz, or at least what is left of him, points a bandaged hand out at Tobias, immediately he seems to have forgotten about the terrifying sight lauding over him. Lorenz looks nothing like Tobias remembered, one of his left arms is a bandaged stump and his face is heavily scarred with what look like burn wounds. Bandages are wrapped around most of the remaining visible skin. When they fled Tobias hadn't stopped for a minute to wonder what the damage would be from Neomi's acidic spheres, but seeing the damage up close was a horrifying reminder of the danger of people having super powers.

Tobias was speechless but it doesn't stop Lorenz from continuing, "I was hoping we would meet again. It's true isn't it?" the man shuffles into a seated position, it looks for a second like he wants to raise himself to standing but lacks the strength.

Tobias' voice comes out weakly and lacks the confidence he felt not minutes ago, he feels guilty but knows he shouldn't, "What is true? What are you talking about?"

"Your powers have not faded yet have they? My men reported that you still have it, the telekinesis." Despite it all the Doctor manages a smile, it looks as sadistic as before but combined with the fresh scarring it looks more menacing than ever. Neomi's head twists from staring at Lorenz to a quick glance over at Tobias.

"I know you have never used before but she has," he strains to nod his head up at Neomi, "even for a first time user your mental powers have lasted longer than anyone we've ever seen. I wondered if this would happen eventually."

Tobias's mind is racing trying to process what is happening right now. Neomi was staring at him and he isn't sure what was running through her mind, he had taken her knowledge as rule. Before either of them can open their mouths to discuss what is going on the Doctor continues his wondering, "Were your parents both heavy users? Where were they from? I'm most curious," the look on his face is certainly not what you'd expect for someone facing down death, he looks invigorated and excited at their reunion.

Tobias doesn't even entertain not answering, or consider that the man might be desperately trying to buy himself time and he answers with honesty and haste, "My parents were from the mid habs, they never touched eliXir, no one in the middle habs does, the punishment is extreme." he begins overthinking everything that has ever happened in his life, questioning everything that is.

"Hmm, that is surprising. Unlikely perhaps." the Doctor trails off, seemingly lost in his own thoughts for a moment before bringing himself back to the room. "It isn't just you, do you know that?" the words ring in his mind, too much for him to understand or process but Neomi reacts almost immediately.

"What do you mean?!" she growls, her shark like teeth only an inch or two from the Doctor's face and Tobias oddly notices for the first time that there is a coating of blood on some of her fangs.

He laughs despite the imminent danger, relishing having even an inkling of power left over the people in his presence. "Well, he is the first person whose powers will not fade, whatever power he has inside him, the telekinesis that my drugs provided, it isn't going to run out, it isn't temporary." Neomi turns and glares at Tobias, even with her facial expression masked by the form she currently resides the angry jealousy in her eyes is unmistakable and the Doctor doesn't hesitate to capitalise on it.

"He doesn't have to be the only one, I gave it a lot of thought and consideration since your," he pauses, seemingly seeking for the right word, "departure, anticipation of you coming back Tobias. Whatever is inside you, whatever you are. I think a small and simple blood transfusion would pass on hmm…" he pauses again and Tobias isn't sure if it's for dramatic effect or if he's once again looking for the words, "let's say, your ability to soak up the eliXir. Imagine it, a world where everyone has powers, no more downtrodden, no more threats from above, no more raids from the so called Angels. Survival of the Fittest. Think of what the world could be, what the human race could achieve with unlimited power. You would be a god in that world Tobias, you managed to get one of the strongest powers imaginable and you have it permanently!"

Tobias ignores the scowls from Neomi and gathers his resolution, "No, we've seen what happens with power. The strong control the weak. Millions would die and the only winners would be those who got lucky with their power set. It's over Lorenz," with that Tobias turns around and walks to leave, he was right that he didn't have it inside him to kill the man, especially not after seeing him in the damaged state he is now.

"Wait… don't leave, you can give me life again Toby, I can help you!" the desperate pleading comes from behind but Tobias doesn't falter, even if he allows Lorenz to live, his operations are destroyed and his power lost. One way or another, it's over. "Don't walk away from me, you aren't too good for the low habs Tobias! We could rule down here and up there."

"Are we just going to leave him here?" the deep yet somehow feminine voice asks, Tobias looks over his shoulder at Neomi and notices the flicker of metal as Lorenz draws a pistol from behind his back, the well-lit room causing it to reflect and sheen.

Neomi turns to the Doctor, following Tobias' eye line and sees the gun for herself as his finger slowly squeezes the trigger, she pounces between the two men as the muzzle flash flickers.

It feels like time slows down as the bullet inexorably spins through the air towards her, Neomi's eyes widen in surprise and she instinctively flinches and holds her hands up as if to somehow deflect the bullet.

Without a sound the bullet falls upon the rugged carpet in the office. The bullet tip flattened where it has impacted the barrier Tobias erected. He tears the gun from Lorenz's hand and crushes it with his mind before continuing to leave, sparing a final look at the Doctor whose face has now drooped and looks truly defeated.

"He's finished Neomi," he states while walking away, grimacing as he hears the man's guttural screams cut short behind him.

Chapter 32

As he slowly trudges through the wreckage of the surgery, Tobias feels a sense of freedom he has not felt for a long time. That perhaps for the first time in his life he is free, that his life is in his own control and not in the hands of others. He steps out into the empty streets of the low habs, with the men he fought earlier having fled or in hiding it is just him. He slumps onto the floor and enjoys a moment of quiet and relief whilst trying to process everything the Doctor told him.

My powers are permanent. It was unheard of and as far as he knew no one in history had ever had powers that didn't fade, he was the first. What would that mean for him, would he be hunted forever? Others were already looking to him for hope and for their future, this would only make things worse he thought.

As if to punctuate his thoughts, Neomi plunges out of the rubble with a crash, having spent her remaining energy and rage on smashing up the building and equipment within. She was starting to regress, her form was a little shorter and her teeth less profound. She crouches down next to him and a little cloud of short hair follows her.

"It's done Neomi, we are free, that man can't hurt us or anyone else ever again," he states, but he can feel the unease radiating from her.

"It'll never be over Toby, but it's a bloody good start." she smiles a wide grin and the blood drip dropping onto the floor makes his stomach churn, "I'm sure everyone else was just as successful, there is no way any of Lorenz's operations were ready for an assault like this. They'll come to you now, they'll look to you for what to do next," it wasn't a revelation for him but it still surprises him that people are looking to him for help and answers. He just wishes he had some.

"So…" she starts and he has a good idea of what is coming next, "you have powers forever, that's amazing. You must be feeling so good right now, that the feeling of power coursing through you is never going to fade, it's like a permanent high!" the more she spoke the faster the words flurry from her mouth, "and to think, if he's telling the truth you can transfer this to anyone! Think of what that could mean Toby, ignore the crap he was spouting about ruling and controlling people, just think of all the good it could do. Medicine. Technology. We could change those things overnight for the better of everyone!"

It was a compelling argument and one he was sure more intelligent people than him had discussed endlessly. He doesn't want to argue with her, he knows what she wants, the unasked request that he doesn't want to fulfil. They sit in silence for a few minutes until groups of people start to arrive and gather in front of them.

He can't tell if anyone is missing or hasn't survived their individual missions, he is frustrated with himself for not knowing anyone's name or how many people had gone, *what kind of a leader was so callous?* He scolds himself, but is thankful there seems to be a bare minimum of injuries, a few scrapes and cuts but nothing as severe as lost limbs.

Everyone looks normal he notes, if anyone is still holding their powers then they aren't physical transformations. His mind wanders and he turns to Neomi, her claws have almost entirely retracted now, "Are some people more likely to get certain powers? Is it truly random? I'm just thinking I've seen you use eliXir three times now and two of those have been big physical changes," he appreciates this is hardly the most pressing concern at the moment but he can't hide his curious nature.

"As far as anyone knows it's random. I'm not sure anyone down here has done studies into it or kept notes. Maybe up the top they have, I dunno." she shrugs her shoulders and a load of hair wafts down her shoulders and shows the skin below and it suddenly occurs to him that she's going to be naked when she fully sheds. He quickly turns his head back to the group and rushes over to a man and asks him for his coat, the man looks at Tobias with a look he has never seen before. A look of admiration and awe. He hands over his coat without any hesitation and Tobias awkwardly thanks him before darting back to Neomi and offering it to her.

"Thank you." her voice has softened closer to her normal tone as she wraps herself in the coat. "It wouldn't have been a big deal down here but thank you all the same." She chuckles and for a moment it feels like it's just the two of them again. "You better think of something to say, they're not going to stop staring at you until you say something," she whispers kindly, he turns to face the group and digs for the words to say.

He raises his voice to the point that it's a strain to talk and it feels like any word might start a coughing fit, "We did it everyone, Lorenz and his operations down here are over. No longer will any of you have to worry about been taken while you sleep, never again will you have to watch as loved ones and family are murdered for his profits. You are in control now, the habs are yours once more, you can live now in peace." He doesn't have much more to add, but no one is leaving, there is some murmuring amongst the crowd but they still stand there waiting for more.

A thin woman, a bruise near one of her temples barely covered by short blonde hair that is unevenly cut steps slightly forward, she raises her voice to be heard but her tone isn't angry or upset. "Only for now, what about the other cities in the low habs? Word will reach them somehow and it'll only be a matter of time until someone hears what happened here and comes to fill the void, they could end up being even worse! We all knew where Lorenz's drugs were going, what do you think they'll do once they find out their deliveries have stopped? They're going to send someone here to take his place." Others were nodding in agreement, concern was rife amongst their expressions. He can't say they are wrong, that they are going to be safe forever, he wishes to the heavens he could but it would be a lie and he hates it.

He feels a tug at his wrist and turns back to Neomi, she is still just about taller than him but most of the fur is gone, her long legs are bared below the coat and he fights to keep his eyes up which means losing himself in her eyes once again. "There is a solution," her voice is lowered and he is confident that no one else can hear her, "Look at these people Toby, sure they are scared and worried, but look past that, look at the hope in their eyes. It's the same hope I felt when we met, for most of them it's the first hope they've ever had in their lives." The passion in her words is overwhelming and he harshly realises this might be the first time he has seen her care so much about the people of the lower habitats. "You can be their leader Tobias, you can empower them all, empower us all, and lead us. I'd follow you and they would too, you've given them a taste of freedom they've never known but you could make that freedom last a lifetime. No more oppression from people like Lorenz, no more being downtrodden from above." she bites her tongue at the end, clearly worried she might have overstepped but Tobias shrugs it aside.

"It isn't up to me to play some kind of evolutionary god Neomi," he was trying to keep his voice lowered but for every passionate word she had, his was lined with equal measures of frustration. "I can't decide who gets power and who doesn't, what if the people I pass it onto can pass it on further or through their children? I could be the catalyst for the end of the world. I can't do that. What happens if someone like Lorenz gets control of something like this? What happens then, the level of escalation is unthinkable." He sighs as he finishes, for the first time since taking eliXir he regrets that decision, hates the responsibility thrust upon him.

Neomi's expression flashes from stunned to rage and he resists the compulsion to step away or fly upwards, any restraint in lowering her voice lost, "At least it would be fucking fair," she spits, "you owe it to these people, to me, to give us a fighting chance instead of what we have now. The next time someone comes at least we'll have an even playing field and can fight for ourselves!" he can hear the muttering behind him, it must have been clear to everyone now that they were in a heated argument.

"It won't work out like that, you can't just up and go to the other habs and take them by force, forcing your own control upon them. I mean that would require passing through the mid habs first and I've told you what it's like up there. It's not like here, the police have weapons and technology designed for fighting back, made to neutralise powers and they all have order to kill anyone who is using eliXir or has at any point!"

A look of confusion furrows her brow "But what about the upper habs? They use eliXir right, how come your police don't stop that?" It was a conversational diversion he was relieved for and he had never thought much about how she was as equally naive about the upper habs as he was about here.

"The people in the upper habs don't live like us, they are rich and powerful and backed by corporations like Pro Life, they are the ones who pay for the mid habs law enforcement, they sponsor our government. They control everything, most of us in the middle habs dream about life up there, but in reality we don't know a great deal about it. What I do know, is as soon as you step into the middle habs, it'll be war. The police, the Archangels, they'll all come for you in force and they'll kill you all. Then they'll come down here and execute anyone who has so much as touched eliXir. We have to stay here, we can both have quiet happy lives here Neomi." he tries his best to put on a warming smile but it is weak and he knows it.

She looks at him, expressionless and it sends chills down his spine "So what then Tobias? We just sit here and farm for a few weeks until someone comes to fill the vacuum left by Lorenz?"

A chasm of silence fills the air between them as Tobias tries to think of a solution, "What if we expose what happened down here? Show the other habs what life is like down here, that the Pro Life Corp is paying for people to be murdered to create illegal drugs that are distributed amongst the wealthy? Show the world what is happening here."

She cocks her head slightly to the side and raises a quizzical eyebrow, "You think they don't already know? You've spent your entire life living in ignorance of what goes on above you and what goes on below you. If it wasn't for an unfortunate series of events, you wouldn't care," she holds up a hand to prevent him from interrupting "I don't mean it nastily, but do you honestly think anyone in the middle habs cares what is happening down here right now? Would you have cared or would you have just switched the news to something else to continue your blissful ignorance?"

She places a hand upon his cheek, it's soft and he feels tingles of warmth radiate from her touch. "You are sweet Toby, naive but sweet. You've given the people here the first hope they've ever had. You've given me hope. You have seen first-hand what happens down here but in your heart you are too good a man to do what needs to be done." She leans in, a hand placed upon his chest and her lips drawing closer to his own. He feels a flash of pain on the side of his head and his descent to the hard floor is the last thing he sees before his world turns black.

Chapter 33

The tyres of his car screech to a halt and it draws the eyes and angry gazes of a dozen of the large group of assembled personnel. The large bulkhead door for the lift to the lower habitats is as solid and closed as it ever is, Russells is thankful that he isn't too late, he has no idea what he can say or do to prevent the wheels in motion but knows he has to try.

His hands pat his waist and pockets in a practised fashion, checking his own gear and weapon are secure and in place. Looking unprofessional or dishevelled certainly wouldn't aid him, his in car communicator flashes to life and detecting that he has stopped, the video screen flickers to life or at least it tries as it takes a small shunt from his fist to bring it fully online.

Mel's expression is one of concern and her optical implant is flickering like crazy, which comes across as a strange sheen over the video link.

"Sarge, something is happening, we've lost a ton of our audio and video feeds, especially round the centre, we tracked some fights and explosions, all of them were escalated through the use of eliXir. Shortly after there was a large meeting of some kind and since then we've started to lose more and more surveillance, it can't be a coincidence Sarge. It feels methodical and whatever they are doing, they don't want us watching."

He isn't sure how to process the information update, it's worrying for sure and it brings everything he had planned into question. "How many people Mel? Is it just a small group of addicts?" He hopes some clarity might make his path clearer.

"It's hard to tell with the footage available and limitations of the surveillance equipment, but I think about forty or fifty powered individuals. They raided the warehouse we saw your man in earlier as well, whatever it is Pro Life are doing down there, they aren't going to be happy about this and you know what they'll want to do with their Archangels."

He knows all too well, they would be the ones pushing hardest to go down there and butcher everyone. But he had to admit things were escalating quickly and spiralling out of control.

He grabs his helmet from the passenger seat and secures it on himself as the video feed instantly jumps from the car to his heads up display, a small feed on his periphery. He storms out of the car and stands himself tall and as authoritative as he can manage, certain that his rank is clearly showing on his chest.

All eyes are on him and he has no idea if his arrival has been communicated ahead of schedule, for all he knows everyone here might have already been told to dismiss him, but he can't let that waiver the confidence in his authority. Not now.

"I'm Sergeant Russells, I'm now in command of this blockade. If you have any questions bring them directly to me." He points to a group of five officers, they aren't familiar to him and they aren't from his squad at any rate. "Officers, things might be escalating down below but that isn't our concern, I want you to ensure all the proper blockades and cordons are set up." They all nod and begin shuffling and he resists the urge to let out a sigh of relief and let his shoulders slump. "The rest of you, I want a tight perimeter but as wide as we can manage whilst maintaining audio and visual contact with one another. As unlikely as it is we need to keep anyone from coming out of that lift, but we also need to keep the public away and avoid drawing attention if remotely possible. If anyone asks what is going on just tell them it's a training exercise." More assent and with practiced training they begin moving into positions, it didn't matter if they knew him or knew what was going on, they followed orders and their training.

"I love it when you're all authoritative." Mel quips into his ear causing him a small amount of relief and is rewarded with a small grin. "I know you don't want to hear this and it's not what you want, but it might be too late. It might be time to let the military down there and to fix this mess."

He doesn't want to admit to himself or her that the outcome was likely inevitable at this point, he isn't even sure if he was right to be resisting it either. But his conscience kept scratching at his mind because he knows that it will end in so much collateral damage, he had seen it on a smaller scale many times with the Archangels and down there with no civilians and no video feeds it would be a massacre.

"I know Mel, but once they go down there, it's over, those people will all be killed. We need to know what's going on, try and find another solution. Those people have their own lives and their own problems, they don't need angels from upon high swooping down and executing them. Maybe I can take a small squad down there and talk to the locals." He would have to do it without telling the Captain and would probably lose his job but it could make a difference he hoped.

"It might be too late Sarge. I'm sorry, I couldn't keep this to between us, it was getting out of our control, the Captain knows about the feeds and the power usage. Everyone is on alert and the military is almost certainly on their way. I'm sorry Russells." With that her feed closes, he doesn't get chance to reply and explain that he isn't upset at her, she had already done more to help him than he should have expected.

His mind was racing, fighting for a solution, trying to puzzle together the information he had with a workable solution. He clenches a fist at his side, he hates the feeling of being powerless, that for all his training and what authority he holds there was nothing he could say and nothing he could do that was going to change the outcome. Like an inexorable force the military and Archangels were going to enter the low habs and destroy an entire district down there. No one would mourn them and no one would miss them, the massacre of the lower habs was inevitable.

Chapter 34

A shudder washes over his body as he groggily wakes up, cold metal against his back, there is a mild throbbing on the side of his head and the whole scene feels all too familiar as he forces down the sensations of panic and fear that he is back in Lorenz's clutches. Mentally forcing himself to note the differences, he can't feel restraints against his wrists and feet. Not that restraints would be required right now, his body feels weak and drained of energy in a very physical way. It's all he can do to sit up straight and he is glad there is no pain, just the strain of expending energy his body doesn't want to spare, slowly opening his eyes as his fears are realised.

He's back in one of Lorenz's surgeries, although it's definitely in a poorer state, the dark metal roof is slightly collapsed and one of the walls is completely destroyed, exposing the room to the near constant breeze and cold of the lower habs, a single flickering light is all that provides any vision from inside the small room. Tobias slides his legs to the side of the table in preparation for hopefully standing to find a tube is left dangling from his arm, he's no expert but he is fairly certain given the few droplets in the tube and from watching his fair share of holo vids that it has been used to transfer blood. His blood, and probably a fair bit given how dizzy and weak he feels, there would be only one reason to do so and the thought itches at his mind, agitating him more than anything ever has before.

With a grunt of pain and a fair amount of rage he yanks the needle led tube out of his arm and immediately regrets it as the pain flares in his arm. He pushes his hand against his arm as he slides off the metal slab that was his bed. The floor rushes up to meet him and denies him of the air in his lungs as he collapses in a heap. Gasping for air he rolls onto his side in pain, noticing for the first time that there was a ragged scrunched up piece of paper on his chest that now blows slowly and gently away in the breeze from outside. He feebly reaches out with his hand, struggling to fully extend it whilst trying to recover his breathing, the note freezes in midair and Tobias is glad at least that his powers still work, even in his exhausted and deflated state.

As the note draws nearer and he pushes himself back up to a seated position he can see the writing is almost childlike, lacking in any elegance or penmanship. He strains to read the barely legible text.

Sorry Toby. You are the nicest person I've ever met but you are too nice to do what needs to be done. I'm sorry for taking your blood but I can't live in fear anymore. We will show the uppers that we are in control.

He cringes as he finishes reading the note and uses his telekinesis to create a cushion of force slowly raising himself to upright, pushing himself to standing and says a small thankful prayer that he doesn't immediately collapse forward afterwards. Rage is boiling inside him, he can feel it in his stomach and he can feel that his mind and thoughts are becoming clouded but focused, like a sniper looking down a scope he could think about only one thing.

"She's going to get herself fucking killed or kill a lot of people." he mutters to himself, his fists clenching at his side, he may feel physically weak but he can feel his power surging through his body. He had considered her a friend, someone to rely on, but she had not only betrayed his trust but was going to do the unthinkable.

The frustration and rage threaten to overwhelm him, the realisation that everything that is happening is because of him that if he hadn't come down here, if he hadn't gone to work this morning. None of this would be happening. People now have permanent super powers including him and it was all his fault. The frustration and self-hatred burn strong as he lets out a scream of rage and his powers respond accordingly, a wave of energy bursts from him and destroys the room, sending everything careening away and it doesn't stop, continuing to push outwards and in a matter of a few seconds Tobias is standing alone, surrounded by the rubble of Dr. Lorenz's surgery, he barely even notices the destruction in his wake as he gently raises himself from the ground. He slowly levitates himself deeper into the empty streets of the low habs, even more abandoned than he had seen before.

It doesn't take long before he arrives back at Shirl's, he has no expectations at this point and isn't surprised when no one is there, not even the thugs from before, and it feels like everyone has left the low habs. As he is about to move forward to continue towards the lift a flicker of light catches his eye and he turns to look down, there is a large pile of spent eliXir vials on the street corner near the cafe. If each of those represented a person who now had lifelong powers the world was about to change forever, he had to find out what was going on and to try and make up for his mistakes he thinks. He flings himself forwards at high speed and is thankful that his body at least can rest whilst he concentrates on the energy surrounding him in order to fly towards the lift up to the middle habs, at least he would be returning home, even if he wasn't about to be welcomed with open arms.

Chapter 35

Russells surveys the scene, it has only been a few minutes since he arrived and took command of the blockade, it wouldn't be many more until someone from the military or Archangels made contact with him, that he was sure of. Until then at least, things were in control here, the officers had set up a wide but tight perimeter and the few civilians that were gathering seemed to be keeping their distance and largely uninterested with what the police were doing.

The remaining officers had arranged their cars in a small semi-circle around the lift exit and were now mostly talking amongst themselves, he doesn't reprimand them, he was hoping that there was no need for them to be doing much more than putting on a show, they had weapons available but they weren't tactically deployed for super powered deployment, just standard police issue gear.

He was starting to feel anxious, it isn't a feeling he is used too or comfortable with, he considers himself a man of action and not having a decisive plan and not being in control was grating on him. It manifested most obviously in pacing, he knew it looked bad to the other officers, that seeing him pace might make them feel on edge or that something was wrong, but all the same he can't help himself as his heavy boots stomp against the tarmac below while he circles his car once more.

He places a hand against the side of his helmet and pings Mel, no answer, either she is busy or doesn't want to speak to him. He believes she is professional enough that she would have answered his call regardless of how awkward things might have become.

He leans forward on the side of one of the cars looking out towards the lift, if a group of powered people came surging through there they wouldn't be able to hold them back he knew, he was probably the only person here who had actually been trained and gone up against eliXir users and has the equipment to engage but even he would be useless without the rest of the Advanced Narcotics Assault Teams here, they couldn't well just leave though, this was their duty.

A red alarm blares in his peripheral vision and a loud distinct tone plays in one of the earpieces, a priority call. He knew it would be coming sooner or later, in some ways it represented the relief of his inaction, a call to do something even it was someone else's plan, but at the same time he isn't sure if the outcome will be one he will like.

"This is Commander Coleman, am I speaking to the officer in charge of the lift police?" The sarcasm in the last few words were clear, everyone knew that the officers on lift duty were usually lazy or put there on a punishment and more than one had been accused of taking bribes.

"I am Sergeant Russells, I am currently in command here." He replies, ignoring the sarcasm and keeping his professional manner at the forefront.

"Russells, me and three squads are on the way there, when we arrive on site we will be immediately deploying down to the low habs, please ensure that the streets have a clear path for us and that the lift is not blocked." It was a clear order, it had always irked him that the police had to answer to Archangel command structure as part of their own, but this was no time for arguments.

"Understood," with that the communication channel closed. He makes his way to the perimeter but his communicator begins ringing again, not a priority call this time at least.

"Sarge, it's Mel. I have some reports that there is activity around one of the Vac Chutes, reports are inconsistent but there are a lot of them. I'm trying to pull surveillance but I'm getting locked out somehow. I think you should head there quickly."

"Thanks, send me the location." a low beep indicates the call is over and he steps up his pace towards the perimeter, he is reluctant to abandon his post here, but it was one he had taken on himself anyway. It's not like the Captain had officially assigned him here, it is a minor technicality but he could live with it.

"Officers, we have Archangels inbound, be prepared to open the perimeter and make sure the civilians aren't blocking the main street." he didn't wait for acknowledgement, he is fairly confident from what he has seen that they are capable of carrying out his orders even in his absence.

He continues past them and jumps into his car, the navigation has already been updated and set to one of the Vac Chutes. The odds of people coming up twice in as many days seemed unlikely, but if Mel was feeding him this he couldn't very well ignore it. He starts the car and the engine roars to life, mimicking the urge for action inside himself.

The chute isn't far but as he draws close to the location the number of people out on the streets suddenly surges, even with his sirens blaring he struggles to wade through the mass of people blocking the way. He pulls over to the pavement in frustration and grunts to himself, "Wouldn't have been able to drive to the chute anyway."

Slamming the door behind him he gently taps the nearest person on the shoulder, a young woman with an outlandish green mohawk turns towards him. "Excuse me, what is going on here?" he asks, doing his best to soften his voice and not sound frustrated.

"Oh man," she begins, her eyes wide are with excitement but her voice quivers with uncertainty "You are going to be busy! Like, everyone here saw it. Forty, maybe fifty of them. All came up from the chute."

The words hit him harder than any dummy round in training ever did, "What?" It's all he can manage as his normally in control demeanour is destroyed.

"Yeah, they didn't start anything, they just all came up and left. Weird man. No one knew what to do, we just watched 'em go."

His headset immediately opens a call, it has to be Mel he thinks, not many people can force calls open.

"Sarge! It's fucking true, we have reports everywhere across town, there is a large group of powered people in the middle habs, latest reports show them gathered at the hospital. The captain is losing his shit, it's chaos here."

"Patch me through to him." he ordered, pushing down his own worries and fears, allowing his training and order to the fore.

"Russells! Of all the fucking people I need to talk to right now you aren't on the list," the voice shouts, he is glad that his earpiece has volume auto correction or he's fairly certain he would be hearing the Captain's voice ringing in his ear for a week.

"Captain listen, we need to deploy all available officers to the Hospital right now, we can't afford to wait for more intel or orders from above, this is time critical. You have to order all forces to converge." he tries to sound suggestive rather than authoritative, he doesn't want the captain to think he is telling him what to do.

The line goes silent for a long time, Russells is on the verge of repeating himself as he gets back in his patrol car. "It's done, get your ass over there Russells and give me a fucking report on what the flying fuck is going on."

He fights against the crowd to get the car turned around but the sirens help disperse at least some of it. "Navigation: City Hospital," a sharp chime indicates his route is updated and he smashes his foot on the accelerator sending the car rushing through the streets, cars and civilians quickly make a path for him and he is glad that at least things seem normal thus far.

The in-car communication system indicates an incoming call from an officer whose name he doesn't recognise, a flick of his thumb brings through call through the in-car speakers.

"Officer Russells? I mean erm… Sergeant Russells? This is Officer Patiala, the Archangels aren't here yet, but the lift is moving, what should we do?" The young officers quivering voice finishes and time feels slower, his mind working to try and calculate the best course of action, what he should say to this young officer and what he should do himself.

Could the lift be a distraction? Or was the hospital a lure for all forces. It certainly isn't a coincidence but he knows nothing of what the lower habs people are doing or their plans. Without Intel he was clueless.

"Shit," he murmurs and swerves the car at a junction, smoke rising from the tyres as they screech around the corner.

"I'm on my way Officer. Prepare flamer units if you have any." He closes the channel and reroutes his navigation. He is yet again making his own orders and gambling that it is the right choice. All he knows for sure at this point is that whatever is happening right now, it is going to end in fatalities, he just hopes he can help minimise them.

"Mel, I need an update, where are the Archangels units deploying right now? We have movement at the lift, do you know how many?" he shouts into his intercom, not angrily but having to be clear over the sirens and roaring engine.

"Archangels have diverted from the lift Sarge, I don't know where right now, they don't share mission data with us. As for the lift, I'm sorry, I have no idea, visuals are completely down. I'm useless." she sounds defeated but he knows she's doing everything she can to help, he knew from experience she could keep her calm under pressure better than most officers could.

"It's fine Mel, keep doing what you can," he closes the call as he arrives back at lift blockade, the perimeter has been tightened as some of the men have moved towards to the lift entrance. He is pleased to see that they have some flamer units and are all now taking the situation very seriously. He pops the boot of his car and grabs a large gun, requiring two hands to carry and glowing green at the sides as it hums to life.

"Officer Patilan?" He calls, not actually sure which officer that is, much to his own disappointment.

A fresh faced cadet with the patchy stubble of youth runs over to him and salutes. "Sergeant, it is good to have you back." Russells tries not to lose his composure as he tosses the heavy two handed weapon over to the other Officer, he barely reacts in time and the bulk of the weapon almost barrels him over. "This is an energy net launcher, anyone caught in this won't be able to use their powers, get familiar with it real quick." He doesn't wait for a response and heads over to the lift, the readout indicates another three minutes until it arrives and he sighs, thankful for the small mercy that the lift is incredibly slow.

"We have three minutes Officers," he calls to the assembled crowd, "Prepare yourselves, we don't know how many there will be but it is very likely they will be using eliXir and may attack without warning. Engage immediately, that is an order." He draws his own pistol and rests his finger on the trigger, the gun beeps immediately as it acknowledges him as an authorised user. Everyone is silent but they share looks at one another and Russells can sense the trepidation and fear amongst them.

A light on the lift panel changes from amber to green, signalling its arrival. "Hostiles inbound," he barks at the top of his burning lungs, not wanting to rely on internal comms as the thundering metallic door slides slowly open.

Chapter 36

The air wisps past him as he flies at a speed faster than he has ever pushed himself before. It feels oddly serene, he can hear the air passing him by while the housing units below give him some sense of his speed, but he feels nothing as the telekinetic shell surrounding him keeps both the cold and the air resistance off him.

The flickering lights of the lift are visible from some distance away, like an antenna or a beacon calling to anyone lost in the habs, it makes sense for it to be almost directly in the centre of the lower hab city. His mind is oddly quiet, just focused on the step in front of him, get up the lift and find out what is going on, for most people the not knowing and the lack of information about the situation might make them nervous or worried but for Tobias it allows him to just forget about what he can't control. The lift closes in quickly and he lowers himself to street level, the rent metal hole from earlier shows him that the lift is already here at the lower habs. It seems odd but he is thankful for the small mercy as he climbs inside.

After pressing a button indicating travel upwards he sits down on the cold hard metallic floor, his back against the wall and taking a moment to let his body rest. Even though his mind feels resolute and strong, his body aches in its frailty and exhaustion. The lift creaks upwards, clearly it doesn't get used as much as it was once designed for, it is slow and Tobias quickly realises it is going to take a while to get up to the middle habs, he internally debates whether he should just tear the roof off and fly up, but the pangs of exhaustion in his limbs keep him firmly rooted.

He stares at the lift doors, the next time they open he will be looking out at the middle habs, his birth place, his home. Will anyone be there or will he just calmly walk out and be another face in the crowd. Who knows what Neomi is up to, it could be a battlefield up there he realises, the police will have had strict orders to engage and given how empty the area around Shirl's was Neomi must have a huge amount of followers now. He suppresses the thoughts and rests his head against the wall of the lift. The minutes drag out and it feels like he's been in here for hours, he starts to drift away as a shout comes from somewhere outside the lift, the sound muffled slightly but still clear enough to be heard. "Hostiles Inbound," it's the last thing he hears before the doors open and the cacophony begins.

Guns roar in the middle habs, he doesn't have time to count the amount of police arrayed in front him, a large semi-circle of them using their cars for cover as they unleash a bullet storm upon him. He can almost feel the rounds, he reflectively holds up a hand to protect himself, but he doesn't flinch or cower, confident in his abilities as each bullet freezes in the air, a dozen at first then maybe a hundred, all floating, unbroken rounds. He is almost caught by surprise as a net comes flying from the side, a bright green glow flickering along its surface as it threatens to engulf him, it closes and wraps as if it capturing an invisible person and Tobias lets the imaginary force form he had created go and the net drops to the street, energy spent and useless against the hard tarmac floor.

Over the roar of fearsome snapping of gunshots he only barely hears as a young officer shouts, "Flame units!" He lunges outwards with open palms and draws them back to his chest. The screeching metal drowns out the gunfire as the doors from the nearest police cars are torn from their hinges by his will, the cars themselves shunting as they are pulled apart against their design. The doors form a barrier in front of Tobias as the flamethrowers unleash gouts of death in his direction. Even from behind the safety of his makeshift shield he can feel the heat from behind it. *Well,* he thinks, *this was probably the reception I should have expected.* After a few seconds the flames die down and the doors are no longer recognisable, they have all started to merge and melt together into a wall of glowing metal, held in place only by his mind. He lets it all drop to the floor with a loud clang and the gunfire doesn't resume, he doesn't lash out at them or go on the offensive. "Are you done?" he shouts, confident that he can at least be heard now the gunfire has stopped, "We need to talk."

The person in charge is almost immediately obvious as every single officer turns to look at one man, the only man still looking at him, staring at him with a penetrating gaze. Long seconds pass and the man sighs visibly before holding up a hand "All units stand down." A flash of familiarity pangs in his mind as he realises that he recognises the officer staring at him, that he was at the bank when all of this began. Tobias resists the urge to levitate forward, thinking it best to keep his power display to a minimum given the company, so he lets his tired legs carry him forward until the two men are almost face to face, only a doorless police car between the two of them.

"Sergeant isn't it?" the other man nods and there is clearly no surprise, he must recognise Tobias he realises, "We have a shared problem, a woman from the low habs, Neomi, she has gained the knowledge to give people powers on a permanent basis, they won't fade and don't have any side effects, well aside from still being random." If his facial expression was stoic and hard before it was the opposite now, the words have clearly spun his world upside down and his eyes are as wide as his mouth is agape. "She isn't evil Sergeant, she plans to find other lifts to the other low habitats and liberate each of them, giving each habitat the freedom that she has so recently tasted."

Sergeant Russells quickly recovers and raises a quizzical eyebrow, his tactical mind working through the information "That doesn't track Tobias," he doesn't manage to keep anywhere near as stoic a face when presented with his own name, he wonders how much the officer knows about him and his lower hab experience, "Not the permanent power part, I believe you, but the bit about the lift, we've been tracking her groups movement and they haven't gone for the lift. They aren't even moving anymore. They've taken up refuge and are currently defending and holding the hospital here. We assume they either got lost or decided it was a defendable location."

Tobias' mind strains and battles with the new information, trying to put what he knows about Neomi together in order to figure out what she could be doing. He looks around at the assembled officers, every single eye is on him. They aren't pointing guns anymore and he isn't sure how much they've heard but there is a sense of disbelief amongst their glares.

The cogs of his mind slowly clink into place and as he looks down at his arm and they snap together with a mental clang, "Fuck." he mutters.

"What? What is it?" concern paints the Sergeants face and he has moved to lean closer over the bonnet of the vehicle. His helmet has some flickering display, some kind of video feed he supposes.

"She isn't hiding or preparing a last stand Sergeant." the time for being cautious is over and he begins to levitate himself off the ground, in an instant the trained officers all have guns pointed at him once more but no one lacks in discipline and he is thankful the shooting doesn't begin once more. "She is going to give everyone in that place powers, whether they want them or not. We have to stop her and quickly."

"How is that even possible? To give everyone powers." The Sergeant is the only person who doesn't have a gun pointing at him right now.

"It's me. Something in me is different, I don't know why or how, but something in my blood causes people with powers to keep them forever, myself included." He was expecting some kind of reaction but instead the other man simply nods slowly, processing the information.

"That explains why the scanner didn't register you properly I guess," he seems satisfied, as if somehow the final piece of some puzzle he couldn't see was complete. "What do you know about your parents Tobias?"

The question comes out of nowhere and smashes into Tobias like a train. For an instant he considers flying away, the urgency of stopping Neomi forefront in his mind, but a childhood longing and painful curiosity grasps inside him, "Nothing. They died before I was old enough to remember them." He looks down at the Sergeant, a longing for more burning in his eyes. "Why?" his voice breaks and the confidence that his powers give him cracks for a moment.

"I met them once, it seems like a lifetime ago. We've met before."

"At the bank, I recognised you too, then-" his words are cut short at the officer interrupts him

"Before that, when you were just a young child, I was barely a cadet then, I was there when that accident killed your parents. I'm sorry for what happened to them." Russells let his head drop out of respect.

Tobias was dumbstruck, of all the times to find someone who had met his parents even for a brief moment was amazing and he longed to know more about them, even a small detail, but something else occurred to him, "Is that why you were protecting me in the bank? Because you recognised me?" it wasn't important he realised but the thought had bubbled to the front of his brain and popped out of his mouth in his usual lack of mental control.

The Sergeant opened his mouth to speak but closes it again, seemingly stopping to think for a moment. "I don't think so, I don't know, at the time my thoughts were that the scanner wasn't working properly and I didn't want to see anyone murdered for a mechanical failure, but I don't know, maybe." Russells seemed uncertain of himself and the look doesn't suit him, both men snap to attention and everyone flinches and jerks as a loud explosion is heard in the distance, a plume of black smoke can be seen rising high towards the SkyCast.

"Shit. That's from the hospital." Russells raises his voice to a near shout "Everyone to the hospital, NOW! Narcotics and Archangels are inbound." he looks over at Tobias who is already floating in the air several meters above everyone else, although for once, everyone's attention is on the horizon instead of him.

"Can you carry two?" the Sergeant shouts up at him, Tobias simple nods his head and raises the man up next to him with a wave of a hand, he is impressed that the officer doesn't seem to be confused or worried, he looks focused and adapts quickly to being carried and moved by an external force.

The pair takes to the skies and flies rapidly towards the hospital, despite seeing the mid habs from this perspective for the first time, it still feels homely to Tobias. He is glad for once that he can actually make out things below him and has a sense of direction that he lacked in the low habs, although from this perspective it looks surprisingly similar to the low habs. He looks up at the SkyCast, he'd never really given it much thought, the illusion, the higher they got the more obvious it was fake, its only purpose to keep a sense of night and day for the people below, to keep the people in line, work and sleep, don't do anything else. He shakes his head in dismay as Russells shouts over to him, "What was it like down below?"

"It was worse than I ever imagined." he thinks back to his ignorance of the lower habitats before he was ejected down there. "They've been abandoned, by everyone above them who put them there. We aren't informed about their lives or how they survive, what they go through on a daily basis," he clenches a fist, rage wasn't an emotion he was familiar with showing but recent events had made it flow more freely now.

"We aren't allowed down there for the most part," the officer begins "we're even given orders not to talk about it. There are people up there and here that don't want the lower habs breaking out but also don't want it maintained."

"People like Pro Life Corp." Tobias adds.

"You saw their logos down there too? I saw it on a video feed, what are they doing down there, do you know?" Russells eyes squint slightly, whether to keep the wind out or from in-depth thought, Tobias doesn't know.

"I met the person, who at least in this district, is responsible for the creation and distribution to eliXir to the upper habs. All the pure stuff he was making was in Pro Life Corp crates due to go up the lift. I don't know if they are directly involved or even know." In truth he doesn't really care, it doesn't matter if it was one corporation or another, only stopping Neomi mattered now, he only hopes they aren't too late to stop her plan.

"I believe they are, they are the main financial provider of the police forces here. You know as well as I that pretty much everything in the middle habs feeds back to them in one way or another. They have their hands in every pie and the man who makes them all. They are the ones that slowly pulled away the policing of the lower habs and let it descend into the shape it's now. Able to survive and produce but never to recover or thrive. It's disgusting."

They fly together for a little while longer in silence and the cloud of smoke draws closer, Tobias regrets there isn't more time to think and plan, "Sergeant, when this is over do you mind if I ask you some questions about my parents?" his voice was tinged with sadness, both for what was to come and what had been, but he did his best to mask it.

"Of course." Tobias feels the field around the officer shift and move as he points out a hand at the drones flying around the hospital, as they grow bigger Tobias realises they aren't drones at all, but men wearing jetpacks with short wings protruding out the sides. "Swooping Angels, they are keeping a very wide distance. We should probably land out of sight so we don't get," he pauses briefly during his suggestion, "mistakenly engaged."

Reacting immediately, Tobias brings them down quickly, his stomach lurches at the sudden descent and he imagines it must be even worse for the Sergeant. They perch upon the roof of a building, the streets below are largely quiet, everyone is probably either recording events at the hospital or sensibly running away he assumes.

"I'm not sure what I can do here Sergeant, even if we ignore the Angels, there are probably hundreds of them now in the hospital and almost every single one would probably risk their own life instead of going back down to the lower habs now." He looks over at the hospital, one of the largest buildings in the middle habs, the parking areas around it create a perimeter of flat ground that most buildings don't get, the building itself looks old, not made out of the same material as the housing units, instead made of older brickwork reinforced with a cold metal framework, smoke rises from the side of the building and there is a substantial hole in the wall where something has exploded outwards. He tries to count the Swooping Angels, twenty or maybe more, they dart and flitter around so much it's hard to keep count, "I mean, I don't even know if I can take on that many or get past them, let alone what waits inside." His confidence wavering in the face of the odds in front of him.

"This is our district Tobias, we were raised here, they are armed and trained for super power engagements but nothing on this scale has been seen in decades, not since Russia. The Angels will react the quickest but with your power, telekinesis, if you hit hard and fast you can get in before they can stop you."

The Sergeant doesn't seem remotely concerned about the idea of Tobias taking down fellow officers of the law, desperate times he guesses.

"They won't pull their punches though, you know the new laws first hand, if they get the opportunity, they'll shoot to kill. Are you sure you want to do this?" Russells looks over at him, his hand is at the pistol at his waist, not threatening just prepared, the fact he looks so ready to act and so steadfast, it's inspiring and helps Tobias regain his sense of purpose.

"I'm well aware the new laws, if the old laws were enforced in the low habs we might not be in this mess right now. What about the upper levels? You going to take that pistol up there and take out all the pure eliXir users up there," he doesn't mean to rant at the officer, but he was on edge and frustrated.

"It's not fair, it never has been." Russells sighs, but doesn't give an answer to a question that is so far beyond his means.

"What about the other people in there? The people like me. It's a safe bet that Neomi has used the hospital as a platform, giving everyone in there powers so that in her mind everyone is level." Tobias feels like the answer is probably obvious given his own experiences.

"The police might hesitate, the military, narcotics and Angels won't. They'll carry out orders on sight and with impunity. She's mad, for all she knows one of them could be a living bomb or lose control and cause some kind of cataclysmic event. She can't surely hope to control this situation? It's a mess," the grizzled officer appears to be speaking to himself as much to Tobias, but he answers all the same.

"She isn't trying to control it, she wants the world to finally be equal. If you, the police that is, are so worried about another Russia then why aren't you stopping the higher ups using drugs? If they weren't paying the lower habs to make it then maybe it wouldn't be so damn harrowing down there. Hell, if they had the SkyCast down there it would be almost identical."

The silence that is the answer hangs in the air and the pair returns their attention to the hospital. Tobias leans over the edge and checks the street below is empty, without warning first he starts moving the officer to the street level, there is no complaint or words exchanged until he reaches the floor.

"I'll help however I can, this is my district after all. Take this," he throws up a communicator that he takes from a pouch at his waist. "I'll be able to keep in touch at least." Tobias plucks the device out of the air with his powers and draws it toward him, lacking any faith in his ability to catch something, he stuffs the small device into his tattered pocket before nodding at the officer below.

"I'll try and keep the Narcs purely on containment duty, I have zero authority over the Angels though, so be careful. Good luck," with that the man nods and begins running in the direction of the hospital, Tobias takes a deep breath before launching himself in the air, it was time for him to get involved.

Chapter 37

This is the highest he has ever flown, he made the decision to fly high to avoid notice from the Swooping Angels below and is hopeful that most people never think to look up.

From this vantage point everyone is tiny, he can see the military vehicles and police cordons around the hospital and although he can't make out the individual people, the border itself was unmistakable. *I could just bring down the entire building from up here*, the thought seeps like an ooze into his brain, even if he could summon that much power there was no way he was going to kill all those people, most of them were innocent and just either drugged against their will or dragged into Neomi's war. Besides, he thinks, I'm not a killer, she had got that much about him right at least.

The slightly larger swirling dots presented the biggest problem, there was no way he could approach the hospital entrance from here with them there, he doesn't have any particular desire to get into a fight with them.

"I need a distraction," he mutters to himself looking around the area below, seeking for anything he might be able to use. There are a lot of people around but he can't think of a way to manipulate them that might result in anything useful, he flies around in a circle of his own around the hospital, careful not to fly into the thickening black plume of smoke rising upwards.

He reaches out with a hand and imagines a small bubble in the middle of the smoke and draws it out towards him, the blob of force swirls with the smoke contained within, if it wasn't for the situation he could stare at it for a while, it looks mysterious but beautiful.

Inspired by the small cloudy ball he summons larger orbs inside the smoke, easily large enough to encompass a human, holding ten of them taxes his concentration and the first few orbs holding smoke wane. He pushes the orbs towards each of the Swooping Angels, some of them stop moving and eye the orbs warily whilst others begin evasively dodging, he manipulates shapes and sizes to surround or create a barrier around each Angel.

It's now or never he thinks as he swoops directly downwards, not just letting gravity carry him but forcing himself towards the ground, knowing that his ability to maintain those bubbles wouldn't last long and the distraction they provide will be momentary at best. He crashes into the ground hard, making no attempt to slow himself down. The tarmac below cracks and shatters outwards.

He's almost certain that people on the perimeter have noticed him but he doesn't stop to look, rushing through the hospital doors into the lobby where he is immediately greeted by a small contingent of people who appear to be guarding the entrance, or at the very least looking mean enough to ward away a few bystanders.

Chairs and tables have been upturned and form a rough barricade around the entrance, he can't tell if the looks on their faces are fear or resolve but they don't run or engage him. One man with dark black skin and thick rolls of hair running down his back points a finger directly at him, there is a dried blood stain crusted onto his denim trousers and the familiar layer of dirt confirms he must have come up from the low habs. "It's him! He's the one who gave us all the power. He made all of this possible." he outstretches his hands and the rest of the gathered people look between the man and Tobias.

He looks over the rest of the people, at least one he thinks must be from the mid habs like him, her skirt still mostly clean and her hair cleanly organised, but her skin is covered in blue lizard like scales, as he looks at her she licks out a forked tongue and smiles at him welcomingly. The other two men have no clear visible powers, both look malnourished and gaunt, and their height difference is staggering, neither look particularly welcoming however and the taller one with animalistic tattoo's Tobias finds quite menacing.

"I need to see Neomi," he decides to go with authoritarian confidence and he is glad at least one person here recognises him.

"I can't allow that friend," the dark skinned low hab man states flatly as he walks towards Tobias, "We have been told to let no one into the building."

With a joking gesture and a cheeky smile he waves back at the door already behind him, "But I'm already in, so maybe we can let it go? Besides, we have to stop what she's doing," he looks over at the lizard lady and back to the dark skinned man "The world might not be perfect, but this is definitely not the way to fix it, it's going to descend into chaos, assuming it even survives tonight." there hadn't been time to really sit back and think about what the ramifications of her actions would be, but he knew there was no positive outcome.

"Chaos?" the animal tattoo man speaks up and Tobias could swear the tattoos have moved since he last looked, the man's voice is high pitched and squeaky and it's all he can do not to laugh as the man starts his tirade "What the fuck do you know about chaos? Sure you've had a little taste of it for a day or two and now suddenly you care? We've lived our whole lives in fear and chaos, Neomi is the first person who has ever tried to do something about it."

The man thrusts his arms out and the animal tattoos swirl to life and a shadowy cloud leaks from his fingertips and takes shape before Tobias' eyes. It looks like an animal from the historic holo vids, prowling on all fours with a smoke like tail whipping behind it.

"You don't want to do this," Tobias growls, letting his rage trickle into his voice. The man seems oblivious to his words however, his face one of stern concentration. The animal dives towards him with the black void like claws taking shape in midair.

He takes a step forward and embraces the oncoming attack, confident in his own concentration and will power, the animal collides into Tobias and the man reels in pain as the shadow is torn apart mere centimetres from his body, imaginary shackles form around each of its blackened limbs as he pulls them apart. The squeaky man's scream echoes through the lobby as he falls clutching his arm, blood pouring through his fingertips.

"What the fuck did you do?" the dark skinned man says as he stares wide eyed at Tobias, he doesn't break his stride, fully intent on making his way deeper into the hospital to find Neomi, the other man's eye begin to glow with a deep purple light which quickly engulfs them while the lizard lady simultaneously charges towards him.

With a measure of frustration that they insist on attacking him despite the consequences of what Neomi is doing, he still shows restraint with his own powers. He swings an arm out in a wide arc and a line of unseen energy swings like a bat towards the mid hab woman's legs, the blow won't break bones but it is certainly enough to knock her off her feet he is sure. He flinches as the woman shows immense agility, jumping adeptly over the obstacle he had created despite it not being visible, the unexpected manoeuvre catches Tobias off guard and he doesn't notice the coalescing in his opponents purple eyes as a beam of energy catches him in the back, breaking his own concentration as his force armour drops. The energy assault sends him flying across the room but he catches himself in midair before he is greeted by the solid concrete of the old building.

Able to catch himself with a thought and being prepared for his own body and weight comes so naturally with his telekinesis, he is still amazed by how easy it is to grasp a power he has never known before. As he floats in midair for a moment having been launched across the room he isn't prepared for the sudden additional weight upon his back as the lizard lady latches herself around him. The pair fall backwards and Tobias is almost expectant for her to release as he lands atop her but if anything she grasps tighter. He can feel her legs wrapped around his waist clenching tighter as her arms rasp around his shoulders and neck. He gasps for air as she constricts tighter and tighter and when he feels her fangs bite hard upon his neck he wants to scream in agony, but his compressed lungs deny him the chance as he flails wildly.

His vision starts to blur and he closes his eyes, digging deep on years of repressed rage and emotion. He can't summon his personal force shield, not with her wrapped around him and being unable to concentrate. He channels his rage into a single action, a lance of pure force thrusts from his back and in an instant the strength constricting him fails, the legs and arms going limp around him. He jumps forward onto his hands and knees gasping for air, his lungs burning to be used once more.

He feels his shirt becoming damp at the back as he hears a cry of anguish from the purple eyed man "You sick bastard!"

Confused and disoriented it takes Tobias a moment to collect himself as he stumbles to his feet, his body feels awkwardly weighted and he feels an overwhelming sense of guilt and pain when he realises why. The force spike still attached to his back, the lizard woman impaled upon it and her blood dripping down onto his back. He immediately forces himself to break apart the spike and hears a slump as her body collides with the floor.

"I...I didn't want to kill her," he stumbles at the truth, it wasn't what he wanted but he had no choice, another person dead as a result of Neomi's action he resolutely told himself. The wound on his neck burns and flashes with pain and his head is swimming but he pushes it aside.

"Where is she? Just please tell me, I don't want to hurt any of you," the words are sincere but the man can't hear them over his own anger, his eyes flashing once more as another beam of violet energy launches towards Tobias. A pointless attack now that they are face to face, a wall of mental energy breaks the distance between them, with a hand outstretched Tobias forces the invisible wall closer and closer, the purple energy doesn't cease as it continues to push against the barrier between them. The man steps backwards as the wall closes in and threatens to crush him against the very physical wall behind him.

"Stop!" a voice cries from behind the counter of the hospital. Tobias holds the wall intact but doesn't push it any further as he turns seeking the voice, the other man, the only one that hadn't engaged Tobias was trembling behind the counter top. "She's down that way, in the blood swapping room. Just don't kill us," the man was pointing towards a side corridor with a wet bloodied hand. He must have dragged the tattooed man behind the counter he assumed. The purple blasts had ceased but the man hadn't moved his back from the wall.

Surveying the scene, Tobias hates what this had become, what he has become. He knew it was necessary, but seeing this man looking at him with pure terror in his eyes reminded him of how he'd looked at the hulk in the bank, he wanted to stop right here, to fall down and cry. To mourn every life lost and every pain caused, but he knew he couldn't stop. That things were only going to get worse the longer they lasted.

He does the only thing he can, puts one foot in front of the next and starts his journey down the hospital corridors towards someone he had considered a friend, the damp patch against his back a stark reminder of the world she is trying to create.

Chapter 38

He walks the haunted corridors of the hospital and looks at all the equipment that has been pushed over or thrown aside. It is evident that a lot of people have been eagerly surging to get away, there are bloody trails against the walls and occasional small drying puddles against the floor. Despite the high tech equipment and professional appearance, he couldn't help but feel an air of familiarity as he walked, it all felt like a cleaner version of Dr. Lorenz's lab, workshop or whatever it was. Tobias can't help but feel reminded as he looks through the opens doors as he heads towards the lifts.

Most of them are empty, abandoned, occasionally there is dead body, either nursing staff or security staff, Neomi has made sure anyone who interfered with her operations was dealt with swiftly and brutally.

He reflects on how much he has changed in a short space of time, in another life the scenes in front of him would have sent him running, fleeing towards any authority who could protect him. The thought of seeing a dead body in real life would have petrified him, but there was no authority he could run to and no one would or could protect him. Not anymore.

The signs for the pathology area are easy enough to follow but the lift going up to that floor is clearly no longer working. The doors bent at an awkward angle offered a glimpse of the damage inside, the lift had met an untimely end at the bottom of the shaft, glass fragmented all over the floor and the walls a scrunched up mess. Not in the mood for diversions or stairs he flicks his hand and the doors screech open, the sound echoes down the corridor and causes him to wince, he levitates cautiously into the lift cab and pulls apart sections of the already damaged roof, letting plates of metal clang against the floor once they are securely torn away.

It only takes a few seconds to fly up the shaft several floors and he counts the doors as he goes to keep his sense of direction. He stops at what he hopes is the correct one, suddenly doubting his ability to count to four as he uses his mind to pry the doors apart.

He barely has time to take in the person waiting in the white washed corridor on the other side before his head becomes a mess. His vision becomes blurry and things begin to move without him doing anything. He can't concentrate and is forced to close his eyes, an overwhelming sense of nausea surges within him as he begins to plummet, unable to maintain his flight.

He can feel his shield waning as he spirals downwards and it disappears completely as he crashes into the rubble of the lift below, adding his own mess of limbs to the carnage.

He rolls over onto his side as his stomach refuses to be contained anymore, retching helplessly as he vomits onto the lift floor. The spinning seems to be stopping however, and Tobias is able to slowly clutch once more at his own thoughts. He collapses onto his back, gasping for air as bile burns his throat, he can feel shards of glass pressing into his already damp back and he pushes down the pain as he looks upwards. Hovering in the open doorway four floors up is a blurry figure, presumably the one who did this too him.

He blinks a few times in quick succession trying to clear out his vision so he can attack the figure, but it's not enough, the blur above outstretches an indistinct appendage and Tobias's mind is churned once more, it isn't painful but it's very overwhelming, a sense of dizziness the likes he didn't know was possible.

As he rolls and writhes he feels the sting of the glass shards against his body. He lashes out with a wave of force. The walls expand slightly outwards but his focus is upwards. He can't see what he's doing but he can feel his success, feel the light wave of force rushing upwards away from him, carrying with it a hundred shards of glass. He hears a scream of pain as his mental claymore explodes upwards and in an instant most of his senses return, the images in front of him are still rotating and blurry but even that is slowly coming to an end. He raises himself to a seated position and his stomach roars in argument as it threatens once more to uproot itself.

He rattles his head, his legs wobbling beneath him quickly proving it is doing more harm than good to his senses. He eases himself up into the air slowly, relieved that being off the ground actually feels more soothing than being grounded. He ascends up the shaft slowly until he tentatively reaches out at the open door for the fourth floor and sees the impact of his glass shrapnel weapon. Tobias recoils at the sight of a teenage girl, her clothes bloodied and her face a mess. Shards of glass prickle her body and she lays twitching slightly as blood seeps from a huge number of injuries, there is no doubt she's dead and it makes him feel more sick than anything he encountered just moments ago. He walks slowly around the young girls body, horrified at what he's done but powerless to change it, for all his telekinetic might, there is nothing he can do and it frustrates him beyond reckoning.

Leaning a hand on the wall for stability, he stumbles down the corridor towards the pathology area of the hospital. Drawn to the sound of voices he at least takes some comfort in being close to his destination, he can make out Neomi's voice and raises himself to his own feet, eager to not appear weak again.

As he strides into one of the large open rooms of the hospital, beds line each wall and there is an unconscious man with a tube trickling blood into his body, three people standing watch over him, Neomi looks as beautiful as ever but the look on her face is pure shock as she see's Tobias walk into the room.

The other two seem to be identical twins, clearly not from the low habs, the two men both have the same short cut dark hair but one has a goatee which doesn't really suit him, in another situation Tobias might have laughed, wondering if the facial hair was purely to distinguish him from his twin. All eyes are on him and Tobias comes to the stark realisation he doesn't really have a plan, but Neomi speaks first and gives him some time to think, her tone is soft but confident and offers the same assurances he leaned into so easily in the lower habs.

"It's good you are here Toby, I'm sorry about what I did to you, I truly am, but it was the only option I had. But look, we are changing the world, you are changing the world. We don't need to argue about this, it's already done, soon there won't be a them or us, it will just be everyone living with their powers in equality, help me guide them."

He patiently listens to her attempt at persuasion, but despite everything he's been through his morality remains unchanged, "Just stop what you are doing, it's already causing chaos everywhere and changing the way people view eliXir, you don't need to carry on and every person you do that too," he points to the man on the hospital bed, "you are consigning them to death."

"They all would have consigned me to death before they had powers, they wouldn't have hesitated, another drugged up low habber, good riddance!" she shouts, her calm reassuring tone lost in an instant and the ugly attitude beneath the facade reveals itself, "The world needs to change Toby and if I have to be the one to do it, then so be it, I've got all I need from you, you can leave, go find a corner to hide in until it's all over, you're good at that. We'll speak again when the dust settles." Her nasty dismissive speech only bolsters his resolve to stay and stop her, and he clenches his fists at his side as he tightens his jaw.

"If this is how it has to be, then I'll make you back down Neomi, the people out there will kill you on sight, I'll take you back home and we can talk about this." he feels a tickle of uncertainty as she starts laughing at his threat, her hair rippling around her shoulders at the motion.

"You can't stop me Toby. You aren't the only TK in town anymore." he tilts his head an instant before the twins lunge out towards him with their hands outstretched, Tobias feels the impact as the power of their combined will collides against his own mental barrier. He loses all sense of surroundings as he goes smashing through the wall of the hospital, certain that if it wasn't for his barrier the impact would have ended his life.

He slows himself down to levitating, the force of the impact having sent him flying into the air. In his periphery he notices the Archangels flying around but keeping their distance as the twins come flying out of the hole in the wall at high speed. He reaches out his own telekinesis and grabs two cars from the ground below and sends them careening towards the twins, one of the twins stops in midair and redirects his focus on the incoming metallic missiles, Tobias feels the man pushing the cars back and the two become embroiled in a contest of mental strength, the cars creep closer to the twin and for a moment it feels like he's going to succeed but then he is sent flying head over foot as an invisible giant fist smashes against his projected barrier.

The blows are unrelenting as both the twins coordinate against him and the two cars he was holding crash against the concrete below. It's no longer a fight at this point, Tobias is returning no blows, simply doing everything he can to keep his armour active against the unyielding savagery of both telekinetics ahead of him. He mentally rallies himself, thinking about everything that is at stake and stopping Neomi from destroying the world, from destroying everything normal that was left in the middle habs. It isn't enough. His armour collapses and he begins plummeting towards the floor as he feels the grip of invisible force around his wrists and waist, holding him upwards in the air.

In silence the two men drag him back towards the hospital, he looks around furiously, looking for the Sergeant or anyone else who might be able to help him, but everything is chaos below, he can see in the distance police colliding with groups of powered people, explosions in a multitude of colours light the streets below. The Archangels bounce from street to street trying to contain a situation that is quickly growing out of their control. Perhaps it is too late, he wonders, even if he stops Neomi, there are powered people everywhere now and her revolution is in full bloody effect in the city below.

The city fades from view as they re-enter the hole in the side of the hospital, Neomi wears a smug grin on her face that makes his blood boil, but he can feel the restraints against him leaving him powerless to make a gesture against her.

"You shouldn't be fighting Toby, you are going to bring around the evolution of the human race whether you want it or not. If it wasn't for your blood this would have been impossible, equality for every man and woman."

"Equality?" the venom in his voice undeniable, "What about Russia? One person gets the wrong power and that's it. No more city, no more revolution, no equality, in the blink of an eye millions dead. That's all it will take Neomi, every single person you give powers to has the potential to kill us all. It's insanity, you're playing a gambling game with humanity."

Her eyes narrow on him and the look on her face is truly menacing, "You've seen the low habs, I would rather die than go back there, I would risk everything to avoid anyone having to live the life I have. You'll never understand that, you only ended up there by bad luck. Hmm," she pauses, "maybe it wasn't bad luck like you thought huh?"

The flippant suggestion sends Tobias reeling back to the events of the last few days, the scanner in the bank, the incident that began all of this, it had given a positive result which had seemed impossible, but now he knew he was different.

The sound of something whizzing flutters past Tobias's ear and he instantly feels the shackles holding him drop. Flicking his head to the side he watches as one of the twins slumps to the ground, a large hole in the side of his head as a scream of agony is released from behind him. The screaming twin stands firm as more rounds fly into the room from somewhere unseen, each impacting harmlessly against an invisible force. The others man's rage reaches a crescendo and in an instant he flies out of the hospital to pursue his brothers killers.

Tobias turns his attention back to Neomi, she's still standing over the unconscious body being added to her super powered regime, totally unphased by unfolding events and how exposed she currently is. Tobias doesn't hesitate, he knows he cannot and that she has to be stopped in the here and now. He lunges out with an invisible hand, throwing her backward and pinning her against the cold walls.

"You think this changes anything Toby? It doesn't matter if I die, I've already won," her voice is strained, the pressure of his telekinetic field clearly crushing her against the wall. She still manages to maintain some element of calm and self-confidence that he can't help but envy.

"Dammit Neomi, in a few minutes everyone still in this hospital and everyone out there you've given powers too, they're going to die, there will be chaos and bloodshed, no revolution, just a lot of fucking death. It's only going to be blamed on the low habs and eliXir which will reinforce the idea that the new laws are needed. Think of the other low habs, how this is going to affect them. Surrender, get your people to surrender, end this." His heated passion gets lost in the middle of his speech and by the end it comes across more pleading and begging than he would have liked.

She chokes a laugh, it pierces Tobias' body and he can feel his rage threatening to take over, an angry storm the likes of which he has never known before.

"Not for long Toby." she splutters, "Soon everyone will have powers." she looks him straight in the eyes and a wicked smirk lines her face as she strains to whisper "Everyone."

He releases the giant hand holding her against the wall, he feels his power surging through him, perhaps stronger than it ever has before, his concentration focused, the anger within him giving it a razors edge. He levitates a few inches off the ground as he unleashes a vicious storm of unseen attacks against Neomi, she wracks and stumbles as each blow hits her. He doesn't notice as everything else in the room begins to float from the ground, the very walls of the hospital warping and expanding outwards from the sheer power he's expending.

Spit flies from his mouth as he angrily shouts at the woman he'd previously felt enamoured with, "What have you done?!" He doesn't relent with his blows, each blunt impact causing her to rock and recoil but she is otherwise silent. "Tell me dammit," he screams as she drops to her knees from the force of his last blow, he stops hitting her so he can focus on picking her up and holding her in the air.

Before he can continue his tirade, a loud explosion rings out on the roof, even levitating as he is, the shaking of the building is unmistakable. Tobias quickly summons a dome around them as it becomes clear the buildings structural integrity isn't going to hold for a moment longer. As if in direct response the ceiling from the floor above collapses upon them and everything becomes dark, the dust and bricks causing a blockade to the outside world. "What the hell was that?" he mutters, Neomi confidently raises herself to standing and takes a step towards Tobias, "That was equality. That was my revolution Toby. You think I didn't have a plan when I came here?" she takes another step towards him as he strains to keep the bubble over their heads, the increasing weight of more rubble becoming evident.

"I knew if I injected enough people I'd get someone with a tech power or some other special eliXir trait I would able to use," she raises a fist and punches him square in the jaw, collapsing him to his knees and he feels the dome around them begin to wane.

"That explosion you felt was my creation, it's going to send spores of your 'super' DNA to everyone who breathes within maybe a two or three mile radius." she plants her knee firmly into his ribs and he collapses onto his back, gasping for air as he holds up his hands in a last ditch effort to keep the rubble from crushing them both to death.

"That's only one of the detonations I have planned for tonight." she lauds over him, seemingly unaffected by his rain of blows inflicted only a few seconds ago.

"Neomi...the rubble...it will crush us both," he strains to explain.

"Don't worry about me Toby, thanks to you, nothing can ever hurt me again." he flinches as her foot comes swinging towards his face, the dome drops and the rubble collapses on them both.

Chapter 39

An explosion rings out from the top of the hospital, normally that might seem like a big deal to him, but given everything Sergeant Russells has seen recently it is just another development in a series of escalating events.

His comms are a hectic mess, so much so he's had to filter out anything not coming from command, the district is in a state of chaos, they felt so prepared for any kind of individual powered attack or small group, their weapons, their training. It had them ready for quick reactions to powered incursions, but this was something else, this was a takeover, an invasion. Gunfire continues to ring out in the distance, broken up by the occasional distinct hiss of energy weapons. People were dying. There was no doubt in his mind, the law was clear and the middle habs were under attack.

A red beep flashes on his wrist panel and he draws it instantly to his chest, it's a signal he hasn't seen since his training and was advised he probably never would. But there it was, a deep red glow lighting up his face.

"That can't be right. What the hell is going on up there?" he mutters to himself as he charges into the hospital, training and instinct has his pistol drawn already, the low hum of plasma is the only thing that feels familiar to him right now.

The inside of the hospital is a mess, bodies lay everywhere and his sense of duty tears at him mentally. He should be stopping and checking each person, calling in the wounded and getting med units on site, but it would be fruitless, with everything going on he'd be lucky to even get a response. He feels himself drawn to the roof, he had watched helplessly as Tobias engaged with the two other powered users, too far away to offer any real support. He has to get up to the higher floors and find out what is going on, to stop this woman from destroying the establishment which keeps order in the district.

Navigating the hospital corridors is treacherous, support beams and brick work are shattered and litter every step. He doesn't even stop to look at the elevator and rests all his hopes that the staircase is still remotely navigable.

"Mel, you there?" he pings out whilst lumbering over a collapsed wall.

The radio is silent for a few second before it clicks to life in his headset "Sarge? Where are you, what the fuck is going on out there?" There was no hiding the sense of anxiety and fear in her voice, although he is fairly certain she probably has greater knowledge of the overall situation than he does right now.

"I'm at the hospital right now, consider it ground zero for the escalation of attacks, I need you to coordinate with command and get them to focus available units here." he pants as he ascends the battered stairs, he knows he needs the fourth floor, but more than that he is hoping will be obvious when he gets to the top.

"Available units?" Mel replies in disbelief, "You have to be kidding Sarge, everyone is deployed, someone said they even saw the Captain equipping a sidearm. I mean shit, even the mech units are deployed, the fucking Mech units!"

He let out a brief sigh, if the mech units were deployed then someone above had decided this was becoming a military affair. He couldn't really deny it was at this point, but it still meant things were escalating too quickly for him to do anything about, a point which always sat ill with him.

"Thanks Mel, speak soon," he signs off as he shoulders his way through the jammed door on the fourth floor, it takes a few hits but whatever is blocking it on the other side gives, causing the door to swing wide and almost taking him off his feet with it.

His worries are quickly alleviated, any concerns he wouldn't know where to look immediately dispelled. The floor is in far worse state than the ground floor, most of the walls are collapsed and debris is everywhere. It almost looks as if this floor and the one above have merged into one as a consequence of the floor being destroyed.

A woman stands amidst the chaos, her clothes tattered beyond recognition leaving her almost naked. Despite all the dirt and destruction there isn't a mark on her. Lying next to her, groaning in pain with brickwork cascaded on top of him was Tobias, he certainly looked worse for wear.

The woman is staring down at the injured man, a contemptuous look burning in her eyes. Russells doesn't attempt communication, he knows his duty and he knows what he morally must do. Gripping his pistol firmly in both hands and softly squeezing the trigger. There is no recoil or loud explosion, the plasma discharge hisses like a den of snakes as it flies from the gun. The woman's dreadful gaze turns to shock as the blast impacts against her and lights up the room with its warm green glow, she stumbles but seems otherwise unaffected as she rubs her eyes and looks at the source of the attack.

Russells doesn't let his disbelief at the lack of impact stop his assault, surging into action as he rushes towards her while shooting one handed, several quick bursts of plasma light the air as he reaches towards his belt. The hiss of plasma hides the sound of the pin dropping and any surprise he has at the ineffectiveness of a weapon that would melt human flesh in an instant is buried under years of specialised training.

The woman holds her hands up against the blasts, more natural response to an attack than an effective countermeasure. He slams his pistol against the mag holster, locking it in place and freeing up his hand before using it to flick a button on his helmet, his visor instantly flicks down and a black filter kicks in, he can barely make out anything in the room.

"Stop alre-" the woman's voice is cut off as the crackle of the flash grenade fills the air, for an instant he can make out the features of the room in normal light before it begins to slowly fade, the tint on the visor compensating for his assault before he clicks it away once more while he kneels down beside Tobias.

"Can you fly?" he calmly asks, the other man is a battered mess but he is still breathing, as Russells helps him sit up his eyes jerk open. "Can you fly Tobias? If you can't, you better get up because we have to go." He wraps one of the man's arms around his shoulder and hoists him up to a walking position, he can feel he's doing most of the lifting but he has no choice. Neomi's vision will already be returning, slowly but certainly, and he didn't want to be there when it did.

"Tobias, we have to go, now, she won't be out for long and I don't have another flash grenade," he shakes his head, feeling a little dizzy himself as the beeping on his wrist display renews. He's taken by surprise but nevertheless thankful when he feels his weight being lifted, both the men slowly raise from the ruins of the hospital, Russells notices for the first time there was another person in there, crushed under the rubble in a hospital bed, certainly dead but not the first fatality of the night.

"She…" Tobias coughs, clearing dust from his mouth and throat, his voice hoarse "she said she was going to give everyone powers… create equality, she's insane."

Tobias doesn't notice the absence of the flying police units, but Russells does, he looks below and quickly finds them, amassed around their own injured and the corpse of the second telekinetic that flew out of the hospital but minutes ago, it's clear he didn't go down without a fight and bodies of uniformed officers litter the car park below.

Realising the person responsible for keeping them in the air is weak and disoriented he points up at the roof of a tall building, just a housing block, but it would offer a good view of the city below and they would be mostly free from observers.

"There looks like a good spot to regroup," he states firmly but calmly, trying not to wriggle or move in fear of overwhelming Tobias any more than he already is.

With a nod they begin a short ascent, he checks his wrist display once more, the same red light flickers away and he worries what it implies.

"Tobias, whatever she did or said, I think it might have worked." he begins as they land on the gravelled rooftop, as he moves to continue the other man snaps to attention.

"What do you mean, she's done it?" the question spurts out rapidly, anxiety lining every word.

Sergeant Russells holds up his wrist mounted unit, "This device, as well as providing communications and other services, is also my DNAAR. What that means is that this device maintains my DNA, or rather it prevents it being adjusted or tampered with by either intake of eliXir or someone with powers. In all my years of service I've never seen this red light flicker, this indicates that something is trying to change me, to give me powers. I haven't taken anything Tobias and I haven't engaged with anyone since we last met by the chute. Whatever she did up there, it's working, it's trying to adjust not just mine, but everyone's DNA."

"To give them all powers." Tobias finishes, neither of them needs to explain what the implications of such an event were, the chaos they've witnessed so far, the destruction and death, it is minor compared to what will come next.

"Oh and another thing, your crazy woman from the low habs, she's completely indestructible. I tagged her with multiple plasma bursts, would've killed anyone else, she barely even noticed."

Tobias points to his face, swollen and cut as he nurses his arm close to his stomach "Yeah. I found that out too," he tries to smile, but his face is just a mess of pain. Explosions ring out in the distance and the lights of a dozen different energy discharges light up the streets like fireworks. The pair would almost consider it beautiful if not for the source of it all.

"She actually did it," Tobias stands tall, his body hating him for the strain and a myriad of future bruises make their presence felt.

He sighs dejectedly and mutters mostly to himself "She gave everyone superpowers."

Chapter 40

Tobias stands upon the edge of the rooftop, Sergeant Russells is still hanging back behind him and can be heard tapping furiously at his wrist device. Screams ring out somewhere in the streets or alleys below but are quickly drowned out by the sound of another explosion somewhere in the distance.

Everything seems to be within the radius of a mile or two he guesstimates, so Neomi was telling the truth, that first explosion was only going to power people up within a two or three mile radius. *Only.* He scolds himself, that's still a lot of people with a lot of random powers, all of them feeling scared and hunted.

The reality of the situation is daunting but he feels certain he has to keep trying to do the right thing, to help if he can, he isn't the scared coward he used to feel like, no longer afraid of confrontation.

"Sergeant," he turns to face the officer, even under the helmet it's clear the events have taken a physical toll, his eyes look weary and tired. "I know this is bad, but we have to be quick, Neomi said that the device she made, the one that is giving everyone powers, it has a two mile radius. So for now, it's kind of contained. If we don't catch her and detain her, she'll keep doing this all over the district."

A simple nod preludes a storm of order the likes which Tobias has never seen. The grizzled officer is making multiple calls and handling multiple heads up displays, it's impressive but he has a very difficult time understanding what is going on but he dares not interrupt. Whilst it has only been a minute or two, Tobias feels like he's been standing around slack jawed watching some technical savant, with a flicker all the heads up displays blink out of existence.

"Right, we have all available units converging and pressing towards the hospital, key chokeholds will be defended at the police headquarters and the closest chutes. That's the best we can expect. What now?"

The man looks at him expectantly and it catches him off guard, he's far from familiar with being asked to lead or give direction. He looks over the edge of the building once more, there is hardly anyone in the streets, he can still hear the sounds of fighting and confusion inside some of the buildings. Glass shattering punctures his thoughts and he watches as an armed officer is flung from a building across the street, Tobias reaches out with his hand and sharpens his mind, slowly lowering the uniformed man to the safety of the ground.

"We can't afford to wait," he speaks over his shoulder as he raises both of them off the ground in a bubble of invisible force. He flies higher this time, he notices above that some parts of the SkyCast have been damage by rogue energy blasts, small black squares in what would otherwise by a beautiful image of the sky when the sun is setting. He makes full use of the height vantage to see what is going on below, the hospital is almost directly below them and like an epicentre the chaos increases as it spreads outwards.

Their position affords them an almost tactical view of the neighbourhood below and it isn't pretty. Confrontations are taking place everywhere and it looks like the area is beyond saving, beyond control.

"Look," Sergeant Russells speaks from behind, he points out at various streets below and Tobias follows his hand. "There. There. There and there." each point is a street section where there is currently heated fighting going on.

"The officers are in formation still, they are pushing against the flow of the untrained powered individuals. It might look like a free for all, but for now, things are still in control and contained."

There is a loud growl of frustration as he points to another location, the flickering lights of almost constant gunfire lighting the intersection. "That's a fucking massacre, god damn military." Tobias squints to see what the other man is talking about, bodies litter every street that comes off the intersection, in the centre stands a large exo suit of some kind. He's seen them on holo vids and the news before, suits that the military use to allow a normal person to use immense firepower, the kind used in the wars in other countries. He'd never thought he would see one in person and as a shoulder mounted weapon spews rounds of death into the streets and crowds below he prays he never sees one again.

"Shit," the sergeant curses as he points back to one of the other streets. There are men in police uniforms attacking the formation of officers who looked like only moments ago they had it under control. They aren't using guns or batons however, fireballs, energy beams and parts of buildings all fly towards the police lines, which almost immediately collapse under the weight of the organised concentrated attack.

Before Tobias can ask the question slinking from his mind, the officer answers it, "Not every beat cop gets a DNAAR Tobias, they are expensive. Given fighting for survival or giving up and being executed under new laws, I guess they don't have much choice. This certainly escalates things, these aren't unorganised civilians cowering or fighting for survival, they are trained and know what to expect. Get us down on that hospital, now." the frustration in the other man's voice is clear but his commanding tone is ever present. "Catastrophic powers are extremely rare, but it's only a matter of time until someone gets one, it's sheer luck so far the city hasn't disappeared in a black hole or vaporized, but the numbers will tell eventually."

As they lower down towards the hospital roof he can make out a small group of people, one is clearly Neomi, her hair bustling in the wind as she is talking about something with a couple of her followers. From their angle of approach they are thankfully unnoticed for now as they see a couple of people tinkering with a machine that he assumes is the cause of all of this.

The Sergeant whispers over his shoulder "We can't hurt her Tobias, what's the plan here?"

"We don't have to hurt her, we just have to stop her. We can't let her do this to every district," he adds as they are now just several meters away from the group below.

"You can't win Toby." Neomi calls out loudly, she doesn't break her attention away from the streets below, watching the fruits of her labours play out in the most visceral fashion. "There isn't anybody or anything that can stop me now. You can hear it can't you Toby? The beautiful sound of revolution. Just stop fighting it, your bravery is attractive but otherwise pointless," she shrugs her shoulders, never really acknowledging his presence with her body language.

She is flanked by two bodyguards, one of who has skin which seems to shimmer in the light, giving it a sort of reflective quality. He bites back at her words as he lowers himself and Sergeant Russells onto the damaged roof of the hospital, "That isn't the sound of revolution Neomi, it's the sound of fear and death."

She finally turns and faces him, ignoring the Sergeant completely as her expression changes from happy to rage in a flash, "You mean the sounds I heard every fucking day growing up down there Toby?" she slaps her open hand against her chest every time she refers to herself, "I never asked to be born in the low habs, I didn't have a fucking bad day and just end up there, I was born scared, I lived my entire life on a knife edge, now the whole world will learn what that's like."

"No matter how much you hate us, how bitter you feel towards the world, this will only end in catastrophe Neomi, there is no happy ending here." He feels a hand gently rest against the top of his arm and the Sergeant whispers behind him "She isn't going to listen, I've seen that look in people's eyes before." there is a short but quiet sigh before he finishes his statement "normally right before they kill themselves or someone else."

He nods over his shoulder and the other man rushes into action, his pistol releasing a rapid barrage of a light green energy into the groups laid out before him. Tobias focuses on creating a barrier in front of them as the blasts impact their targets, one of the men who was standing next to Neomi drops onto his back immediately, his chest cavity melting as his gargled cry screams out into the night, she doesn't flinch or seem to even care about what is happening around her.

The reflective man smirks as the blast impacts him, the shimmer around his skin taking on the same bluish hue as the plasma dissipates around him. The final wave of energy collides into the device itself, a glow of its own indicating some kind of energy field, it doesn't seem to take any damage but the two men who were tinkering with it recoil in fear as the crack of the two energies collide.

"Stay tight behind me." Tobias commands to the Officer, surprised a little at his own presence. Quickly rallying, the two men at the back begin to approach them, but he keeps his focus on the shimmering man, who with hands held out unleashes two streams of the same plasma energy that Russells own pistol used. His barrier holds firm against the blasts and he finds himself more focused than ever.

"I have no sight Tobias, no targets." the frustrated call from behind comes, hastily looking around he begins gathering together bricks, at first just ten or twenty from around his feet, but soon hundreds of bricks from the damaged rooftop and the exposed rooms below. He begins moulding them into a half sphere and holds it between the two groups as the plasma flames, at least for now, are contained within, he doesn't drop their force barrier, not knowing quite how long the physical shield will last.

Seizing the opportunity, Russells rushes to the side and dives behind some battered old stack of brickwork, the function long forgotten. Within an instant he's unleashing a tirade of normal rounds into unseen foes. Over the noise it's hard to tell if the plasma has subsided, but he starts moving his way towards the Officer as a spear made up of some kind of red energy pierces through the brickwork, narrowly misses impaling Russells. Tobias feels frustrated not being able to see the source or go on the offensive himself, he does the only thing he can, smashes outwards with the bricks, mimicking his earlier strategy in the lift whilst simultaneously creating a tight barrier around his ally.

Another spear of energy thrusts towards the Sergeant and leaves a trail of nothing where it has touched, disintegrating everything it contacts, including his barrier he realises much to his dismay. Locking eyes with the officer, Russells holds a hand close to his chest and points upwards with a single finger, Tobias nods and pulls up a ring of the roof below the other man's body, raising it up in to the air with incredible speed.

There is no surprise or shock on Russells face as he sails through air, his pistol roaring round after round into the people below, his accuracy is remarkable and despite some rounds going wide, enough find their targets. As he reaches the zenith of his ascent, he braces himself for what looks like a painful fall.

With his sphere of bricks smashing outwards Tobias can finally see their adversaries, at least for a fleeting moment before each of them slumps in a pile on the floor, perforated with the powerful rounds unleashed from the pistol of the Sergeant.

Neomi still stands firm, laughing as the bricks he launched simply drop at her feet. Her disregard for human life sending a chill through Tobias' spine.

The hiss of burning plasma cuts the air as the balls of energy pass by him, each finds their mark masterfully, three glowing balls of fiery death disperse against Neomi's chest, the smirk on her face doesn't flinch in the slightest as her new clothes disintegrate in an instant, exposing her to the mid hab air as a few droplets of green ichor hiss against the brickwork below.

"Have you forgotten so soon? Did Tobias not explain? You. Cannot. Hurt me," she teases them, her arms spread wide as if inviting them to try.

"I know." the Sergeant quips in returns "I was just testing." He moves to stand shoulder to shoulder with Tobias, both of them facing down Neomi.

"There is more to your blood than you ever had chance to learn Tobias." neither of the men take their eyes off the woman, keen to learn whatever they can but also to hopefully get support from inbound units.

"Do you know that your blood is capable of holding more than one power at a time?" her smile was more taunting than ever, she is clearly enjoying lauding over them the information and power she currently wields.

"You see I couldn't help taking another hit. I had power, but the cravings Toby, I don't know what they mixed with eliXir down there but the cravings never stop biting at me, clawing at my skin. I had to have more." she moves to the edge of the building, looking down once more at the battles below, the carnage and destruction that super powers have wrought.

"No one else knows of course, I couldn't trust anyone else to lead this revolution." she tilts her head and looks over her shoulder, "Well, I could have trusted you Toby if you'd only had the guts."

"Wait, what are you saying Neomi?" Tobias asks, taking a small step closer, he wants so much to reach out to her, to stop all of this.

"I'm saying, I'm not just invincible, I can do an-" her speech is cut short as a huge blast of bright green light explodes the floor out from under her, she tumbles from the side of the building in silence, not a scream or a whelp as she plummets down to the hard tarmac below.

Tobias snaps his head to look at the officer, unsure what just happened.

"Overload shell." he states flatly as he discards his weapon to one side, a raised eyebrow in surprise causes the man to continue "It's useless now." he rushes over to the odd device sitting unguarded on the roof.

"There was no time for her speeches Tobias, we have to get this device out of here. Fly off with it, take it to another district, the low habs, hell throw it through the SkyCast and into the upper habs, I don't bloody know, just go!" the unexpected impetus the man is showing is sign enough that he needs to hurry, his first instinct is to simply crush the device with his telekinesis, but he finds himself unable to do so, something around it is preventing him from using his powers on it.

Thinking on his feet, he instead cracks away a disk of the roof itself, dragging that upwards with him, the device sitting firmly atop his floating improvised structure.

He launches upwards, glad for once that he doesn't have to worry about carrying or protecting anyone else as he leaves the hospital below him. His speed makes the sudden jerk to a stop all the more painful, his limbs and neck snapping to a halt as he feels some kind of force wrapping itself around him like tendrils, enveloping his body as they pull him back down towards the ground.

He tries to scream in frustration but his mouth is covered by a deep purple tentacle, a thin smoke rising from whatever it is. He finds himself unable to do or move anything as the bindings slowly turn him around, facing him towards the ground.

There he sees that familiar smile that makes his body shudder in disgust.

"Before I was so rudely interrupted," she chuckles as he looks over to the Officer, purple vines looks equally binding and constricting as they make eye contact and a sense of futility fills them both. "I was trying to explain just how many powers your blood can handle." She grabs the device from the brick disc and after a brief inspection nods in satisfaction. Turning to him he feels the tendrils loosen around him, "Let's go for one last flight together Toby, just you and me, we'll go to the police headquarters, then maybe you'll see sense and join me." Her expression changes and for an instant he sees the soft warm smile he was charmed by in the lower habs, "Don't try anything silly, it won't work, now be the good man I know you to be and fly us away from here."

Tobias sighs and spares a last glance as Sergeant Russells before lifting them both into the air, ascending quickly and heading towards the police headquarters.

Chapter 41

Tobias flies them over the streets of the middle habitats, he had been looking forward to seeing the familiarity of his home once more, but there was nothing like that here now, it was a warzone that was completely alien to him, people were diving from the alleys and hanging out of windows to launch powered assaults against the slowly expanding police presence. He can't help but feel like the entire situation could have been handled better had it not been for the new laws the Mayor put in place.

It had left the military and police with little choice but to execute every powered individual on sight, a fact that everyone was well aware of and which was now forcing people who would have otherwise stayed clear to fight for their lives. Desperation was a powerful catalyst for the fires burning below, if someone had reacted quicker, tried to calm the people or detain them, then maybe this wouldn't be happening. But then, it had all happened so fast and was continuing to do so that the escalation was the likes no one could have expected.

He looks over at Neomi as the police headquarters draw near. She doesn't do so much as even acknowledge him with a look, her focus off in the distance and her mechanical doomsday device is clutched close to her bare chest.

It feels like they have passed a border of sorts, as things seemed to return to normal and people are out on the streets, talking and pointing as police cars occasionally stream down the streets. Her device obviously hasn't reached this far and there is obvious confusion about what is going on elsewhere in the district.

"They'll all experience it soon enough Toby," the malicious voice chirps from beside him, as if in response to the question not asked.

He doesn't bother trying to argue or dissuade her, she has proven already it is too late for that. He points over to the police headquarters as they close within a couple of hundred meters. For a moment he considers turning around and blasting her as high as possible, through the SkyCast with her device but there was too much unknown. *It wouldn't even kill her,* he resigns.

"We can't go down there, it's suicide." he very much feels that way now they are close enough to see what the situation is. The police headquarters is surrounded, not by people wanting to get in or the usual reporters but by military units. There are tanks which Tobias has never seen before alongside more of the mechanised suits and armed officers everywhere. Someone has clearly decided a stand would be taking place here if things escalated. They have turned the police station into a fortress.

He peers back at Neomi to see how she will react to the scenes below but she just gives him another smirk, the smugness of knowing something the other person does not. "It might be for you, bye Toby," she flatly ends as a black egg appears in front of her, growing in a fraction of a second to encompass her entire form and leaving a large black shape darker than anything he can imagine, like peering into some sort of void. As quick as it appeared it shrinks back into nothing, leaving no one in the space behind but the empty air.

Tobias doesn't hesitate or sit there dumbfounded like he certainly once would have, he begins scanning the rooftops down below, trying to figure out where she might have reappeared, assuming she hasn't teleported into the building itself, but he believes if she needed to be on the hospital roof with the device before then surely the same is true again.

Unfortunately his searching is interrupted as bullets begin to fly in his direction, they are no threat to him and he holds out an open palm and redirects each round off into the SkyCast somewhere, the realisation that he is just hovering here as an obvious target and powered person slowly sinks in.

He watches as a small group of Archangels break away from the cordon around the ancient building, flying up on wings of steel to intercept him.

He doesn't want a fight, doesn't want to engage them but they are closing quickly and leaving him little option as he spots a figure moving on one of the buildings adjacent to the police headquarters. Shunting his body into looking downwards he dives head first towards the Archangels.

With practiced precision the squad breaks apart to avoid collisions but they don't simply let him pass. Plasma rounds flicker past him, with more than one impacting against his telekinetic armour. He certainly doesn't feel confident he can take many more impacts before his armour fails him, but he refuses to lose sight of the woman on the rooftop, he has to stop Neomi.

He launches a wave of energy out from himself, hoping to force the flying troops away from him but he can feel his boundary dissipating as it impacts them, something absorbing his focused will power.

Tobias doesn't get to think on it for long as he sees first-hand what the device below looks like when it activates, a shockwave ripples outwards silently but unmissable, the building shudders with the impact and unlike the hospital, the fabricated housing isn't as firmly made, walls explode outwards as floors collapse down.

Instinctively he curls into a foetal ball and surrounds himself with his own energy as the shockwave crashes into him and the Archangels. The blow is more than he could have anticipated and it sends him reeling upwards, it takes a few seconds for him to grasp enough control to bring himself to a stop and survey the changes below.

Neomi has already gone and the device with her, the slowly deteriorating and collapsing building void of her presence. The Archangels below seem to have had the impact cushioned somehow, they have recovered quicker than he has and seem to have barely moved. He knows there is no way they have forgotten about him, he is after all only a short distance above them, but they pay him no mind at all. To Tobias they seem to have frozen, looking to the rooftop and one another before checking wrist mounted devices and simultaneously diving back down towards the ground, a direct path towards the police headquarters. They regroup with the mass of uniformed officers and military below and are lost to his sight, he begins to start scanning the other buildings below and mutters to himself, "She can't have gone far. Shit. Shit. Shit." Each curse is progressively harder and more pronounced.

His search doesn't last long however and before he can lower himself to take a closer look a shot rings out from the police headquarters rooftop, it cracks loud enough for him to hear even from here, a large calibre sniper round of some kind. He tries to trace the target of the shot, a quick glimmer of hope that perhaps the military have some kind of ammunition that has taken Neomi down, as seems usual for Tobias the hope is quickly dashed as he watches helplessly as a young woman slumps out of a window in one of the hab buildings, it isn't a long drop but she crashes to the pavement below as some of the few remaining people on the streets rush towards her. Tobias instinctively begins flying downwards, he can hear the wind but not feel it inside his thin energy shell. The scene below becomes clearer as he closes, the woman who has a small hole piercing her chest also happens to now have blue skin and her ears have grown in height. It's obvious to him and he presumes equally so to the sniper that this woman has or had powers. Tobias didn't have to wonder how long until the people below him demonstrate their own powers, none of them would be protected against Neomi's device.

An explosions rings out against the building Neomi was previously standing atop. This time it isn't from the deployment of her device but from a shell fired from a tank into the core of the building, shattering what little structural integrity it has left as it crumbles to the ground, sending dust and debris into the streets below. The cloud would be choking for those below and would force people indoors momentarily, but it also served to block line of sight to the police forces as it billows outwards into their organised cordon.

For a moment the district is quiet, the sounds of engagements far away too low to hear and in his elevated position everything seems calm, as if the brown dust cloud below has calmed everything. Two more people rise from the mist below, other people with powers of flight or some form of kinesis he assumes, they look scared and confused, clearly unsure what is going on or how they gained these powers.

Small black figures take to the sky, the Archangels making the most of their tactical gear to try and get a better vantage. Seeing other fliers and Tobias they immediately engage, metal shells with a light blue glow about them cut the air. He doesn't wait to see if his shield can take the hits from the unknown ammunitions. Extending his will to feel each round in the air as they approach him, far faster than his eye can follow or his mind comprehend, he exerts his will, his force over the bullets and each losing its momentum in an instant before dropping harmlessly into the cloud below. The other two fliers either aren't as powerful or are caught by surprise and like the rounds he just stopped, they vanish into the unknown below, their lives coldly extinguished in a moment.

Unable to combat Neomi, the familiar feelings of helplessness threaten to return and overwhelm him, he roars in frustration, his angry scream piercing the quiet below. He refuses to be powerless, to be helpless. He lashes out at the only people he can, the people actively trying to kill him. There is only five of them and his rage is fearsome, the closest Archangel levels his rifle at Tobias for another round but never gets chance to unleash it as the rounds explode in his magazine, causing a blue fiery explosion which sends what remains of the officer careening downwards in a spiral of smoke looking like a swatted insect. The other troopers try to react with trained precision and reactions but the mind is quicker, he isn't thinking about his actions or trying to prepare anything, his mind is his weapon and it is fuelled with years of repressed anger.

Lances of force fly from his hands and impact two of the remaining fliers, he can feel their custom armour resisting the force and he pushes harder, exerting his anger into the weapons as they pierce through the stomachs of the pair, dragging them downwards in silence, their screams of pain quashed by their helmets.

As he flies forward eager to engage the final two enemies, he notices the clouds below are taking shape, in a way he'd only ever seen on holo vids about nature outside, a whirlwind begins to coalesce, dragging the dust and smaller debris from the streets and directly towards the headquarters.

The creator of the weather change isn't clear but the cordon below reacts with brutal force. The quiet near silence from before broken with the roar of gunfire and energy weapons being expended, aside from the few quick enough to duck into alleys or buildings the citizens in the streets are swathed down in the hailstorm of bullets.

Tobias quickly swats aside the two Archangels in front of him with a backhanded wall of energy that sends them head over foot with broken wings into the distance. He doesn't know where to engage, where to focus his energy, the civilians in the buildings are beginning to wake up, knowing that their lives are forfeit if they don't fight. From an array of windows come energy blasts raining down into the gathered combination of police and military whilst elsewhere a huge chunk of building crashes into the organised line, crushing several officers as the streets predictably erupt into a warzone.

The small black void that opens atop the police headquarters catches his eye as soon as it appears, the absence of anything in a tiny area signalling the arrival of Neomi on the roof. She is looking down and surveying the scenes below, he can't make out her face but he's certain she is smiling and feeling pleased with herself, the snipers previously on the roof lay around her, their bodies burned or contorted into broken looking positions, as the purple tendrils slowly release from their corpses. She has her hand covering her brow, trying to keep the dust from her eyes even though it doesn't hurt her he supposes.

He hovers there for a moment, not helplessness holding him but indecision, he could help the people with powers defend against the military, but that would just be ultimately helping Neomi, he grits his teeth in disappointment, if he helps the police, he'd be fighting against innocent people who didn't ask for any of this and at the end the police would still want his head. As he stares down at Neomi, her body covered in another new thick jacket she'd acquired from somewhere he realises that is just as fruitless as the other options, he can't hurt her or the device from here, or maybe at all.

He has to do something, if he can't stop the events below, if there is no way he can stop the wheels in motion Neomi has pushed, then he can at least prevent her continuing to do so.

He surrounds himself in a bubble of energy and lunges it downwards towards the rooftop, he approaches at spectacular speed, the military below barely have time to see or react and a lone plasma burst launches from the crowd below and hisses harmlessly past him into the SkyCast above, adding another black square to the rapidly increasing number. Neomi reacts way quicker, whether she can sense him somehow or is expecting him, he doesn't know and doesn't care. She smirks as she waves up at him during his approach as if warmly greeting a friend. Her snarky expression is replaced with surprise however as Tobias crashes into the side of the police headquarters, destroying a substantial chunk of the wall as he forces his way into the building. He focuses on his barrier, shrinking it to the size of the corridor so as not to destroy the floor and walls as he flies around the building.

The building feels almost abandoned, most of the officers already stationed outside or elsewhere in the district. He is sure he can feel what he seeks, is drawn to it almost. He rushes through the headquarters with the imperative to succeed pushing him further, he bursts into an open office area and the few people still there jump to attention as Tobias flies through the centre of the room. None of them engage or do much of anything, too stunned and slack jawed to react.

It hasn't even been a minute since he entered the police building but it already feels like he has been here too long, the building wracks under the barrage of explosions and power expenditures outside, the battle between eliXir fuelled civilians and the military now in full swing. He tries not to think about how high the body count will be as he flies down a staircase, and as he enters a lower level he finds what he has been seeking and a pang of doubt begins biting at the back of his mind.

Two guards look at him and within an instant have their pistols drawn, there is no hesitation or confusion here. The sound of gunfire echoes through the long narrow corridor as he levitates rapidly towards them, bullets frozen in the air and harmless. With a small swish of his hand both of the men collide with the walls of the corridor and collapse in a heap, he doesn't have time to talk over the merits of his plan with himself let alone two people who he doesn't know and who would want him dead. He hovers over the unconscious officers, the imposing vault like door they were guarding wouldn't have looked out of place back at the bank he oddly thinks for a moment.

He is fairly certain there is no amount of force or weaponry that would put a dent in the entry, he is also equally certain he won't need too. He reaches out with hands, his mind sharp and focused as the walls begin to shake and buckle under the strain of his pull. Chips of old paint fall to the floor as cracks begin opening in the wall. His telekinetic force is too much for the old structure and it quickly gives way, huge chunks of masonry crumble and Tobias realises he doesn't have a plan for the door itself, he flies backwards and drags the two officers with him before releasing the door and leaving it to crash downwards with as much noise as any of the explosions outside.

He steps over the vault door into the almost warm familiar glow of eliXir in front of him, seized and yet to be destroyed in the police headquarters evidence room. As he steps closer he hears Neomi's voice ringing in his head.

'There is more to your blood than you ever had chance to learn Tobias', he can see her taunting smile in his mind's eye as keen as if she were right in front of him, *'Did you know that your blood is capable of holding more than one power at a time?'*

Chapter 42

Bolstered by his mission, Tobias stands in front of a dozen vials of confiscated eliXir. As he holds one syringed vial in his hand it occurs for a fleeting moment that he has no idea if this is pure or mixed with other drugs. It was a passing thought and one he doesn't have time for, he forces down any doubts and anxiety, clutching the vial a little tighter in his hand.

Neomi's words echo in his mind once more, the image of her beautiful face marred by the acts she has committed fill his thoughts as he considers what is at stake. He would never have thought for a second he'd be fighting for anyone else's life, let alone that of the district or even the world itself. He slams the vial into his arm and the self-injector begins pumping the drug into his bloodstream.

He doesn't wait to see the effect, doesn't pause to feel the high, the clink of the vial dropping to the floor reverberates in the room as he grabs another.

Tobias grits his teeth as the second needle finds its way into arm, he can feel the rush of eliXir burning through his blood, there hasn't been enough time for the powers to manifest and he doesn't stop to think about what is going to happen to him, only that he has to stop Neomi. "Have to stop her stupid revolution," he mutters as four vials float in front of him, levitated with his telekinesis.

He roars in defiance as he slams all the vials into himself at the same time, the quiet hiss of the auto injectors lost in the din.

Blood trickles from his nose as he falls to his knees, his body feels like it is burning from the inside out, Tobias convulses as he struggles to find breath, his lungs immolated in pain. His body forcibly trying to reject the changes, bent over double as he vomits all over the floor. The pain shoots upwards and he cradles his head, it feels as if someone is sending electricity directly into his skull causing his teeth to chatter as he rolls around on the floor, a coarse scream coming from a haggard throat echoes through the halls.

He has no idea how long the episode lasts but in an instant it is over, his body feels more alive than he's ever known as he spits out a mouthful of blood onto the floor. Wiping his face with an already dirtied arm, he adds blood to the plethora of mess.

It isn't the same as before he knows, when he took the eliXir for the first time he felt at one with his telekinesis, as if it had always been a part of him, as natural as walking. He assumed it was something to do with taking so many vials at once and the powers being possibly permanent, but it doesn't feel as natural to him anymore. He can't sense properly what his new powers actually are and he mentally curses as there isn't time to find out.

He holds out a hand upwards, intending to fly directly to the roof when to his surprise a white beam shoots upwards, a light so bright that he has to wince against its power, with a clenched fist it immediately cuts short, nothing remains where the beam of energy travelled, a large hole leads directly upwards to the roof and Tobias wonders for a second if he has burned a hole into the upper habs, he doesn't dwell on the matter as he raises himself from the ground upwards through the breach he has created. Flying through the multiple levels of the police headquarters he notices that the circles he has created have left singe marks where material has been burnt away. *Did I just kill anyone?* He panics for an instant, that if the beam had caught someone there would be nothing left of them, he callously pushes the terrifying thought aside, the stakes are greater than him and his actions and he has to find Neomi. His single minded determination pulls him ever upwards and out of the building.

Hovering just above the rooftop the sounds and sights around him confirm all of his worst fears about what would be the consequences of Neomi's actions. The streets of the middle habs have become a war zone, military and civilians alike are darting between buildings and alleyways as they exchange gunfire for powers. The organised lines around the police headquarters have broken, whether intentionally or not is unclear, to his untrained eyes he doesn't know if the small squads rapidly moving around are being defensive or offensive.

"Glorious isn't it?" the soft voice catches him by surprise but he finds himself somewhat relieved as he turns and sees Neomi casually sitting on top of her power spreading device, her expression looks almost playful and it makes him want to scream.

"Soon there will be no government. No rules. Everyone will be equal and the strong will survive. I will survive." She looks him up and down and tilts her head and her expression flips from mirth and excitement to genuine concern. "What has happened to you Tobias?" she enquires gently as she stands and takes a step towards him as their eyes lock together, "Your eyes, they are white. You did it didn't you?

You took more eliXir. That's where you went!"

The sudden switch in demeanour confuses him, but his body feels like it is getting hotter and hotter, conflagrating from the inside, he can't allow himself to be distracted.

"I'm sorry." he states calmly as he breaks eye contact, "You left me no choice."

Conversation ends as he holds out his hands, two thin crackling beams of white extend outwards but find only the void as Neomi reactively teleports away, he hovers himself higher, looking for the telltale sign of where she may have gone and finds her on a nearby burning building, he unleashes another attack forcing her to stay on the defensive as she bounces to another roof, small circles of black appear again and again, engulfing light and vision where she leaves them in her wake as she jaunts from roof to roof.

He is taken back when a void appears less than a meter in front of him, everything turning to black as a growling woman lunges outwards with a fist, he rotates his body in the air at the last moment and feels the sting as her knuckles graze his jaw, the force behind the blow stronger than anything a normal human would be capable of.

Reactively he flies himself backwards away from the attack but it is too late, she's already pinged to another location. He spins around looking for her distinctive void but can't find it, her machine is still on the roof though and he knows she won't have left it undefended. He cries out in pain as a foot catches him in the back and sends him tumbling towards the roof of the police building.

He shakes his head, trying to force out the dizziness and burning from within. He tries to use his telekinesis to pull himself up from the rooftop but feels another kick smash into his rapidly failing barrier, the impact is strong enough to leave him winded despite his protection, without it, the attack would probably have broken most of his ribs if not his spine.

He launches himself forwards and upwards, flying at high speed in a tight circle over a few of the buildings in the area, hoping that if he maintains the speed she won't be able to continue her assaults. After a few moments of being left alone he spots Neomi sitting atop a bright neon sign, damaged from the fighting below but still flickering its adverts into the dark. He slows down and flies in her direction, she makes no move to attack but he readies himself all the same.

"Come on Toby, this is fun and all but what's the point, eventually I'm going to overwhelm you and you'll die." he launches another blast at her, wider than the previous but in an instant she's gone again, leaving only the after image of bright white where the beam just was, the sign nothing but a fizzing memory.

Refusing to be fooled the same way twice he snaps himself quickly around and reaches out with a hand, grasping Neomi in midair with his telekinesis as she appears behind him, her face tightens in a grimace of anger and rage. Before he can launch another attack, a purple tentacle lashes his face and he reactively holds up a hand to try and pull it away but it's gone in an instant as is Neomi, having disappeared from his grip, flittering to another rooftop below.

"I can do this cat and mouse game forever Toby," she shouts up at him, "Just give it up, even if you hit me, you can't actually kill me, shit, you can't even hurt me!" she laughs as she blinks away to another rooftop slightly higher up.

He screams in frustration as he allows the burning inside him to overwhelm his senses. He can feel it tearing him apart, but it isn't painful, if anything it gives him some relief. He opens his eyes and watches as two reflections of himself appear next to him, then two more, within a few seconds, there are twenty copies of himself all in a line. They are all standing to attention in the same way he is and he can sense each of them as if they are a further extension of his will.

"Oooh," comes the approving sound from below, "I always loved duplication, so much fun." she lets out a high pitched wolf whistle.

He isn't in the mood for humour however, launching another pinpoint attack of energy in her direction and as he predicts she teleports to another roof, but this time Tobias isn't alone. His manifested clones sweep out around him, each of them launching their own independent attacks, forcing Neomi to keep teleporting quicker and quicker, giving her no time to rest, no time to quip or hurt anyone else.

"You" comes the single word from a rooftop below, "can't" another black void, "hurt" she comes to stop above the police headquarters, directly next to her DNA adjusting doomsday device, "me," she stands resolute as three beams of white burning light impact her torso, her arms thrown to the side almost as if she wasn't sure what was going to happen herself.

After a second he ceases the attack and grits his teeth as the woman who he had found himself attracted too still lives and taunts him with that smile. "I'm bored of this now Toby, I have work to do, bye!" she ends cheerfully.

The taunting only serves to make him more frustrated and he focuses his mind to a single point, attempting something he isn't even sure if he could do. In his mind's eye he imagines her heart, like he had seen in the medical holovids, creating a small bubble inside her chest, attempting to sever her hearts attachments to the rest of her body. It was severe and fatal, something Tobias would never have considered himself capable of doing.

Neomi clutches a hand to her chest, her eyes widening in shock before allowing her arms to drop to her sides, "I can't believe you actually did that Toby, I'm not sure if I'm impressed or hurt. My actual heart. You bastard. Enough of this cat and mouse."

He looks down on her from his floating vantage point as he gathers all of his manifestations around him. "You are right, enough of this."

His clones all dive towards him, plunging into his own body as they evaporate, each one making him shine brighter, a beacon in the sky that is visible for miles, Neomi is forced to cover her eyes as the display of raw power takes place.

He outstretches his arms, his power unable to be contained and demanding to be used. A vortex swirls around him, it builds quickly and within moments debris and chunks of building are orbiting him. Within seconds entire buildings are crumbling, being sucked into the swirling morass of power with Tobias at its heart. Neomi tries to teleport away, fluttering from building to building, but it's not enough, he watches as she tries going faster and faster, but no matter how quickly she teleports, her range is limited and she is drawn inexorably into the chaotic storm he has created.

He singles her out, pulls her closer through the maelstrom and within seconds they are face to face. She writhes and struggles but ultimately knows any chance at escape will only end her back here. A dozen purple tentacles thrust from her hands and arms towards him, a last ditch effort to strike back and to regain control. With a single back handed gesture a short thick white beam like sword cuts them short with ease.

She screams to be heard over the sounds of buildings being torn asunder, cars and market stands alike are sucked into the storm and ripped apart. "You are so powerful Toby, you can lead at my side. You are my revolution," she smiles softly at him, all the venom and hate lost in those beautiful eyes.

His own eyes glow pure white and despite it all, regardless of the deaths and turmoil she's caused, he can't help but offer a smile of his own.

"It's over," he gently states, placing an open palm on her head as the storm reaches a crescendo, the power surrounding him glowing brighter than ever before. She convulses under his touch, her body writhing under the power he can command.

Like an exploding star, his light pulses outwards a final time. His energy expended, the vortex slows, wall sections and cars heavily begin crashing the ground. Tobias can feel himself losing his very essence, he looks at his arms but he can't recognise them, they are simply energy, bright and beautiful but beginning to disperse.

Neomi yells out once more as the whirling storm releases her, gravity ceasing control as she plummets to the ground. The sound of bones crunching is masked only by her screams of agony as her legs break upon the impact.

Through the tears and screams, she looks upwards at the white humanoid form floating above as it slowly fades away and crumbles apart, little wisps of light breaking up and floating into the distance or fading entirely.

Tobias can feel his form losing shape, but he manages a final smile as he looks out over the middle habs and feels no fear, closing his eyes and allowing himself to dissipate.

Chapter 43

Sergeant Russells watches helplessly as Tobias and Neomi fly off towards the police headquarters but as they drop off onto the horizon the bindings pinning him release. He taps his communicator, "This is Sergeant Russells, currently on site at the hospital, the main threat is moving towards the police headquarters at high speed, be prepared for incoming powered individuals."

There is no reply on the channel, he taps a button on his wrist mounted computer, selecting a broader channel of communication "This is Sergeant Russells, can anybody read me?" whilst waiting for the silence to break he begins clambering his way down the rubble and back into what remains of the hospitals structure.

"Sergeant Russells, this is Commander Coleman, this is now a military matter, regroup at the police headquarters and keep off the comms until you have been told otherwise," the familiar click of the channel being closed does nothing to assure him that de-escalation is possible. He was hoping to try and buy Tobias some time to fix things but at least now his path is laid out in front of him.

He rushes out of the hospital entrance, in the distance a small group of narcotics officers are engaged with a group of powered civilians, it isn't obvious who has the upper hand and he feels drawn to the conflict but at the same time he doesn't even know what he would do if he got there. Even in the face of the greatest threat to life he's ever known, he doesn't agree with executing these people but at the same time he swore to protect the city and its people.

The moral battle rages inside of him almost as fiercely as the battles in the streets, like it has so many times in the past, so he resolves to push it aside, to dedicate himself to action. He begins running down the street, not towards the conflict but towards a nearby police vehicle, it isn't his own but at this point it doesn't matter.

He hops inside and taps in his personal code as well as placing his hand on the biometric reader. The car hums to life and he slams his foot on the accelerator, the vehicle screeches in the direction Tobias was flying, towards the police headquarters.

He weaves the car through wreckage and bodies, sirens drowning out the chaos from the outside, several minutes pass and he checks the navigation panel as he slows the car to carefully drive through an abandoned blockade.

A voice hisses through the in car sound system "This is Commander Coleman, the weapon from the hospital has been deployed here, powered individuals are on all sides, engage at will and with full force. Coleman out."

Russells rams his fist repeatedly against the centre of the steering wheel, cursing as he throws caution to the wind, smashing through what remains of the barricade, something bouncing under the wheels of the patrol vehicle as he bears his teeth in frustration.

The streets quickly become hostile, he sees people flying overhead, both Archangel and civilian alike, the sky above becoming a light show of plasma and a myriad of other explosions. Realising too late he should have turned off the cars sirens, something blasts the side of his vehicle and the force of the impact flips the police cruiser, sending it careening into a building with a crash of metal and concrete.

Russells wakes to an angry beeping on his wrist panel, his DNAAR has been going off for a while, he feels a wetness trickling down his neck and reactively places his hand there, blood is dripping from somewhere, the flaring pain in his arm suggests something has gone wrong there too. It takes a moment for him to orient himself as he unfastens his safety harness and kicks out what remains of the windscreen.

The dust has already begun to settle in what remains of the building he's crashed into, but some still lingers in the air, a positive sign he hasn't been knocked out for long. Given his near scrapes with death the last few days he's glad to be walking away from this one with just the burning in his shoulder.

A crackling comes through on his communicator as he stumbles out into the main street, it's a clumsy move he realises, his assailant could easily still be here but he needs to assess the situation. The street is empty with not an officer or civilian in sight. He taps the side of his helmet trying to fix the signal of his comms.

"This is Captain Rodriguez. Cease all attacks. Regroup at the station. Repeat, do not engage." A short beep and the message replays, having been set on a loop before being broadcast on most of the official communication bands. He dismisses it and begins running in the direction of the police headquarters, or rather where it would be if his way wasn't blocked by the large hulk of a military exo suit, lying on its side with huge furrows rent in the metal, something huge or strong had obviously engaged the unit in close quarters.

Russells strains to climb over the husk, but what he sees on the other side almost sends him tumbling back over. At first glance it looks like a war has taken place, tanks lie in ruin and the streets are unrecognisable, tarmac ripped apart and huge pockets of wall and roof missing from the station itself. However, that's at complete contrast to the goings on around him, groups of officers intermingled with civilians, which in and of itself wouldn't be odd if it weren't for the obvious power usage on display. Overhead people are flying around, a few of them are even in police uniforms. For the first time Russells finds himself speechless, there is no fighting, no threats of executions, everyone seems to working together to clear the area.

Seeing him standing aloof on top of a damaged exo suit, a man comes flying down towards him on feathered white wings, instinct kicks in and Russells goes for his side arm but forces back the trained impulse and watches as the muscular figure draws closer and he can't fight back the smirk than lines his face.

"Captain Rodriguez. I might have known you'd still be alive, just my luck." he snorts as the large Hispanic man lands firmly on the wreckage in front of him, Russells notices that the man is missing his wrist mounted DNAAR, an obvious observation he supposes.

"Well, if it makes you feel any better," he laughs "you were right. Shouldn't have been executing powered people. Although I guess I might be a little bias."

"You in charge here?" Russells asks, keen to restore some sense of order in the chaos of the last few hours.

"Captain Avalos killed himself, at least I think he did, it's a fucking shit show in there. The military that weren't taken out have fled, narcotics refuse to surrender and are still engaged elsewhere in the district. So as far as your question goes, I'm in charge of this little slice of heaven I guess. Figure it's as good a place as any to rally the people, both powered and not."

"Do you know what happened to the woman responsible for all of this? She has a machine that was spreading powers. These are permanent you realise Captain? They aren't going to fade." There are so many questions and so much disarray, but he needs to know the immediate threat is contained before he can figure out what to do next.

"She's in custody, couple of officers brought her in after some kind of power vortex," he shrugs as the pair share a confused look, "I don't fucking know, anyway, she's over there," he points to a half destroyed armoured transport, three officers standing over a woman on a stretcher, her hair distinguishes her immediately despite its dirtied appearance.

"As for the machine," he points over to a convoy of trucks, not police, but well-guarded by private contractors, the cleanliness of their uniforms implies they haven't seen any of the action here. "They said it belongs to them and I'm not about to start another battle right now. I have enough on my plate trying to keep everyone calm and trying to restore some sense of order around here."

"Who are they anyway?" he has a fair suspicion, especially if Captain Avalos was dead, looking over Rodriguez' shoulder at the remnants of the police station he hopes Mel is okay, he has no idea if she has a DNAAR chip or not.

"Pro Life," the man shrugs, not really understanding the importance of the question, or simply not caring.

Russells only nods in reply before dismissing himself to go and talk to Neomi, hoping to get some perhaps slightly less disconcerting answers. He nods at the guards standing over her but from the look of her they aren't needed. He's surprised to see she isn't in any bindings, her legs both in splints. He's apprehensive at first, worried he may have walked into a trap, but the woman's face is lined with tears, trenches of clean skin where they have run.

Through soaked eyes she looks over at him. Muttering half sentences with no air of her previous confidence. "Burned it out of me. Weak. Normal. Forever," the words splutter out and she trails away, staring at the SkyCast above as if no one exists, her lips quivering and occasionally repeating the same words.

Russells kneels down beside her, his words measured and calm "In many ways you won Neomi, the world will never be the same again. You've changed everything you wanted, but it seems you aren't in the place you wanted to be. Where is he Neomi? Where is Tobias?" his last questions had all the firm but calm authority he was so well versed as using.

The tears renew, following the path of the previous ones, despite not breaking her attention from whatever it is she is focused on. Her whimpering breaks for a moment and despite her rugged throat a single word comes out with clarity, "Ascension."

Sergeant Russells shakes his head as she descends back into muttering and rocking her head back and forth. "We'll talk more later Neomi. You have a lot to answer for," he gets the impression his words are falling on deaf ears as he looks out at the scenes around.

Civilians with super strength are helping to lift up huge chunks of debris and broken vehicles with the direction of his fellow officers. A man flies over head, carrying two injured officers to some kind of medical station where a burly woman is tending to the wounded as a glowing aura cascades from her hands. People helping people, it seems so natural and casts such a different light to everything he's ever been told and enforced, but as he watches the Pro Life Corp trucks pull away and drive into the distance, he can't help but feel a chill down his spine for whatever will come next.

Epilogue

A man in an expensively tailored suit sits at his desk, light fighting to break through his blinds as he pours over the various reports scattered around the table.

He grimaces as he swallows a mouthful of his barely warm coffee, opening the first of many small cardboard files. As with most of his files, this one contained a small greyscale picture of a person from one of the colonies, he flicks it to one side and pays it no mind as he begins skim reading the person's biography and what led them to the point of taking eliXir. Feeling his head getting heavy and bobbing in the heat, he decides to skip to the end, flicking past pages of personal history to get to the section of displayed powers.

With a sigh he slams the folder closed and slides it to one side, adding it to the pile of reviewed case files.

The knocking at the door draws him out of his stupor and he quickly shuffles the folders to look at least slightly more professional. "Come in," he calls out, the door flies open as an excited subordinate practically jumps into the room.

"Sir, we have an issue!" the worker cries, holding out another brown file, his anxious tone only exacerbated by the almost shaking of the file.

Straightening his back and putting on a stern tone the man replies, "Out with it erm..." he has to look at the man's name tag to recall his name, there were far too many monitors for him remember them all, "Phil is it?"

"Yes sir, Colony 37 has become unstable." Phil begins and he can't help but roll his eyes at inevitable paperwork and meetings this was going to create.

"But," the worker continues, "it may have yielded results!" the anxiety of reporting the bad news was clearly lost by his eagerness at the latter.

His smooth leather chair almost tumbles backwards as he stands up, his knees jerking it back, "What do you mean, results? Be clear." he states, leaning forwards on the table as he expresses his own eagerness.

"The people in Colony 37 have demonstrated longer term power usage, definitely hours and possibly cases of days. We have reason to believe that they may in fact be permanent." the worker physically slumps as his news is told and spent, the tension and anxiety lost in an instant.

Standing upright and composing his own anxiety he assumes his command. "Get a sample immediately. Let's say a sample size of twenty, should be more than enough. An additional sample of ten non powered individuals as well. Do we know what or who might have started this?" This was going to make his career, not only would this change the political landscape here, but globally. *Fuck the Russians*, he thinks to himself.

"We are still compiling data and reviewing footage from the last few days, it's a bit of a mess over there, however we have received word that one of our subsidiaries, Proliferation Corp, have secured a device that is believed to be responsible for spreading powers amongst the populace." suddenly remembering his station, Phil stands straight with his chin held high.

"Perfect, get that device over to the R&D boys as soon as possible, keep me posted on what is happening over there and tell the other monitors it's going to be a long night." he sits back in his chair and casts aside all the files on his desk as the other man begins to leave.

The man turns tentatively, obviously reluctant to ask, "Sir, sorry to ask, but what shall we do about the situation once we have the samples secured?"

After swallowing what little remains of his coffee he waves his hand dismissively, "Purge sections two and three, hell, purge section one as well if there is evidence of use in the upper sections. Dismissed."

Enjoy the book?

I would love to hear your thoughts!

Please drop a review over on Amazon or Goodreads

You can find me on Twitter @C_Rook_Official

If you would like to be the first to hear about future projects or would like to join a review team, please email:
chris.rook.official@gmail.com

9 781999 308308